GIALLO FANTASTIQUE

Other books by Ross E. Lockhart

Anthologies:

The Book of Cthulhu
The Book of Cthulhu II
Tales of Jack the Ripper
*The Children of Old Leech: A Tribute to the Carnivorous Cosmos of
   Laird Barron* (with Justin Steele)
Cthulhu Fhtagn! (forthcoming)

Novels:

Chick Bassist

Critical Acclaim for *The Children of Old Leech:*
A Tribute to the Carnivorous Cosmos of Laird Barron,
edited by Ross E. Lockhart and Justin Steele

"Lockhart and Steele collect 17 original stories from some of the shining stars of modern horror, constructing a worm-riddled literary playground from elements of the fiction of horror maestro Laird Barron. The results come across with a coherent feeling of dread, without feeling derivative of the source. [...] Hopefully Barron will enjoy this tribute; his fans certainly will."

—Publishers Weekly

"This multifaceted grimoire, and the talent associated with it, is staggering to behold. [...] The tales, while sometimes recalling certain tropes or characters from his fiction, can be enjoyed in their own right; and, I must say, the range of styles on display is consistently impressive."
—C. M. Muller, *Chthonic Matter*

"Lockhart and Steele have a winner on their hands, I think; this is one I'll keep coming back to, much as I do with Laird's work. Reading TCoOL was like standing in that Tree beside that lake in the hills, up to my ankles in smoky rot and grey grubs, unable to move, while the sun dipped down to dusk. Recommended."

—Martian Migraine

"The Children of Old Leech brings horrific joy from start to finish."
—Rue Morgue

"Some of the best horror short fiction I've ever read into one book."
—Cthulhu Slippers

"A reader new to the whole Barron cosmos won't feel excluded at all, though familiarity with those totems obviously will help. What they will feel is entertained, shocked, stimulated, rewarded, upset, disturbed, and sometimes very scared."

—TeleRead

Critical Acclaim for Ross E. Lockhart's *Tales of Jack the Ripper*

"*Tales of Jack the Ripper* manages to walk that fine line between entertainment and exploitation with real finesse. It's a gripping group of stories about one of our most enduring mysteries, and well worth your time."

—*FEARnet.com*

"...there are enough original and inventive approaches to this most bedeviling of true-crime mysteries to suggest that Jack the Ripper and the Whitechapel Murders of 1888 will continue to inspire imaginative speculations for some time to come."

—Stefan Dziemianowicz, *Locus*

"You need to get up off your lazy duff and buy this collection."

—*Shock Totem*

"...there's enough variation of theme and style here to interest almost any crime or horror reader..."

—*The Big Click*

"Readers interested in Jack the Ripper will love this anthology. Horror fans in general should be quite pleased."

—*Tangent*

"Most of the authors explore the Ripper's mind, and it is indeed a place of grue and madness. [...] Yet, taken one by one, the stories show a remarkable level of skill and power."

—Richard A. Lupoff, *Locus*

"*Tales of Jack the Ripper* marks a strong debut for Word Horde. Lockhart, in usual fashion, has managed to put together a strong, multifaceted anthology that explores the Ripper legend at length. If this book is indicative of what's to be expected from his new press, than readers have much to look forward to."

—*The Arkham Digest*

"Judging from the author lineup in this book, Word Horde will not have time for your Mickey Mouse bullshit."

—*HorrorTalk.com*

"The bottom line is these are all excellent stories, all about Jack."

—*Hellnotes*

GIALLO FANTASTIQUE

DIRECTED BY
ROSS E. LOCKHART

WORD HORDE
PETALUMA, CA

Giallo Fantastique
© 2015 by Ross E. Lockhart
This edition of *Giallo Fantastique*
© 2015 by Word Horde

Cover art © 2012 by David Palumbo
Cover design by Scott R. Jones

Edited by Ross E. Lockhart

An extension of this copyright page appears on page 228

First Edition

ISBN: 978-1-939905-06-2

A Word Horde Book
www.wordhorde.com

TABLE OF CONTENTS

Giallo Fantastique is dedicated
to three maestros of cinematic terror…

Dario Argento

Mario Bava

Lucio Fulci

YELLOW: THE COLOR OF DECADENCE, STRANGENESS, AND FEAR

ROSS E. LOCKHART

Throughout history, in many cultures, the color yellow was considered fortunate. It is, after all, the color of sunlight, of grain in the fields, of gold. But by the late 1800s, the color yellow, particularly in combination with literature, became much more evocative of decadence. When Oscar Wilde referenced a corrupting yellow book in *The Picture of Dorian Gray* (1891), scholars now know he is evoking Joris-Karl Huysmans' infamous aesthetic novel, *À rebours*, but at the time, Wilde's novel inspired publishers Elkin Matthews and John Lane to create their own decadent yellow literary journal, *The Yellow Book*, in 1894, and American author Robert W. Chambers to craft his story cycle *The King in Yellow*, a collection of weird tales centered around the corrupting and sensational influence of a forbidden, yellow-bound play, in 1895. Both of which were far stranger works than Huysmans—or Wilde—could have imagined. Yellow, it seems, was primed to enter the twentieth century as a sinister force.

The title of the anthology you hold in your hands is derived from terms demarking two literary traditions. The first, *Giallo*, is the Italian weird crime genre, originally known as *Il Giallo*

Mondadori, or "Mondadori Yellow." It was named for its publisher as much as for its lurid yellow covers. *Giallo* began in 1929, not too terribly long after the Yellow Decadence of the 1890s, as a series of cheap pulp paperbacks comprised primarily of Italian translations of American and British mysteries and thrillers. Over time the sensationalist covers and ghastly content of these paperbacks evolved into a highly stylized filmic genre, one that would revolutionize horror cinema in the 1960s and 1970s. The second literary term, *Fantastique,* is a far older tradition, a French genre of fantasy and horror dating back to the Middle Ages and *The Song of Roland.* Literature of the *Fantastique* typically involves the intrusion of the supernatural into an otherwise realistic and mundane world, one in which the primary characters within the work are often unwilling or unable to mentally correlate and accept the strange events which are occurring. *Giallo Fantastique,* therefore, is comprised of stories at the intersection of the crime and supernatural horror genres. Stories to surprise, titillate, frighten, shock, and, above all, entertain.

To that end, I have asked a collection of some of my favorite authors to bring you their own takes on *Giallo* and the *Fantastique,* and on decadence, crime, horror, and strangeness, building their stories upon written and cinematic traditions alike. The result is a paranoiac descent into a dark world of literary *Grand Guignol* like no other, an anthology of both style and substance, on the one hand grim and fantastic, on the other, pure (if grotesque) cinematic fun.

That said, many readers who discover this anthology will have been drawn to it based on an operating knowledge of *Giallo* cinema, rather than its lengthy literary roots, so I would be remiss were I not to leave you with the following recommendations of some of my favorite silver screen *Gialli*: Mario Bava's *The Girl Who Knew Too Much* (1963) and *Blood and Black Lace* (1964); Lucio Fulci's *A Lizard in a Woman's Skin* (1971) and *Don't Torture a Duckling* (1972); Dario Argento's *The Bird with the Crystal Plumage* (1969),

Deep Red (1975), *Suspiria* (1977), and *Tenebrae* (1982); and Michele Soavi's *Stage Fright* (1985). I would also highly recommend Mario Bava's *Black Sunday* (1960) and *Black Sabbath* (1963) as a pair of proto-Giallo films that elegantly evoke the *Fantastique*.

So put on a Goblin soundtrack, pour yourself a glass of blood-red wine, and settle back into a comfortable chair. After checking behind the curtains for black-gloved intruders, of course. What's your favorite shade of yellow?

MINERVA

MICHAEL KAZEPIS

Where Leona Pardi was murdered was on odos Apollonos, outside of an old bookshop that sold expensive rare editions. Pardi had been en route to her partner's home, a studio near Makrigianni on the collapsed side of the Parthenon. Approaching 0300, everything on the street was shuttered, revealing a series of intricate and sometimes profane or political graffiti murals you only saw in daylight on holidays. Her killer had stopped to admire the work.

When Pardi never arrived, the boyfriend was devastated. Her phone went straight to voicemail. He'd thought she was ignoring him. But when he didn't hear from her after several days, and it appeared no one had been to her place in some time, he went to the police. They contacted him days later after a Jane Doe matched the description.

He was the one that identified the body. Pardi had no immediate family, at least no one she'd told him about, anyway. She'd been stabbed forty-three times. That night he mourned, drinking in his third-floor apartment until he was unconscious—he'd planned to propose to her that week up in the mountains near Arachova, where they'd first met during a ski holiday.

Nearly six weeks later, the boyfriend, whose name was Quentin

Marrast, was found in an abandoned construction site, one of many in the city suspended by archeological digs, after some passersby noticed the smell.

"This all seems obvious enough," said the naked detective, sitting alone in his office, scanning through photographs of the crime scenes.

***

Quentin's sister, Celia Marrast, arrived a week after their family was notified by the embassy. Enough time had passed that her brother's unclaimed body had been cremated. And the case was more or less cold. Their mother was too ill to make the trip, and in any event, might not have wanted to.

Back stateside she worked as a photographer. Mostly she chronicled weddings and staged portraits of young and still excited families or couples. But she dreamed of bigger subjects. Walking the streets and seeing so much to capture, she was kicking herself for having left her equipment on another continent. Still, at least she had her phone. She snapped photos of anything that caught her eye, which was much.

No one had heard from Quentin in years, like he'd simply dropped off after moving abroad. There'd been only a mailing address and the few postcards he'd sent her. However, this was understandable—there'd been something of a falling out, an argument between him and their mother. Neither ever revealing to Celia what it'd been over.

Marrast booked a bed at a hostel on odos Menandrou, locking what few things she'd brought in the cage beneath the bunk. She had a hard time sleeping in the room, with only another traveler's unmade bed as company.

The following morning Marrast met with her brother's landlord outside the building and he gave her the key to the apartment. Had he been flirting?—this infuriated her. Marrast told him she was surprised he hadn't already rented it out. The landlord, an older man in his fifties, said things moved slow here. He wiped sweat from his forehead with a handkerchief. "Well, let me know if you need any... *help*." But she shook her head. "The more you can take the better," he'd said.

She walked up the spiral stairwell to the apartment and found the place rifled through. The smell of mildew, hot stale air. Drawers pulled partway open and in some instances torn out entirely, papers and clothes scattered. Like thieves or the landlord or the police had ransacked it for valuables. She asked herself why she'd even come. There wasn't a body to mourn, not anymore, there really wasn't anything here for her at all. Maybe it was the late gesture, an attempt to know something about him as the man he'd become. To disentangle her from the idea of who he used to be. Marrast opened the windows to let everything breathe. She found bin liners in the kitchen and started to fill them with the most obvious trash. She began with the empty bottles and takeout bags on the counter. There was something about this which felt like peeling off a cooked layer. Marrast tied the bags and took them to the dumpster to drop them. She looked down the street, feeling she was being watched.... Marrast shook her head and reentered the building and climbed the stairs slowly. She walked around the apartment a while doing nothing else. Once she started to feel tired she stepped onto the balcony and sat on a wicker chair that was there. The balcony was the only part of the apartment where she felt at ease. Jetlag took hold. Soon she was dreaming of the building's ghosts.

***

Detective Alex Halkias dropped by the decedent's apartment just after sunrise, hoping to catch the sister there. The Marrast woman hadn't been at the address she'd given and the hostel clerk that greeted him had been less than cooperative. Accommodations are like that, he thought. They never want you looking around. Thing was, Halkias had been disturbed by the deaths of the young lovers. He thought speaking to her about her brother might help him somehow.

He knocked, then noticed the door was unlocked. He opened and called out and no one answered so he let himself in. Ransacked shelves and cabinets. Curtains lifting wraithlike from open windows. Halkias stepped over some stacked books and looked around a bit before walking out onto the balcony. He was alone here.

Later he sat in his car and watched pigeons scrambling across the sidewalk. He looked up at the same balcony from this vantage, then around the street. He got out of the car again and looked at the dumpster. He cut open a bag. Magazines and books in English. Papers. The smell of beer and spoiled food. He glanced at the balcony again, backing away from the dumpster. Halkias held his fingers up in the shape of a rectangle and scanned the scene. A blind man walked past him with his service dog, tapping his cane along the grooves in the sidewalk. The pigeons moved to a power line. Two riders on a motorcycle sped past. All movement was a spell. The trick was to manipulate the correct trajectories....

He walked up the street until he found an alley entrance from which he could see both the balcony and the dumpster clearly. He looked down and noticed the several spent cigarettes. He tapped the freshest remains into a plastic cylinder with a pen. He wondered if any had belonged to the killer. "Probably," he thought. "Probably."

***

Marrast arrived back at the apartment an hour later, having been briefly lost in the winding roads, searching for breakfast. The early morning air smelled of oranges and burnt petrol.

She stopped in front of the first pastry shop she saw and browsed. The currency here looked strange to her, like play money—different sizes too. She'd changed some of her dollars at the airport in Berlin, then again at the airport in Athens. Someone on the plane had told her that not everywhere took a card, and certainly not without a high minimum charge. They'd warned her about pick-pockets. Already the wad of bills in her bra was dampening from sweat, from the heat, what felt like opening an oven every time she left a place with air-conditioning. The pastry she was eating was called a *kasseropita* and had a flaky crust and cheese filling, and went well with a strong espresso. Her things were still at the hostel and she found herself wanting to stay instead at her brother's place, to be closer somehow. She was paid through the week; she'd return when she needed to.

Marrast cleaned some more, throwing stacks of films and books into a garbage bag. She fumbled a paperback and a photograph fell out, a picture of a woman she didn't recognize standing beside her brother. Who was she? They were smiling. What had she meant to him? "Hm."

She tossed the paperback and put the photo atop a pile of the few things she intended to keep.

She moved the bed and lifted the mattress, leaning it against the wall to get at the things beneath it. When she lifted the frame, a mobile phone fell out. The battery dead. Marrast searched around for the charger and couldn't find it. She scrunched her face and held it in her hands. Breathed slow.

"It's okay, it's okay." There was liquor in the kitchen. Half-empty bottle of Russian Standard. Marrast rinsed a glass from the cupboard and poured a few fingers. But she couldn't bring herself to drink it and poured it out, then the entire bottle and all the rest of it—these were his things. She couldn't enjoy them. Not when this had happened to him.

It occurred to her that maybe someone had been here while she was out. The apartment somehow different, some variable within *shifted* enough that she had noticed, though nothing seemed blatantly out of place but what she'd moved herself.

Marrast locked up and went out, feeling thirsty.

In the main square, where the entrance to the market was situated, a film crew had set up. Actors choreographed a scene with the director. Marrast didn't recognize any of them. They spoke Italian. Marrast entered the gathered crowd and watched for a bit.

The cameraman choreographed his own movements around the scene. The director shouted something to one of the actors, a young woman, certainly younger than Marrast. The young woman leaned her head down and muttered, cursing the director or maybe herself. The director grabbed one of the other actors by the shoulders and moved him to a different mark. He announced that they were starting again. A bearded man in the crowd holding a trumpet said, "Is this that witch film?" The actors changed positions a few more times. The director grew increasingly frustrated by a lack of progress.

Quickly bored as a spectator, Marrast moved on, walking until she found a pub full of expats and spent a few hours drinking vodka lemonades. She was finally letting herself grieve.

She listened to an older British man talk to the bartender about island real estate. About his time in Bahrain working in oil. How he always loved visiting Greece, that is, if you could get past all the Greeks. How this had been his home away from his home away from home, if you got him. After a while his mouth only continued moving, the same sounds coming out, none of it making much sense to her. She stared into her glass and stirred the straw. Someone found a spot beside her and asked her something.

"I'm sorry, what?" replied Marrast.

"I said, are you just visiting or do you live here?"

"Oh." She looked up; the man wore a shirt with a maple leaf on it. "Just visiting," she replied, after a beat.

"I live here," he said. "Is this your first visit?"

"It's my first visit anywhere."

"Where are you from?" He finished the last of his stout and signaled the bartender for another. Marrast talked about Cincinnati.

About her mother's condition and her brother's death.

"I'm sorry," he said. "He was murdered?" He squinted as though scanning her reaction.

"…he was."

"I don't mean to pry."

"It's okay. Well, it's not okay. But it's nice to talk."

Marrast talked about what she'd been learning about her brother, after going through his belongings. Truth was, this felt as much an escape from the bullshit back home as it did a family duty.

"I don't have any stories like that." He was from Montreal or just outside. He visited the States a lot, mostly when he needed clothes. He'd been married once, but they hadn't been right for each other and it ended after a few months. For Marrast, it felt strange and also a relief to open up to a stranger. They soon ordered another round and the more she drank, admittedly, the more it began to show they had a lot in common. Mostly it was just music and some books. But it was almost enough to start separating from why she was here. And she still found herself getting sad even laughing at things the stranger said.

He told some jokes he'd heard from some backpackers on a ferry to Mykonos.

"Do you go to the islands a lot?"

He nodded and leaned in, visibly feeling his drink, and tried to kiss her. Marrast turned away.

"Don't do that." Something about the way he said it made her turn back, and the second time she complied. Soon, they were back at his place, which wasn't very far from the pub. He pressed her against the foyer wall and pulled up her dress. She said "Not here," and he walked her into his bedroom. Before she knew it their act was ended and she was looking up at the ceiling while the moon shone in and she felt hot inside and the stranger smoked.

"Killer," he said.

"What?"

The Thiseio metro station still bustled outside. The stranger

snored loudly and Marrast went dizzily in and out of conscious-
ness for a few hours. When the stress returned she slipped out
from under his arm and gathered her things. The floor creaked
loudly as she tiptoed and she held her breath hoping he wouldn't
be up before she was gone, not feeling she'd made a mistake but
not wanting to punctuate it with further contact either. Then she
was out into the early morning gray blue sky crying most of the
walk back.

***

Alex Halkias spent the night in his car, parked a few blocks down
the street from his home in Pangrati. He hadn't felt like going
inside and decided to rest his eyes, then he'd fallen asleep, miraculously, something he hadn't done well in weeks.

He dreamt he was sitting in the only row of a darkened cinema, perhaps a private screening, where the screen was projected
footage of himself watching it. His face was relaxed. He seemed
unconcerned. There was a figure emerging slowly behind him, a
silhouette, as though frozen in time, walking toward his seat. As it
got closer, all he could see were the eyes—glassy cat's eyes or ser-
pent's eyes, maybe the eyes of a person blind from cataracts. The
word "PAIN" droned through his mind as though spoken. But
also the words "APPLAUSE" and "MURDER" and "EMPIRE."
He saw the knife emerge in the hand of the shadow figure on the
screen and shut his eyes tightly, wanting to cry out.

Halkias opened them to daylight and a dashboard covered in
food wrappers, and clothes that were saturated with sweat.

He'd had nightmares since he could remember. When he was
younger there was a recurring dream where he would be chewing on broken glass. Sometimes his teeth were the glass shards.
Other times he'd be looking in a mirror and watching his mouth
bleed. Watching the blood run down his chin and neck, staining
his shirt. Most nightmares he didn't remember and he never knew

if he had pleasant dreams. He had a wife then and they stayed together for several years. She had insomnia, and when she was unconscious it never really felt like sleep. Because of this she would log his behavior during the nightmares. Mostly it was words he whispered or the way his eyelids moved. There were often screams. Halkias wasn't good at being a husband, lacking in many respects, specifically the attention he gave her, and eventually his wife left him for a professor at the university where she worked as a librarian. He no longer remembered where her logs were, if he had them or if she had kept them. This hadn't seemed important. He hadn't had the recurring dreams since she'd gone.

He had left the windows down. He was lucky no one had robbed him over the course of the night. He walked to the kiosk at the corner and plucked two canned beers out of the refrigerated display, and a small bag of ketchup chips.

"That looks like heartburn," the vendor said.

"If that's the worst it'll get, it's a good day."

"I know the feeling." But Halkias wasn't sure he did.

Halkias locked up the car and went for a walk. The city was making the transition toward morning. He stopped in front of the Panathinaiko stadium and sat on the marble, watching the early-bird visitors. He drank his beer and stared at the cylinder filled with cigarette butts in his hand. He kept telling them, "I'm going to figure you out," though it wasn't clear to him what that meant.

He'd check on the decedent's sister again, he figured, hoping she was okay. Hoping maybe she left on a flight home already. From what he could tell, everything around the expatriate was a real shit storm. He finished the first beer and crushed it under his shoe. The second one he drank slower, making it last. With the sun rising in the sky the city began getting progressively louder, more crowded. More buses unloaded elderly tourists and families in front of the stadium. To them he must have seemed a drunk or a tramp, though maybe he was only feeling that way, looking like another tourist, one enjoying a beer unusually early.

He couldn't remember the last time he'd been back to the station.

"The station," he said.

Before he ever thought of becoming a cop he had wanted to be a magician. He wasn't any good at tricks, even simple ones. He lacked quick fingers, the sight. But he obsessively watched magic shows and occult documentaries on television and he read books about different kinds of magicians. He'd read somewhere that the poet Pessoa had assisted the magician Crowley in faking his death. Becoming police was just something that happened after everything else didn't. He finished his breakfast and stayed a while before returning home to have a shower.

***

Marrast arrived back at the building in time to have the wind knocked out of her at the top of the stairwell, as someone in a hooded shirt shoved past and sprinted down the flight. She struggled to regain her breath before it occurred to her that the apartment had just been robbed. The door was open.

She cautiously approached, holding the key between her knuckles. The locked wasn't forced, which meant they'd had a key. It crossed her mind someone else could be waiting when she went in, but no one was.

The picture of her brother with the person that had probably been his girlfriend was now mostly ashes in the kitchen sink. What remained of it was the bottom corner, her brother's shirt sleeve and part of his arm. The smoke alarm, thankfully, hadn't been triggered. That would've been the last thing she needed, she was sure.

Marrast remembered the mobile phone was still in her purse. She got it out and held it to the light. There seemed nothing special about it except that it'd been his. "What were you getting yourself into, Quent?" She half-expected someone to respond.

Down one of the side streets off odos Athinas, she found an

electronics shop that had a compatible charger. She paid and asked if she could plug it in somewhere, just to turn on the phone. The clerk nodded his head upward *no*, then sighed when she slid a wad of bills across the counter. He let her come around to where an outlet was. Marrast waited for the phone to charge, only just noticing how sore she felt.

When the logo flashed on the touchscreen, she swiped the bottom to unlock the phone and was greeted by a numerical password screen. "Well, shit."

Marrast tried 1-2-3-4, then 4-3-2-1. She tried his birthday. Started to look at the letters associated with the numbers. Four-letter combinations her brother might have used. Her stomach was starting to feel the way it did right before she was going to start her period. Things she remembered Quentin liked or talked about... crime films, fishing, music, science... she tried C-A-R-P, then B-A-S-S, then P-U-L-P, and several others until she typed N-A-S-A and the phone clicked over to the home screen. Something fell in the shop, startling her. The clerk looked up at her impatiently from a bin of spare parts he had knocked over.

There were messages from a woman labeled "Hara," revealing an affair that had ended badly. There were mentions of another woman, Leona, who seemed unaware. Hara was furious that he'd been indecisive or that there'd been another, which wasn't clear. But why wasn't it with the police? She checked the directory. Only the one contact. Most of the recent exchanges between the two were hostile—"so ur following us"... "please stop"... "is there something wrong with me"... "why did you do that"—revealing a side of Quentin she'd never seen. The first messages on the phone, and the last chronologically, read "can't wait to see u tonight, have something to show u," then, "shit. ignore this. not for u." But the further back the dates of the messages went, and it'd gone on for the better part of a year, the less antagonistic they seemed. The more explicit too. There were photos, some that had him in them, and this made Marrast hate him some. One photo was different from the rest, a photo of an old, indigo door with the number "3" on it. The door looked familiar, like something she'd passed in the old town without a second look. And there was something about it she found beautiful, the way the paint was bubbled and peeling, the color that contrasted the graying rot of the wood.

Her eyes lit up and she unplugged the charger and left.

***

Elsewhere a shadow drifts along the paths of the market, invisible to everything around it. Time moving slower here. It has named its pieces on the board. It has nudged things in a direction they otherwise would not have gone. A series of interlocking parts to be arranged any which way it sees fit. Millennia ago it was gifted hecatomb by those who understood its existence. Men have since forgotten it, but it has not forgotten them. It caresses the face of a teenage girl looking at a shop window. For her the contact is so brief she will not understand that this is the moment her destiny shifted. In two years, they will meet again as she sleeps in a bathtub, draining a feeling that seems linked to the blood inside her. The shadow continues its drift, uncertain if being a secret is better than being known.

***

It took over an hour wandering through Plaka, crisscrossing back and forth along the maze of side streets, before she found the right building. The flier on the door read "MINERVA 13:15," with a poorly drawn image of a figure in black brandishing a knife, blood dripping off its tip. Marrast opened the door and stepped inside.

An usher sat on a stool beside a popcorn machine and a cooler filled with refreshments. He told her the price of admission and she paid him and he handed her a bag of popcorn. Marrast followed the corridor down to the two great doors at the end of it. Darkly-painted plywood floor shifted with each step. There weren't many people inside the auditorium. Maybe a dozen or so, their heads contrasted by the light from the screen. She found a seat at the back of the auditorium.

The film opened with a progressive rock soundtrack heavy with synth over a black screen. The music like something she'd heard before, in some other film. Slow, steady drumming. Title card.

Exterior shot, handheld: a restaurant, a couple sitting outdoors. The footage was grainy, but she could make out the faces. Marrast mouthed "what the fuck"—her brother and his girlfriend, eating.

Whispered narration she couldn't understand—it was in Greek.

Cut to the couple elsewhere, dressed differently, having ice cream by the flea market. Shot of an angry dog barking at the camera. Pan up to reveal a lone figure walking down the street, closing in to reveal it as Leona, wearing different clothes again. This was happening over a series of days, maybe weeks or months. Leona checking her phone and texting. Turning down side streets and looking back. Suddenly aware she was being followed.

Heavy breathing, synth, more whispering. Cut to close-up of Leona's face: she was very beautiful and very terrified. Cut to a hand holding a knife. Knife entering skin, clothing. Blood, lots and lots of blood.

Marrast nervously ate popcorn, looking around at the people there. Everyone immersed in the footage. The stabbing continued, excessively.

A steadier shot of the empty street at night, the body prone and bleeding into the cracks of the marble, out front of the store.

Scene change: shot of a coffin, elsewhere, maybe a crypt. But it looked more like a room set up to seem like a crypt. Everything lit red and violet.

Marrast looked over at the exit. The doors were shut. She didn't hear them shut. She wanted to run out, but knew she had to stay because there was more.

The coffin lid raised. A ghoul inside, face covered in gray makeup and rotting-effect prosthetics. Still, there was something about it that offended Marrast. The combination of this more steadily filmed footage and the hastily filmed murder. Marrast checked her phone discreetly; no service. Checked her brother's phone, the same.

The synth playing increased in tempo, drums still steady. The old woman in the coffin opened her eyes synchronous to a cymbal crash, startling Marrast. The scene changed to the exterior of a bar, shot from a distance. Her brother staggered out, visibly upset. Orange lit streets. He looked worn out, resembled little of the man she knew.

Marrast looked down and noticed the popcorn was nearly gone. She laughed to herself. Someone in the theater whispered *"Shhhh."*

The killer started to follow her brother, stopping to look in a glassy display. Marrast could tell she was a woman, the person from the affair, the one who loved her brother. Head-on reflection. But where was the cameraman? Her gloved hands covered the face on the glass and the camera resumed following Quentin. From there, the footage became static, like a flawed transmission, jumping frame and dissolving into noise and back again. Her brother being strangled in the ruins. Looking helplessly up at the viewer. Eyes pathetically wide. This was almost comical; Marrast was surprised to find herself enjoying this. The footage continued to cut from shots of the coffin to shots of the murder. The ghoul began to change through lap-dissolve, until she resembled their mother somewhat, until she was their mother. The killer plunged the knife into Quentin's chest over and over, then cut his throat. Celia Marrast started to think that this was great, this could have been the greatest, most hilarious thing she'd ever seen.

"I never want this to end," she whispered.

***

At the detective's house, crime scene photographs were a collage on the wall of his bedroom. The cigarette butts were laid out on the nightstand and he presently sat, staring at them. Across the floor, photos of the body of Leona Pardi, from multiple angles. He had an envelope filled with a lock of her hair that he kept beneath his pillow. Sigils marked various points on the ceiling. He concentrated, trying to levitate the cigarette butts, but he couldn't get them to move. He couldn't help but feel he'd never truly understand magic.

Outside, the sky flashed red, then yellow, then everything went violet and stayed that way. He pulled the curtains shut and looked at his body in the mirror. His mutilated penis was hidden beneath a thick mound of hair. Reminding him of what he used to be, what he was becoming. Halkias opened a drawer on the nightstand, the one where he kept his gun. For a moment he was sure he'd use it, but he reached instead for an open pack of peppermint Chiclets and chewed two, wondering how long it'd been since he'd last smoked.

IN THE FLAT LIGHT

ADAM CESARE

Are you sure you want to set up there?"

"*Scuze?*"

Sergio pointed to the small digital camera and made a line with his finger that transformed into an open hand as he indicated what part of the room the lens was going to catch.

"You're shooting white walls, straight on. It's just that it—It won't look very interesting, especially as we approach noon, when the sun comes through there," Sergio said and indicated his office window.

"Signore, where would you like us to set up?" the reporter asked, putting her hand on her cameraman's shoulder, like she was preparing him for a move.

Sergio was about to say that it didn't matter, that he was already sitting and didn't want to move his ass out of the chair and find a new spot in the living room. He didn't get to say any of that because the cameraman spoke first.

"We can use the space on the bottom of the frame for a bumper and the white space on the side for any split-screen. To show clips or stills from your work, Maestro. Don't worry."

Sergio wasn't worried, didn't worry about things he wasn't getting paid for, other people's work.

The cameraman was young and when he called Sergio *Maestro* he meant it. The boy's voice was heavy with reverence and Sergio guessed that somewhere in his equipment bag was a DVD, maybe a videotape, that he would be asked to sign after they wrapped. The kid might even try to do it surreptitiously, keep it from his boss who might consider that type of thing unprofessional.

"Can you talk for me?" the girl asked, and Sergio was roused from his thoughts, his presaging of a possible fan interaction.

He didn't ask her what she meant, just looked up and arched his eyebrows. He was not used to being commanded to speak, he didn't even make his dog do that.

"You can count, or say testing. It's just for levels."

He cleared his throat and spoke, trying not to look like he was playing towards the small microphone clipped to his lapel. He knew that these things were designed to hear without any of that.

"One. Two. My name is Sergio Martin—"

"Perfect. You can stop," she said, turning away from the small lighted console she'd been watching and sitting down in the chair opposite him. She was short with him, but Sergio didn't blame her. She wasn't just talent but the producer of her own piece and quite busy from the look of things. He understood and empathized with the pressure, even if he'd never worked in television himself.

The girl—*young woman*, he corrected himself, most people were girls and boys to him at his age—was beautiful and Sergio noted that she used that beauty as an asset, an embellishment to enhance her professionalism and intelligence, not detract from it.

She was a woman who knew that all eyes were on her at all times and she'd acclimated her life to it.

Her name must not have been nearly as memorable as her face, otherwise Sergio would have been able to recall what it was.

The signal that she was ready to begin went unspoken, she hadn't even looked at the cameraman but still his eye was pressed into the viewfinder and there was some kind of chirp from his device, the red dot under his pointer finger illuminating.

Sergio had been impressed by her on the phone, her tenacity, but watching her work up close he had a whole new appreciation. She would have been great on set, if she'd been born to a different time.

"The first thing I notice, Signore Martinelli, is that your apartment doesn't look at all like I'd imagined it would."

If this question was going where he thought it was going, he was ready to mark it as a demerit against her. *I expected it to be a dungeon, skulls and spider webs and skeletons, but you're such a nice man.* But he decided to give her a chance and listen to the rest.

"While we were setting up you commented on your white walls, I have to admit that I was expecting something more," she invoked a pause, not to think but for effect, "dynamic. Colorful, maybe. In more than one way."

The interview was beginning by focusing on style over content. That was good, he knew there was a reason he'd said yes, even if he couldn't remember it now, their phone call subsumed by the fog in his mind.

It hadn't been because he was familiar with the program; he owned a television but it wasn't connected to the outside world, even the antenna had stopped working and he hadn't gotten more than the local stations when it had.

"Have you not heard of the virtues of a *clean, well-lighted place?*" Sergio answered her non-question with a question, saying the last part in English. He was trying to keep cool but his self-consciousness kept him wondering if any of this would be going into the final program, or if these were merely warm-up questions.

"Clean and well-lighted," she said, repeating his words back to him. "Hemingway?"

"Correct. If I were going to quote an American you were expecting Poe?" Sergio asked, doing on his own what he'd been expecting her to do: shackling himself to a genre.

"Not necessarily, I may have went to France first, though, maybe de Sade?"

Sergio laughed, not sure whether it would sound fake or not, once it filtered down through the microphone. Second chances in the recording booth were one of the many advantages of never rolling live sound, but he guessed that she didn't have that option. Gathering his words, in his own voice, was the point of this whole exercise.

She didn't ask a follow-up question, kept still in her seat while he felt himself shift in his. The folds in her skirt were immaculately demure, sexy without being revealing, and her stockings were so smooth, the fibers so finely woven, that it was difficult to discern if she was wearing any at all.

Without her talking, he felt compelled to. On a conscious level he knew this must be a fairly common interview trick, withholding, but he admired her and opened up anyway.

"People often ask why I don't throw up some color, how I could have been such a stylist on-screen and not at home, but I always answer that movies should be more exciting, more exotic than real life, especially mine."

"You said 'could have been.' Do you not continue to be a director, even into retirement? If that's what we're calling it."

"What we're calling it? I quit," Sergio said, not even knowing he was hot until he felt the air against the cool sweat on his brow and felt the vibrations of his own raised voice bounce back against the walls of his office.

"I didn't mean to upset you," she said and leaned forward in her seat, her hand appearing on his knee.

"Of course not, I," he paused, embarrassed. "Next question, please." If there was a way to mop his face without looking even more distressed for the camera he would, but there wasn't, so he opted to stay still and focus on his breathing.

"As you wish. Continuing on the theme of literature, I was browsing your bookcase in the other room. I didn't see much in the way of the phantasmagorical, the horrific; are those kinds of stories not to your tastes anymore?"

He knew she'd taken too long after she'd asked him where his bathroom was, she'd been snooping.

It was a fair question, he tried to tell himself that before answering, but it was hot in here and he was getting agitated, confused.

"I don't know how closely you looked," he said, more attitude than he wanted, "but there are several mysteries there, crime stories. That's what my films are, crime stories. Just because they look fantastical, that doesn't make them fantasies."

It was a permutation of an answer he'd given several times, it made it easier to say, as if he had a script to guide him along, through the gas bubbles in his stomach, the wetness under his arms.

She didn't bite, didn't believe the stock answer.

"That's not entirely true. Your last film, *The Black Concerto*, dealt heavily with the occult."

Sergio didn't remember all the conditions but he did remember that she agreed not to mention the accident. But that didn't mean that her questions weren't going to try to fly as close to the sun as possible.

"I," he searched for the words, "I don't consider that a supernatural film, its horrific sequences can all be attributed to the protagonist's deteriorating mental state. There is nothing explicitly supernatural about it."

There was no curl to her lips, her mouth an unreadable line, the rest of her face just relaxed enough to match it.

"Come now," she began and smiled, "even your mysteries aren't really mysteries. Mechanically. They aren't tightly plotted who-done-its. Frankly, most of them don't add up, you put the emphasis on all the wrong clues. They work on dream logic, do they not?"

"*Si*, I guess they do," Sergio said, impressed even further, but walking into a trap.

"So if they are dark dreams—nightmares—are nightmares not fantastical?"

How did this girl know exactly the word to say? he thought.

It was his last cogent thought before he felt his back go limp, the word 'nightmare' emblazoned on the office carpet as he slumped and plummeted face-first into it.

***

"No TV," Sergio said, wielding the words like a shield. Shields are only effective for so long, though, especially when you're backed into a corner.

"It wouldn't even be like TV. No studio, no fixed cameras. You could shoot it like you would a movie, only shorter," Andre said. "It's one hour, a pilot for a series you have to have no involvement in outside of your name. Why not take the money?"

"Give up my name, you mean. Have no involvement either way, you mean. Even if it's shit, it'll be shit presented by Sergio Martinelli."

"Is that so bad?" Andre said, so tired he was almost panting. They were stuck in a closed circuit, running through a version of this same conversation all afternoon, every angle exhausted for both of them.

"One for them, one for me?"

"Of course, they're excited about your script," Andre said, looking like he was going to break out in tears, the way marathoners cross the finish line sometimes.

"Payment upfront. I get to do *The Black Concerto* first?"

"They may never go for that, but I can try," Andre said, willing to agree to the impossible just to make this meeting end.

This stipulation, this impossible clause, was the reason that Sergio Martinelli had never done TV.

***

Sergio was not so much rising up out of unconsciousness as he was bobbing, the water he was treading too thin to support him, his body too dense to float.

Above him, twisting as if buffeted by a strong wind, was a light fixture he recognized as belonging in his office.

Only no, someone had replaced the bulbs or thrown two strong gels on either side of the light and the ceiling and walls were coated in vibrant purples and greens.

The lights began to flash, no flicker, as the flames of his nightmare ate him up.

***

The budgets were getting smaller. It was nothing that was Sergio's fault, the industry wasn't doing well, was on life support, but he couldn't help but feel a responsibility.

That was the other side of the double-edged blade that was the auteur theory. If a director wanted to take credit for the beautiful shots of the D.P., the script's best lines, then he also had to take responsibility for what didn't work. Therefore Sergio could not pass the blame even if the problems were out of his control, were due to the nation's economy.

This was a philosophy he would spend the second half of his life regretting, but on set of *The Black Concerto* it hadn't yet begun to erode his stomach lining, only spurred him into the breach, trying to make the best film he possibly could with limited resources.

It was the last day on set, had to be because they were about to burn the place down.

The script called for a cataclysmic fire. *His* script that he'd adapted from a garishly over-written draft by some toady fiction writer who would now have to take 'story by' credit.

Living a film for whatever span of weeks and months you could squeeze out of your budget, your stars, could give a director an odd form of tunnel vision. Highway hypnosis, how you get so intent on watching the lines in the road flash by that you don't see the approaching turn until it is too late.

Six weeks into *The Black Concerto*, no second unit, only Sergio and his small crew, too few of them with their union cards, he was feeling that hypnosis, that numbness of living half-in and half-out of a fantasy world.

Most of the money had gone into the sets and although they weren't overly expansive, many of the backings needing to be re-dressed and doubled, the rooms were real to him when he was standing in them.

Around the second week the tracks and wires underfoot became invisible, the draped windows ready to be thrown open to let the sunlight in, even though they were in a dim warehouse outside of Terni.

He'd tried to find a real hotel, preferably one facing an opera house, but none of them were able to shut down for the amount of days required. So they'd built one. Movie magic.

"Natalie, you stay inside this mark," he said, indicating the taped-off circle surrounding them, "and you only run towards the camera when I tell you to. All your lines, all your emotion, inside here."

The girl nodded. She'd been so eager a month and a half ago, and although she was tired, she'd rallied for this last day. He could see the excitement of having her first feature in the can apparent in her eyes, her smile.

She was in her early twenties, barely the Lolita detective that he had her playing, but still he couldn't help but feel she'd grown up during *The Black Concerto*.

Sergio remembered thinking something along the lines of: *my camera has taken the youth from her, she may do many more films, have a long career, but she will never look as beautiful as she does under my lights.*

It was a thought he was glad he'd never vocalized, something that could have tipped the scales in court and still haunted him, internally.

Natalie looked up to where the two men on ladders were painting their flame jelly, the fumes from the chemicals only just starting to make the warehouse reek like a petrol station.

Every man who wasn't helping move the camera had a fire extinguisher clenched in their hands.

His assistant director, a fresh-faced kid who'd worked with stunt coordinators before on big American shows even though *The Black Concerto* didn't have one built into the budget, had offered Sergio an extinguisher, but he refused. He would be busy directing, as the flames were growing.

They'd reloaded just for this, had seven minutes worth of film in the camera, ready to roll out or get as close as they could to it. Sergio put a hand on his D.P.'s shoulder, let him know that he was behind him, ready to ride the dolly rails together as they pushed in.

They would begin in a wide shot, catch the beginning of the blaze, then press close to get Natalie's reaction and finally her panicked flight.

They'd already shot the exteriors, her character falling into the arm of a firefighter and whispering something cryptic before passing out, but they still needed to film the model of the hotel going up in flames.

With these three shots and a handful of inserts of Natalie's hands fumbling with doorknobs, Sergio would be able to cut them together into true art: an ambiguous climax that challenged the audience to decide for themselves whether the blaze had supernatural or terrestrial origins.

There were callbacks to his earlier work, masked figures in black gloves spying on his protagonist, but there were also those nightmare sequences. Like Hecate and the Weird Sisters in *Macbeth*, their strange non-bearing on the events of the play. The meaning of the film was so illusory that Sergio himself had not yet decided where he stood, probably wouldn't until the workprint.

"Remember: emote, don't be afraid to go big. We need to get it in one," he told Natalie, the girl nodding to him, looking nervous.

He didn't know if her fear was stemming from the two men dismounting their ladders and grabbing their hand torches or the fact that she had only one take.

Sergio was only concerned with the take.

That night blindness you get on a set blocks out the real world. The knives aren't real, the guns aren't real, not even the walls or the sun is real. Nothing on set can hurt you.

"You there," the D.P. said and looked up from the viewfinder, yelling to one of the grips, "take two steps to your right." He put his face back in the camera. "Better."

"Good?" Sergio asked.

"As it's going to get," the cameraman said.

"Roll camera."

"Rolling."

"Cue fire," Sergio said and the men touched their open flames to the wet spots on the walls, the D.P. moving his hand on the focus ring to compensate for the new light.

"Action, Natalie."

She screamed, cheating her body out slightly as she faced the corner, her face and the silhouette of her figure highlighted by her position to the camera and flame.

There would be such dimensionality to the shot, the furnishings of the room also brushed with the firestarter, igniting in an elegant line as the camera began to track forward in one smooth motion.

Sergio wished he could see what the D.P. was seeing, had to use his imagination to cut out everything around him that wouldn't be in the frame.

"It's you, it's you," Natalie yelled, forming the words with her lips more than she had to, she'd be speaking at least three different languages once they recorded the dialogue and that was only the territories they'd presold. "Why are you doing this?" she asked no one.

Sergio liked the dialogue, wondered how it would translate. There was something profound in her revelation, even if the audience wouldn't know what she was referring to, who she was asking these questions of.

The curtains caught fire, the blast of heated wind causing them to billow out at just the right moment, Natalie turning to look, her character maybe catching a glimpse of the arsonist's gloved hand, maybe not.

They were almost to the end of the track now, Sergio's hand still on the cameraman's shoulder, the man's polo sticky with sweat under his fingers. Around them, men cursed and yelled.

"Quiet on set," Sergio yelled to them, even though their shouting hardly mattered. The noise wasn't damaging Natalie's performance as she dashed to one edge of her circle, then the other, looking for a way out.

The sweat caked her, giving her so much of a sheen that she herself could be counted as a light source if they were as tight on her face as he wanted to be.

A few more seconds, he told himself, saw the D.P.'s hand move the zoom back, in-camera zooms were something they could hide with cuts, if it came to it.

There was a puff of cool air behind him, one of the crewmembers letting off a controlled blast of fire extinguisher dust.

"Not yet," he cried, not turning to admonish the man, still watching the set in front of him, some of the plywood beginning to show under the bubbling wallpaper, not looking very much like a centuries-old hotel anymore.

Two more seconds, they could use the coverage.

That's when the first ember touched Natalie's hair, the orange blob tumbling down and brushing against her ear.

Natalie turned as if she'd been slapped, looking Sergio in the eye, which was bad but at least she hadn't looked into the camera.

She was at the edge of her mark, breaking character and looking more perturbed than frightened.

This is the exact moment that Sergio would scrutinize the most heavily, in the days and years that followed. It's hard to remember what you feel from moment to moment, attitudes shift and change, are especially volatile on set, but in his nightmares he could remember being angry at Natalie for having her ear scorched, for allowing herself to feel pain and letting it shake her performance.

It wasn't fair and it shamed him later, but it was what he felt and he can't take it back.

She pleaded with him using her eyes, not breaking her mark. He held a finger out, giving her the one-second sign. It could have been one minute, it wouldn't have mattered.

A piece of flaming molding peeled off the top of the set wall and hit Natalie just above her nose. Embers flew off the wood and ignited her hair and then her blouse. The top was a polyester blend that she'd been wearing all shoot and was soaked through with perfume because they couldn't properly wash it.

The crewmembers that had been so quick with their extinguishers when it didn't matter stood around her, stunned as they watched her flare, their hands frozen by inaction.

"Cut," Sergio yelled after a moment's delay that would become a longer span of time in his dreams, in a prosecutor's notebook.

It took the men another second to realize that he meant they should put her out, that the show was over.

***

Sergio awoke on the floor of his office, the light above him not yet back to normal.

Not true: it was dark now, the neon from the clubs and takeout joints across the street painting his white ceilings orange and blue, as they always did.

It was a nice composition, something he would have worked for hours to achieve, in his younger days.

The tripod was no longer in the room, the boy's camera bag, too.

They were both gone, the young woman and her servant, the girl who'd so impressed him with her professionalism.

Sergio turned onto his side, not noticing the pin until he attempted a push-up and drove the sharp end into the flesh of his midsection.

He hadn't been harmed on purpose, left booby-trapped. There was a note pinned to his shirt. He stood before reading it, daubing the pinprick on his chest, letting the fabric of his shirt soak up the blood, the tiny pattern something he would have killed for in a macro shot.

Sergio moved to his desk to switch on the lamp, but instead opted to angle the paper against the window, the colored light from the street being ample to read by and having much more character to it.

"Thank you for giving us what we needed. You look to be making a full recovery."

The note was signed with a flourish reserved for celebrities and football stars, completely illegible, the signature meant as its own pronunciation. Even with the hint, he still couldn't remember the name.

Sergio tucked the note away in his desk drawer and sat down to try and remember what the young woman's name had been and what network she had been employed by.

It was a mystery he would turn over in his mind for the rest of his life, if not his career.

TERROR IN THE HOUSE OF BROKEN BELLES

NIKKI GUERLAIN

error in the House of Broken Belles... Terror in the House of Broken Bells...

Yeah, that's pretty much running nonstop in my head. Any time now I full expect someone to jump out of a bush and lunge at me. They're probably not going to look like Traci Lords. I'm guessing like maybe a thin creepy dude in a Steve Buscemi mask or maybe Cher. Cher in a Cher mask—now that would be good.

Terror in the House of Broken Belles... Terror in the House of Broken Belles...

I wonder if by bells they mean like bells that ring or whether they mean like belles like girls, you know, southern gals all pecan pie and iced tea and biscuits? Are we talking about broken instruments or broken women? Both prospects sound oddly arousing. It could be both. It could be. Now I'm just getting greedy.

Terror in the House of Broken Belles... Terror in the House of Broken Belles...

***

It's raining, a fine phantasmagoric mist, and the wet street shimmers with the neon lights vibrating above it. The lights throb, vibrant and buzzy buzzzz like insect zappers. The air is salty and thick and cold while my blood is hot and pheromone-y, sticky with something weird in it. It's making the ME part of me feel like hot goo swimming through cold bones. I feel nommy. I feel like I want to get inside something and have something get inside of me. Where am I? I'm here. I'm pretty sure. Interstitially speaking.

Eyes open real wide to catch all that delicious cold mist. Membranes love misssst. I slake off the water that my face skin has warmed to allow it to be kissed by cooler misssst. The air tastes complex like sea salt, pine trees and smoked meats.

Meats.

Rain ssstopssss.

Meatsssss.

I'm on my tippy toes, inhaling sharply, my tongue and face thrust into the air to get more of whatever it is I want to get—I don't know. I don't think I care. I just want more.

The street is desolate except for a handful of smokers securing shelter under the cover of a tattered bar eave. They pay me no mind. Just continue smoking and vaping, smelling like cherries and tobacco, their eyes glassy and red. They should really wet them.

After some time I locate the building I want. It smells like the coast even though it's over sixty miles away. A group of seagulls has flown inland. They land all at once, surround the building, block the stairs descending down to the bar. A giant porn emporium called The Horny Piggy takes up the first three floors of the building while the unmarked bar takes up the basement. As I approach the building the seagulls evaluate me strangely. Their movements are too slow, too languid, too intelligent. Their eyes glint neon light like little slicks of motor oil. They caw to each other in feminine voices. Makes my skin rise in prickles of gooseflesh and my head goo grow chilly spilling down my spine into the stirring heat of my pelvis. There's a dancing neon sign of a pig wearing a horned berserker helmet and a pitchfork hanging on the front of the building.

Here piggy! Here piggy pig! Here pig! We'll make you squeal like the horny pig you are! Just step right in and we'll take care of you for suuuuuuey!!!

Some sort of motion-activated recording, obviously. Bags of popcorn and cotton candy as well as long rainbow suckers like unicorn horns hang in the windows. I'm a horny piggy. I want to go!

Juice firssssst.

Hmmm. Juice. Downstairs first then. The seagulls shriek excitedly as they part down the middle to allow my passage. Their loud caws and powerful batting wings send ripples of terror and exhilaration through me. I stand there a moment, unsure of my bearings, trying to collect my thoughts which seem to slip away from me in some sort of euphoria, replaced by *I want more* and *caw*. The rustle of their flapping wings as they take flight sends new ripples through me as if every action of the seagulls is a rock thrown into my waters. My pelvis grows heavy, the flesh nestled within it taut with fresh hot blood. It gets heavier, more engorged with each step I descend like I'm being pulled down pelvis first.

Get your peanuts! Fresh hot peanuts!

Carnival music begins to play on the porn store speaker.

I open the door to the bar. A warm whoosh of humid air comes at me. The room is dark and dank like a cave lit by candles. The candles flicker strange shapes onto the plaster ceiling as if they are shimmering up from the bottom of a tide pool. The coastal smell is more prominent down here. The tables are made of rough-hewn wood and are decorated with shells filled to the brim with black shiny things like beetles without legs. There's an empty, slightly elevated stage at the back. Ocean waves mix with the low murmur of intimate conversations. The patrons wear beautiful primitive clothing clasped with gold fasteners in sea creature shapes. The women turn away from their conversations to stare at me, mutely, their shifting black eyes boring into me and my extremely casual wear, I am sure. Very suddenly and quite simultaneously they turn their attentions back to their men. All except for a woman with shiny black hair, glowing mother of pearl skin and eyes that even under this low light radiate like creamy jade lamps.

Severine.

Her eyes pull me hot goo first across the strange room, straight to her. She does not move from the table but waits for me to slide into the seat next to her. I slide in. Her dress is made of a luxurious metallic crimson material that flashes subtle green and blue fire like a boulder opal. The shoulders and waist are fastened with ruby-encrusted seahorse clasps. Her hair is pulled back with gold coral-shaped combs lined with fuchsia tourmaline. Her cheekbones are severe and her nose has a bird-like quality to it. There's a milky glowing fluid moving like a cloud billowing within a delicate glass sitting in front of her. That's the juice. That's the shit right there. I've already had me some of that tonight. She lifts her drink in one long languid movement and parts her seashell-pink lips to sip from it. She gracefully places the drink down on the table and pushes it my way.

"Drink."

I eagerly lift the drink to my lips, smell the strange yet familiar scent of licorice and other herbal essences. As it touches my tongue I feel the sun upon my shoulders, the cotton candy melting on my tongue, the crashing of the sea upon my rocks, the blast of shotguns wash through my wind. I drain the glass completely. The colors of the room grow more marine, the movements of the others in the room more alien. Everything vibrates in and out, lulling me into a simple-minded hot mess sitting next to her. Buoys bob, foghorns roar, water splashes against anchored boats, waves crash upon rocks echo inside cave… conversations turn into a smattering of seagulls coo.

"What is this place?" I have forgotten why I am here and what here is.

"It is everything you deserve and more," she replies. Her voice is strange and shimmery, delicious and entrancing. I grow oozy and anxious. My heart pounds heart pounds madly but it feels strangely dislocated and I worry that I will pass out.

"I think I've had too much to drink," I say, though I can form the words just fine. I'm seized with the mad desire to smash my mouth into Severine's and take her right here in front of everyone. I feel rapey. Scared. Confused. Lost. Out of control.

"I think you have not had enough," she says. She motions to the bartender for another round of drinks. "Fear is good."

The waiter brings our drinks and I use the opportunity to more closely observe the other patrons. My initial assessment was wrong. Not all of the patrons wear the beautiful primitive clothing that Severine wears—only the women do. The men are all dressed casually like me. The women move strangely, their faces and bodies blur and flicker in and out of focus into beastlike forms. The men start to cry. I shake my head and rub my eyes to ensure that what I am seeing is actually what I am seeing and it is. My vision has never been so clear, every detail delineated so clearly. I can see all the individual jewels in the women's clothing. The men sob louder and begin to wail while the women smile at them.

"I need to get out of here," I say. I can't breathe. I need to get a grip.

"I need you inside me," she whispers. Her skin seems to ripple. Her image blinkers in and out into something sponge-like and holey. I lean into her. She smells like warm sand. The scent makes me quiver and stiffen beneath the table. "You look like a man who has lost someone special."

"My son," I say, tears streaking hotly down burning cheeks. My throat knots. Severine takes my face into her hands and forces me to look straight into her green lamp eyes. Ashamedly, I feel the meat between my legs pulse and strain against my jeans.

"You feel guilty, responsible. Why?"

"Because his spine slowly rotted from cancer and I couldn't stand to be around him so I drank myself into oblivion and buried myself in my work." My body shudders with sobs but she won't let my face go and I can't make myself break free, can't break free from those eyes. "Just let me go—"

"You don't really want to go, do you? There's more."

"I wasn't there when he died. He called out for me as he lay dying but the hospital couldn't reach me. My wife was there but he wanted his daddy and I wasn't there. I wasn't there for him."

"And why couldn't they reach you?" Severine's grip on my face grows stronger, more severe. "Your child lay dying in the hospital, Michael, and he's calling for his daddy but you aren't there. Where are you? What is daddy doing while his child gasps for life?"

"I'm drunk, in bed with another woman and my phone is turned off."

Severine pushes my face into her breasts, coddles me, strokes my hair, rocks my helpless form. "There, there. Get it all out. Shhh."

Her breasts are warm and soothing. I hear her heart reverberate queerly through her chest. It's more a murmur than a steady beat. Slow. Calm. Peaceful. I no longer cry. I feel lighter, deliciously disconnected, and the only part of me that aches is what she's stroking beneath the table. The men at the other tables are similarly being comforted by their women, but the women have grown grotesque, undefined, more beastly. I realize that these she-beasts aren't washing away our sins, they're reveling in them. Surely this isn't going to end well.

Just then strange bells ring queerly through the room and vibrate everything. The ringing wavers in and out, first close then distant then close again like the ringing of bells carried by wind. There's an overall staticky sound to their rings like they're being heard through a bum radio. I feel electric and hungry, so violently hungry.

Terror in the House of Broken Belles... Terror in the House of Broken Belles...

There's that again. The bells quit ringing and when they do crimson stage curtains open into a dark stage and I don't know how but we're standing in the front row. Eyes like a cat's at night reflect black and hollow from the darkness. Severine is behind me, stroking my meat and breathing hotly into my neck. Slowly she begins to undress me. The stage is suddenly bathed in hot pink light like we're looking onto some foreign karaoke bar. The stage contains an electric potter's wheel. A she-beast sits at the wheel. A man enters the stage. He's silent, completely naked. His penis is erect and his eyes are hollow. The she-beast beckons him to her wheel. A large metal spike protrudes from its center. She takes his swollen meat into her mouth and performs fellatio on him to the groans and sighs of the audience. Severine fondles my balls. Everyone always forgets about the balls. It's strange that I haven't come already. I feel like I could go forever. The air is steeped in the smell of sex and rain on stones after a long summer. The she-beast's skin takes on a stone-like appearance, her features becoming more rigid and stern. The blowjob grows angry and the scent of blood wafts through the room electrically. But the man, the man continues to pump into her face, oblivious.

"That's Leda and her potter, William. He failed his child too but much more intimately, if you catch my drift."

Hot anger rises in my throat as I watch the potter thrust in and out of Leda's rigid throat and imagine what he did to some poor little boy or girl. The man groans and spasms, driving himself deep into Leda. Her throat visibly expands. Leda removes her mouth from the twitching man, looks out to the audience with blood, jissom and meat dripping down her chin and her front, her eyes like black lights set into her skull. The blood, as well, appears black under the heavy pink light. What's left of the man's penis hangs limp, shredded, dripping blood and cum. It looks like he stuck his junk in a belt sander. She pulls him down to kiss her but when he bends down she rips his head clean off. Blood spurts out across the audience, the stage, painting the air with wings of black crimson. The women lick their lips and coo while the men continue to groan under the hands of the women. The man's body falls to the ground with a dull thud. A black mist rises from it and I want it inside me. I'm hungry. I pull it to me with my need and take it inside my mouth, inside every little part of me. I want more.

Leda impales William's head on the wheel's spike, then triggers its spinning using her foot. She calmly uses her stony hands to mold the head. Her hands are strong and make the head appear as if it's made of cream cheese rather than muscle and bone. The sound is wet and gristly as his face is torn and worn away by her gritty touch. The broken bells begin ringing once more as the curtains close to the smell of hot bone. The women clap vigorously. The men groan under the women's touch. His death feels beautiful and poetic and the memories of his murder flicker brightly within my blood like an old-time movie played at the wrong speed.

The bells stop ringing.

Everyone is abuzz and festive and it's beginning to feel a lot like Christmas. Christmas music begins to play in the background. Drinks are brought and bodies momentarily disengage to receive them. Everyone tosses them back in one fell swoop. Bodies meld once more. The flavor in my mouth shifts from licorice spice to sugar cookies to eggnog to cordial cherries like some boozy everlasting gobstopper. Severine licks my throat with her long, very thin tongue. "I can taste him inside of you."

"I want more."

"And you shall have it." My meat is purple and achy and slick with blood. Severine brushes her fingertips lightly down its shaft sending sparks of electricity throughout my goo.

"I want you to kiss it," I say, feeling more demanding.

"Not yet," she says, placing one of my hands through a secret slit in her gown, guiding me to her slippery gash. She grinds her pelvis against my palm as my fingers penetrate her. There's something large and foreign up there, and it has the texture of a hot beef tongue. She pulls my hand away. "Just a taste. Don't get greedy."

I lift my fingers to my mouth and suck her juice off of my fingers. She tastes like copper and brine. Severine removes my fingers from my mouth, then places them inside her mouth, suckles them too. "Good."

Once again, the bells ring and the curtains open to darkness and a set of night cat she-beast eyes. The stage floods with red light.

Blood and gore still cover the stage but the potter's wheel has been replaced by a hammock set in some kind outdoor barbecue scene. A man enters the stage. Like the last man he is naked and has a boner but is a bit more on the plump side. The she-beast beckons the man to climb into the hammock, which he does. The she-beast plants kisses down his fat stomach. Dark hairs sprout from her skin as she goes down on him. The smell of wet grass and something faintly insectile permeates the room. And blood. Everything still smells like blood. Severine runs her fingers through my hair, whispers into my ear, "That is Camille and her weaver, Sammy. He shook his girlfriend's baby to death. Now she'll turn him into a shake and he will die." These words excite me terribly but Severine won't let me come. But the lucky bastard on stage does and real quick too. A real two-pump chump. Camille removes her mouth from Sammy's twitching meat. Jissom drips off of her fangs, down her chin. She spins the hammock around Sammy so that he is cocooned except for his head and his penis which she has carefully parted the fibers to reveal. She opens Sammy's mouth and regurgitates a stream of blood, cum and venom slur into it. His flesh sizzles upon contact and he scream-gurgles madly, sending waves of euphoria throughout the audience. Bravo! Bravo! Sammy's cheeks sink in as they're enzymatically digested. Camille moves down to his still-erect whang and bites down on it, begins to noisily suck out his stewed flesh while he's still alive. The audience goes wild with applause. His form caves in and he finally dies, his black mist rising for me to take it inside me. Sammy's bright death images strobe between William's and I want more.

The bells break and ring once again as the curtains close.

Another round of drinks is passed around and everyone is handed a sparkler. Music turns to Black Betty and flavors turn go from cherry pie with vanilla ice cream to baked beans and barbequed ribs. The room flickers festively with burning phosphorous. Everybody smiles.

"Tell me, ghostwriter, why are all of these men artists?" she asks.

"Because only artists deserve such beautiful deaths," I reply.

Severine laughs. "And why are all that are chosen are men?"

"Because we're disgusting cowards and we take solace in flesh and we deserve this," I reply.

"Tres bien, Ghostie. Tres bien."

"Can I come now?" I ask.

"Not yet," she replies. "You have so much more to take in."

"I want more."

The drinks work on my flesh and I let the music, the scents, the colors and bells and she-beasts, blood, cum, murder and black mists go into my every fiber. Over and over the broken bells ring as my world becomes a spinning kaleidoscope of desire and terror. No space for thought or talk, just the flicker of flesh and death and sense. I am Michael, I am William, I am Sammy. I am any man. I take all of the death inside me until I can take no more. I am lost in the strobe of murder we. I have become every man. I am we. And we are full.

The broken bells ring again, more urgent and disjointed this time, and the curtains open once again but this time we are on stage and there is no one in the audience. All is darkness except the shining hollow eyes of Severine pulling us to her. It's just us and our fat meat and our mad desire to come all over Severine's flesh. To make the bitch taste all of our death and pain and fear and lust. Suddenly, we are bathed in purple light. The entire stage has been transformed into a satin-covered bed scattered with pillows. Blood and gore drip from everywhere. Severine lies naked and beautiful on a pool of satin. She beckons us and we crawl beside her. We want to cave in her head with a ball peen hammer and fuck her tight ass while she screams in pain.

"Are you ready to die?" she asks.

"Ghosts gotta ghost," we say, and we take our fat meat into our hand.

Beastly, disembodied hands rise through the satin and part Severine's thighs, stroking the slick purple roast between her legs.

"You can come now," she says.

Her lilac skin ripples with movement, her flesh languid and surreal as if it's warm mercury rolling over bone. A million little mouths open up across her skin, gaping like a legion of hungry baby birds calling for a fat worm and that fat worm is us. We can feel the pull of all of those hungry little mouths. The bloody hands around flanking Severine's thighs pull her flesh open, exposing the inside meat of her pussy. Severine rubs her penis-like clit until her inside meat splits open and something inverted and meaty looking thuds onto the satin. We pump our bloody cock over her writhing mouths.

Hairs on neck rise, tail bone grows cold, eyes grow cold and sink into skull.

Severine's face grows slack and her eyes become dead channel snow tinted red. Fear runs electric through our flesh that just wants to fuck her, to kill her, to bathe in her blood. We pump away completely mad and half blind. And we're coming hot and thick and endlessly, covering the bitch with our meaty goo. Brains sink into skull, as we pump our gooey bits out with each ropey spasm. The meaty jissom falls across Severine's hungry skin and the thing that fell out from between her legs raises up into what looks like the giant red head of a sea slug. It sprays us back with a fine pink mist that smells like roses. Our skin hisses as the mist hits it.

We grow cold, terribly cold.

We can feel the broken bells ringing but can no longer hear them.

We hover over our discarded meat sack. Our flickering ghost light bathes Severine's body in murder. Her skin has gone smooth again, no more hungry little mouths. Her face narrows, her mouth becoming more beak-like, soulless eyes shift iridescently with murdervision light. Her lower jaw drops suddenly. Too wide.

Caw.

THE STRANGE VICE OF ZLA-313

MP JOHNSON

A golden fembot pranced naked into her bathroom. She turned on the pressure shower, but did not step in right away. She preferred to let the steam build up first. It trailed her as she wandered through her sparsely adorned apartment, condensing on her cool surface and forming beads of water. She picked up a statuette of a human child with comically large ears. Whispering into these ears, she smiled. Then she walked in front of the window, bathing in the light of the moon.

She did not notice the black-gloved hand manipulating the lock on her front door, pushing the door open. She was oblivious to the gleam of the moonlight on the electro-razor as the intruder stepped inside and silently approached. She simply stood, staring out the window, as if waiting for the blade to slide across her neck.

And it did.

Blue sparks danced from the blade to the surface of her throat, forcing her entire body to dance with them—a stuttering, halting dance that resulted in her limbs being ejected from her torso. Black lubricant poured from her metal lips, forming a pool on the floor for her to dive into when the intruder finally let her fall.

***

ZLA-313 and her husbot, the Ambassador, arrived in Silver City on the eve of the sixth murder. The Ambassador had hired security bots to accompany her everywhere, but she refused them. Murders or not, she would not be tethered by such nonsense, not on a visit to Silver City, of all places. Having a security detail follow her every move would be nearly as much a hindrance as having her husbot by her side at all times. Of course, that wasn't going to happen.

Immediately upon stepping off the transport tube platform, she and her husbot were swarmed by politicians. ZLA-313, Zeela for short, played the role of ambassador's wifebot perfectly. Her silver surface shined brighter than the city itself. This was necessary. Silver bots were standard issue, but rather than bemoan her membership in the majority, she did what needed to be done to stand out. She adorned her facial seams with bejeweled bolts that accented her beaming, lavender-tinted vision sensors. A sleeveless, red A-line dress covered her curved frame.

The click of metal on metal echoed across the tube platform as the handshakes commenced. Zeela made certain that her face remained configured in the most sincere smile. She touched upper arms. "It's been too long," she said. "How have you been?" she said. "Your flexi-steel is positively iridescent," she said.

When the mob finally dragged the Ambassador away, Zeela's motors whirred in relief. She had fulfilled her primary duty. Soon she would be free to go off on her own. Silver City was her favorite place in the entire world. It was among the oldest of bot cities, built upon a once-thriving human metropolis. Remnants of human civilization still lingered on the edges, serving as homes for artbots and defectoids, little hubs of wonder and darkness that infiltrated the city proper, forming shadows around otherwise pristine skyscrapers. She had dipped her toes in those shadows on previous visits. Perhaps she would slide in a little deeper this time.

Her driver led her to the hov-transport. She climbed inside, eager to get to the apartment the Ambassador had rented so she could wash the day of travel off her and delve into the night. Parties awaited. Drinks. Manbots.

The hov-transport had barely left the platform before it reached a checkpoint and a policebot forced it to stop.

"What is it?" the driver asked the policebot.

"Another fembot was murdered," the policebot replied.

"The port fiend again?" the driver asked. "Still using the electro-razor?"

Zeela leaned forward to listen to the conversation. The mention of the electro-razor made her flexi-steel surface tingle. She pictured the weapon in a black-gloved hand, blue sparks emanating from the blade. Leaning back again, she surreptitiously put her hands between her legs, touching her port.

"Yes, very sordid," the police officer replied. "You check out. Go ahead."

When the hov-transport arrived at the apartment, Zeela dismissed the driver and ran inside. She stripped out of her dress and slowly peeled off the matching red gauntlets. She walked naked through the apartment, feeling the air on her surface, letting it touch her everywhere. But its touch was far too gentle.

She slid into the pressure shower. The water hissed on her metal surface, and her mind drifted back to the rendezvous she had the last time she was in Silver City.

GORG-9 had taken her past the border, to one of the few areas where green still thrived. She pretended to be put out. She feigned disinterest as he parked the hov-transport amidst the trees. Without warning, GORG-9 slapped her and she exited the hov-transport, fleeing into the forest. Rain poured through the bright green leaves, soaking Zeela, soaking GORG-9 as he followed. He pushed her to the wet ground and smiled. She smiled too. She knew what was coming next.

He had a fistful of screws, jagged and rusty. He poured them onto her as she squirmed on the bed of emerald moss and dying foliage. Then he kneeled over her. He pressed himself into her port. He wrapped his arms around her, pulling her chest to his, trapping the screws between them. With every thrust, the screws scraped her surface, scratching deep, causing pain, sweet pain. Oh, how she craved pain. She couldn't understand why bots had bothered to equip themselves with pain sensors, only to do everything possible to avoid the sensation.

Pain, when coupled with pleasure, had a dizzying effect on her. Pressed closer to expiration, she felt more in-the-moment, more acutely aware of everything. She saw every color, felt every gear turning within her, and just lived harder, better.

The buzz of the doorbell pulled her from her reverie. She turned the shower off, wrapped a towel around herself and answered the door. A deliverybot presented her with a bouquet of roses. No tag. No note. Just a dozen deep red roses.

***

The party began wonderfully, as VRNCA-99's parties typically did. The fembot was the heir to a great fortune, and loved to spend it.

Zeela drank enough hydrocarbon fizz to give her a buzz. She danced with a dozen random manbots, including VRNCA-99's handsome cousbot. He was the only one who came close to meeting her standards. Perhaps she had become spoiled. Even a night with the Ambassador seemed better than a night with anyone at this party. She laughed at the thought. The Ambassador. So sweet, but so reserved. So unable to give her what she wanted.

Maybe VRNCA-99's handsome cousbot though, with his sleek bronze body, his jaw so square, his bolts so even. She made certain to let her vision sensors linger on him long enough for him to notice, but not long enough for him to be sure.

She didn't need to worry about that at the moment though. All she needed to do was dance. Dissonant beeps rode a rhythmic drum machine out of the sound system, infecting Zeela's actuators. She turned off her vision sensors and let her body become one with the rhythm. She swayed and gyrated wildly, ignoring the cheers of the crowd. Of course she became the center of attention, as always.

When she reactivated her vision sensors, she saw GORG-9 across the room.

She grabbed VRNCA-99. "Veronica, who invited George?"

"I think he invited himself, dear," Veronica replied.

"I don't want to see him!"

Zeela stared at her former lover, trying hard not to look at his perfect hands, gray and dulled with use. They had no shine. They scraped with every touch. Oh, but she mustn't think of that touch.

She ran out of the party and into the street. The moon reflected off so many surfaces, it was hard to tell whether it originated in the night sky or behind some wide window somewhere here in Silver City.

George followed. "Wait!"

Zeela turned to him. "What was between us is over. Don't be a fool!"

"I'm no fool. You cannot turn your back to me."

Zeela accepted the challenge. She turned her back. George grabbed her and spun her around. He clutched her bare silver shoulders with those hard, dull hands. She tried with every circuit in her body not to show her true reaction to that touch.

Mercifully, her hov-transport arrived. The Ambassador stepped out and, without a word, pulled George off of her. Then he shoved George. Zeela could hardly believe it. She had never dreamed of such aggression from her husbot. Her circuits buzzed at the thought of that aggression being turned on her. Dare she hope?

"Take me home, darling," Zeela pleaded to her husbot. "Now."

***

The next day, Zeela found herself at Veronica's apartment once again. The place was in perfect order, as if the entire night hadn't happened. Zeela wished that were the case. The confrontation with GORG-9 had already tainted her visit and left her with un-shakeable images of past trysts that had lingered during the disappointingly tepid hours spent with her husbot that followed.

"If you're afraid, surely the Ambassador could provide you with a security detail," Veronica said, sprawled out on her sunshine yellow couch.

"To tell you the truth, I don't know if I need protection from GORG-9, or from myself," Zeela said, thinking back once again to that day in the forest, in the rain.

"Who needs protection?" Veronica's handsome cousbot asked, standing inside the door. Both Veronica and Zeela started, not having heard him enter.

Zeela regained her composure. "Oh, it's nothing."

"I was riding around on my hoverbike and thought I'd stop by to see if Veronica wanted to join me, but there's only room for one. Veronica, would you be terribly upset if I invited Zeela instead? May I give her a tour of Silver City?"

"Zeela, are you going to steal my handsome cousbot?" Veronica asked.

"Of course not," Zeela replied with a devious flash of her lavender-tinted vision sensors as the manbot dragged her away by the wrist.

She followed him out to the street and slid on the back of his hoverbike. He climbed in front of her and she wrapped her arms around him, realizing she did not yet know his name. "What should I call you?"

"7-JAX," he said as the hoverbike launched forward.

They sped past street vendors selling flashchips, through the financial district, where all the bots were augmented with auxiliary monitors. They weaved around a childbot running and laughing with a pack of pupdroids nipping at his heels. They rode so fast that the mix of languages—English, Binocomp, Dialex, German, French—all blurred into an aural fog that swirled around them. Downtown, the buildings penetrated the sky, claiming it for all of botkind.

As hard as Zeela tried to absorb every detail, she found that her focus fell on the back of 7-JAX's head, the little divots and dents in his bronze dome. When she played connect the dots with them, the scenes she saw made electricity crackle between her legs. She wondered if this manbot had ever held an electro-whip. Or an electro-razor. The thought excited her and scared her.

As if in response to the increased pace of her motors, 7-JAX pushed the hoverbike to go faster. Faster. Faster.

Zeela clung tighter. "Please slow down."

"Do you feel that you are in danger?" 7-JAX asked.

"Please slow down."

7-JAX accelerated.

When he finally stopped, it took Zeela a moment to regain herself. Her components seemed to have become jumbled inside her, circuits crossed, motors in reverse. 7-JAX grabbed her by the wrist again, harder this time, and pulled her up cracked concrete steps into a garish brick building flocked with dust and grime.

"Where are we?" Zeela asked.

"Human ruins," 7-JAX replied.

Zeela stopped. "Are there humans here now?"

7-JAX—so clean, so smooth, so unlikely to be lurking in a place like this—turned to her and said, "Hopefully."

Zeela shuddered, but strange thoughts crept into her head, thoughts of warm, organic hands on her cold silver surface. She shook the disgusting thoughts away and focused again on 7-JAX. "I don't think I'd like to see a human."

"They linger in the shadows, but I like to come here."

"I can see why," she mocked.

"It's funny, really."

"Funny?"

"Our ancestors fought to make us superior to the savage meat globs, and now here we are, so many generations removed, trying to emulate humankind."

Zeela laughed nervously, not prepared for this turn in the conversation.

7-JAX continued, "We've modified ourselves to feel emotions and pain. Human weaknesses."

"These are not weaknesses," Zeela said.

"They are, and they've led us to primitive vices—lust, addiction, jealousy. I myself find that I am envious of my cousbot's fortune that she spends so frivolously. And of your wealth as well. Why do I have to feel that? It does not benefit me. And that childbot we passed. Why do we make childbots?"

"To deliver newschips... and flowers?" Zeela replied.

"I have a friend who keeps them as pets."

"Childbots?"

"No, humans."

7-JAX led Zeela into a hall filled with bots that had seen better days. They clinked with every movement. White noise distorted their voices. Some had bored holes into their hulls so they could inject a dark purple fluid. Bot drugs.

7-JAX ushered her safely past these vagrant bots and into a locked and clean room, a room with nothing more than a bed.

He pushed her onto it.

"No," she said, but even she didn't believe it.

He held her wrists down. She kneed him, but not convincingly. He tore through her red dress, ran his bronze fingers around her sparkling silver port.

"Please," she pleaded.

"I love you," 7-JAX said as he moved on top of her.

Outside the window, a camera snapped pictures unnoticed.

A camera held by black-gloved hands.

***

The following morning, Zeela lay silently in bed, watching as the Ambassador dressed in his finest. She could count the time her husbot had spent with her since arriving in Silver City in minutes. But she had expected this. He was here for work, not play. Not that he ever played.

The Ambassador asked, "Do you feel neglected?"

She responded, "I am more than content."

***

That day, Zeela ran errands. Or rather, she shopped mercilessly, with Veronica at her side, until she found a gorgeous gown that seemed perfectly suited to her shiny surface. She was back at her apartment trying it on, gazing at herself in the mirror at every angle—getting Veronica's second, third and fourth opinions—when the phone rang and a distorted, masculine voice told her he was in possession of pictures of her that she would not want her husbot to see.

"Pictures of what?" she asked, playing coy not because she didn't believe it, but to learn specifically which liaison this mystery manbot had photographed.

"Last night."

"And I suppose you want something for these pictures?"

He wanted digicredits. A meeting was set. However, Zeela wasn't entirely certain she would appear at this meeting. She wasn't entirely certain she cared.

***

In the bathroom, she discussed her options with Veronica. Zeela sat on the hamper, her flexi-steel legs crossed. Veronica soaked in an oil bath, rubbing the liquid all over her body with a thick pink sponge. Zeela admired her friend's curves, and her attention to keeping them properly lubricated.

"The truth is, I think the Ambassador already knows," Zeela said.

"About last night?"

"Not about last night specifically, but that I have…"

"Now listen, Zeela. You have the digicredits. Just pay."

"But…"

"Let me do this for you. Let me meet him. I could use the adventure."

Veronica stepped out of the bath, oil running down her nickel-plated surface. Zeela threw her a towel and said, "Okay."

***

In Veronica's hov-transport, they drove to the meeting place, a greenpark not far away. The green made Zeela nervous, brought to mind that meeting with GORG-9 in the forest. But surely GORG-9 had nothing to do with this. Or had he become so enamored with her that he would attempt to destroy her life after being rejected?

Veronica took the digicredit chip with the payoff. "Wish me luck."

"Be safe," Zeela said.

And then all Zeela could do was wait and hope that this would be over soon. She would move on with her life and be faithful to the Ambassador. She would not get entangled in anything else like this. She promised this to herself. Promised.

Then a scream.

Zeela lunged out of the hov-transport and ran toward the sound, telling herself that she was mistaken, that it wasn't Veronica's voice pattern. Perhaps a childbot had seen a meat rodent and screamed, unused to the organic life that still festered in places like this. Veronica was too tough to scream like that.

But then Zeela saw her, crumpled up on the lush emerald grass, as if already halfway through the recycling process. Veronica did not move. The electro-razor that had been dragged across her throat had been turned up so high that blue flames still burned across the scar. Zeela kneeled down and shook her friend, as if that could somehow repair her, bring her back to life. But it couldn't.

"Help!" Zeela screamed to the sky. "Someone help!"

***

As she sat in the police station, Zeela had trouble locking onto the questions the policebot asked. Her thoughts were occupied weighing her options. Should she reveal the blackmail attempt? If she did, she'd have to explain the reason for it. When they had offered to call the Ambassador, she had told them no to prevent him from learning anything, but that was naïve. Whatever she said in this room would find its way to him, confirming suspicions he most certainly had. Then what?

No, there was no point in revealing this detail. The blackmail had been a pretense, a means to lure her someplace where she was an easy target. Only she had not appeared, and Veronica died in her place. Or perhaps it had been a coincidence. Perhaps the slasher, whose murders up to that point had taken place at night in the victims' homes, had simply been wandering the greenpark. Perhaps he saw an opportunity and seized it. Perhaps the blackmailer watched on, taking pictures.

Ridiculous. Zeela didn't believe in coincidences. She had been the target. The more she thought about it, the more she became convinced that she knew exactly who was targeting her, who had been targeting her ever since she arrived in Silver City, as his surprise appearance at Veronica's party confirmed: GORG-9.

She could feel it in her circuits. GORG-9 was the slasher. Who else would have followed her and taken pictures of her porting with 7-JAX? Who else was so jealous, wanted her so desperately, that he would kill if he didn't get what he wanted?

But she couldn't tell that to the policebot grilling her. If she did, she would have to tell him everything, and she was not prepared to do so.

Instead, she feigned ignorance and was eventually allowed to leave.

***

Zeela drove Veronica's hov-transport home. As she sped through the glimmering streets of Silver City, her thoughts of self preservation faded and she realized she had lost her best friend and confidante, the only bot in the world who knew about her strange vice, aside from the manbots whose beds she had shared.

But what selfish thoughts! Poor Veronica. An amazing fembot—so pristine, so many years in front of her. Such perfect parties! All gone, because Zeela didn't have the courage to deliver the blackmail digicredits herself.

Oh, how this terrifying business made her head spin. Her circuits felt murky. She wanted nothing more than to power down for the evening.

She pulled onto the magna-lift that carried her to the docking annex—a massive structure that floated like planetary rings around the uppermost floors of her apartment building. When she parked the hov-transport inside, the lights in the annex went out. Fear—that curious bit of programming that made her thoughts race and her flexi-steel surface seem somehow too flexible—took over. She ran toward the intra-building transport tube. Were those the slasher's footsteps she heard behind her? Or merely echoes of her own?

She stopped running and forced a laugh, a loud laugh she hoped would make her more comfortable. Instead, it echoed through the annex, growing distorted, turning into something too dark and organic. Still, she told herself not to worry. The lights had simply gone out. It didn't mean that the slasher was waiting for her.

She calmed herself as she walked toward the tube.

The doors parted as she approached. Just enough light seeped in from outside to reflect off the electro-razor that moved out of the tube and toward her throat. She ducked it, miraculously, and the body that wielded it moved past her, out into the dark annex, while she slid into the tube and clicked her pointer finger against the door close button. Safely sealed inside, she entered her room code. She could hear the blade slash against the outside of the door, until the tube finally energized and transported her to her apartment, into the Ambassador's open arms.

"He's here!" she screamed.

"Who is here?" the Ambassador asked, voice gruff but not mean, just urgent, just in need of clear answers as soon as possible. Although he rarely showed it in their relationship, this was a manbot who knew how to take charge. He did it every day as part of his job, and now it showed through.

"The slasher! GORG-9!"

"Are you certain? Did you see his face?"

"I didn't see his face. All of the lights in the docking annex were out, but it was him, I know it was him. You must believe me!"

The Ambassador nodded. He unlocked a desk drawer and pulled out a handheld circuit disintegrator. With his thumb, he pressed a button on the weapon, testing it. The end radiated a purple light. "We will end this once and for all."

With the Ambassador leading the way, they transported quietly back to the docking annex. The lights had re-engaged. They found nothing.

Except a bouquet of roses on the hood of Veronica's hov-transport.

"Enough of this," the Ambassador said. "Get in the hov-transport."

They drove to GORG-9's house on the edge of Silver City.

Zeela stood close to her husbot on the doorstep. How dashing, she thought. She wondered what she could do to get him to behave this way in the bedroom. Did she merely need to feign danger? But stampeding around with a circuit disintegrator drawn was one thing. Doing the things she needed him to do in bed, things that she didn't like to speak aloud, was something entirely different.

Nobody answered the door, so the Ambassador kicked it in.

Zeela had never been inside GORG-9's home. If she had, she may never have spent time with him in the first place. Or perhaps she would have been more drawn to him. Cages hung from high ceilings. Each contained a wild, poorly groomed human. Upon seeing visitors, they reached out their grubby hands. When had they last been fed? She didn't like the noises they made, as if they were trying to reclaim their language, but their tongues wouldn't allow it. It was hard to imagine a time when these creatures ruled the world. She remembered what 7-JAX had said about bots impersonating human traits and shuddered.

Did GORG-9 feel the same? Did he study these humans? Were they his pets? Did he take them out and chase them around? Did he do strange things with them? Sexual things? The thought simultaneously turned her on and repulsed her. What violence were these beings capable of? Could those meat hands damage her flexisteel surface? She imagined the beasts being set free to ravage her. Were their parts compatible with her port? The thought was so wonderfully vulgar.

"Do you hear that?" the Ambassador asked, interrupting Zeela's burgeoning fantasy. She would have to come back to it later.

"Is the oil running?" she asked.

The Ambassador pushed open the door to the bathroom.

Indeed, the oil was running. The bath overflowed with the slippery, brown fluid. But it was not completely brown anymore. Black muck rode on the surface, emanating from the open mouth of GORG-9, who lay in the oil bath, unmoving.

Killed by the slasher.

***

"Clearly, he is after me, and is starting with those who love me," Zeela argued, back at the apartment, curled up on the couch.

"Those who love you?"

"Yes, VRNCA-99. And GORG-9 loved me too… Unrequited, of course."

"Of course. Still, there is no actual proof you were the target," the Ambassador said. "The murders began before we arrived in Silver City."

With those words, all the gallantry he had displayed earlier became void. She whispered, "I need to get away from here."

"My business in Silver City is not yet finished."

"Then I will go without you."

***

But Zeela would not go alone. 7-JAX, Veronica's handsome cousbot, happily accompanied her on her journey to Old Mexica. No one, not even the Ambassador, knew of her destination, nor of her travelling companion. She and 7-JAX went to a resort far off the beaten path, far from Silver City and all of its movement. The resort echoed pre-bot civilization, and the bots that lived there reveled in antiquity.

In their bungalow near the beach, Zeela and 7-JAX were closed off to the world. There was no televideo. There were no newschips. If there were, Zeela would have been interested to see the next day's headline: "Would-Be Victim Slays The Slasher." She would have read about the wily fembot who, while stripping for a pressure shower, was set upon by a black-gloved man. This fembot was herself quite skilled in the use of a blade, and managed to engage her personal surge-dagger and jam it into her assailant's control panel as he lunged at her with his electro-razor.

Zeela did not learn this news. Still, she managed to push the thoughts of her presumed stalker, whoever he may be, out of her head. He was of no threat to her under such a bright, all-showing sun. He would never find her here.

***

In a tiny wooden antique boat far from shore, Zeela stripped. She removed her clothes, her red gauntlets, even her bolt covers. She wanted 7-JAX to see all of her. She wanted him to see the scratches in her silver and get ideas. But she couldn't tell him the ideas she wanted him to get. If she told him and he did as she said, she would be the one in power. She didn't want that. She wanted total loss of power. She wanted to be pushed, and hurt, and surprised and made real. For her to feel what she so desperately wanted to feel, these ideas had to come naturally to 7-JAX.

But they did not. Yes, they ported as the waves rocked them, and it was beautiful and intimate. But beautiful and intimate could never truly satisfy her, no matter how adept 7-JAX was at displaying them. And he was very adept.

When finished, they lay together, holding each other. She felt safe and she realized that, perhaps, that was not the feeling she preferred.

***

Back on shore, she walked slowly through the dirt streets of the little resort town. She didn't even know the name of the place. So rustic. 7-JAX had gone to run some errands, leaving her with time to explore the dirt streets and little tech-free shops selling hand-made trinkets by worn-out bots. Her baby pink bikini drew more than a few lingering glances, and not only from the manbots. She didn't mind their vision sensors on her. She could speculate about the thoughts behind them.

Did any of those thoughts involve an electro-razor?

As if unleashed by her violent fantasies, a spear whisked past her head, lodging solidly into the door of a nearby shop. She spun to see where it came from, but saw nothing but screaming Mexibots running in all directions, as if they were in danger, as if they were the target.

She knew otherwise. That spear was intended for her. Wasn't it?

She tried to tell herself that it might not have been. After all, a spear was a far cry from an electro-razor. So distant. So impersonal.

What would compel the slasher to make such a dramatic switch of weapons? Desperation probably. She had run, but he had found her, and now he simply wanted this finished. No more games.

"Where are you?" she called out. "Show yourself, you bastard!"

A childbot stepped forward, handing Zeela a bouquet of red roses.

"Who are these from?" Zeela asked, throwing the flowers to the dirt.

The childbot pointed to the far end of the street. "That manbot."

But there was nobody there.

***

"I'm not crazy!" she yelled at 7-JAX back at their bungalow.

"But nobody knows you're here," 7-JAX insisted.

"You're right. Nobody…" She paused as a horrible thought occurred to her and she gave it voice. "Nobody, except you."

"Don't be ridiculous."

Was she being ridiculous? Probably. 7-JAX wouldn't kill her, and he certainly wouldn't have killed his own cousbot. But why did he seem so stoic? Had his emotion chips failed? His cousbot was dead and Zeela was next, unless the slasher got to 7-JAX first. She couldn't take it. All she could do to express her emotions was pound her flexi-steel fists on the wall and wail.

"It's too much!" she cried.

"A stray spear, nothing more," 7-JAX pleaded. "I will go to the police and they will get to the bottom of this."

"Damn your calmness. You don't even care!"

She stomped into the bathroom. Before she could slam the door behind her, she saw the color of the liquid dripping from the sides of the bath. Black, just like from GORG-9's tub. The curtain was drawn. What body hid behind it now? Who lay dead and soaking before her this time? Was it 7-JAX? Had she been talking to his ghost? Or maybe it was her body and she was the ghost. She couldn't bear to pull back the curtain to find out, but she had to know. She fell to her knees and slapped her hands against the floor. "Please! Please! Please!"

"I don't know what you want me to do," 7-JAX whispered.

"I can't even move. It's too much," she wailed. She pointed at the bath.

7-JAX pulled back the curtain, revealing the source of the discolored liquid: his spare arms, soaking. Black muck percolated from their hinges. Still, Zeela screamed. Could those hands ever have been wrapped in black gloves? Could they ever have held an electro-razor? A spear gun?

"I'll go to the police now," 7-JAX said.

Zeela merely blubbered and whined.

And then 7-JAX left Zeela.

Alone.

***

She remained in the bathroom, staring at the bath.

She wondered if this was what it felt like to go mad. Bot delirium. Circuit rot. Maybe she had always been defective. Her strange vice seemed proof of that. But still, her fantasies continued to swell and overpower any other thoughts.

And now here she sat, in the bathroom, waiting as the day faded.

She rose to her feet with a forced slowness and simply stood there.

When she realized she was not alone in the room, she did not turn around at first. How long had she been standing there, lost in her thoughts, oblivious to all around her? She thought that not turning around would be best. Letting death take her from behind would be easier, a relief almost. To some extent, she anticipated the slice of the electro-razor on her throat, invited it.

But then she heard the growls, the distinctly un-bot-like sound of air passing through constricted tunnels of meat, and the fear that filled her forced her to look. There, waiting for her, were a half dozen humans, naked and coated in their own filth. They showed her their mouths full of crooked yellow teeth as drool foamed out onto their mite-filled beards. They clawed at her with ragged fingernails, but they couldn't get to her, restrained as they were by collars, collars attached to leashes, leashes held by familiar hands—gray and dull hands.

GORG-9's hands.

Zeela gasped at the sight of this ghost.

"Surprised to see me, lover?"

"You're dead. I saw your body. They took you for recycling." Zeela backed away, staying just out of reach of the savage human hands.

"Nah. That was a bit of a show for you."

"But why, George? Why kill me? Why Veronica and all the others?"

"Ah, you've mistaken me for the slasher. I'm afraid I can't take credit for all his work. The best time to get rid of someone is when there's a homicidal maniac on the loose. You and Veronica needed to be gotten rid of."

GORG-9 moved closer. Zeela stepped back into the oil bath, but could retreat no further. She pressed herself against the bathroom wall. The humans could reach her, but couldn't get a grip. They could merely scrape their nails across her flexi-steel. They scraped so hard their nails came off, just flipped off their flesh, leaving bleeding nubs. This only seemed to drive them further into their frenzy. They kept clawing at her, leaving streaks of blood on her silver surface.

Despite their softness, Zeela had no doubt these humans could damage her. They could pry off her panels and gnaw through her internal cords. She could hardly imagine the pain. It made her motors buzz. She screamed, not entirely out of fear.

"You like this, don't you? The anticipation of pain," GORG 9 asked. "I'm glad the real slasher went and got himself killed, so I didn't have to bother with the impersonation any longer. This seems more fitting for you than an electro-razor."

The lavender light from Zeela's vision sensors dimmed as she turned them off. She was ready to take whatever those meaty hands had to offer her.

But then another voice demanded her attention.

"Step away from her!"

Zeela re-initiated her vision sensors to see 7-JAX standing behind GORG-9, pointing a spear gun at the murderer's back.

"What do you think you're doing, 7-JAX?" GORG-9 asked.

"Saving the girlbot."

GORG-9 laughed. "Why?"

"I'm afraid I've fallen for her."

"Join the club."

"I'm serious."

"I killed for you," GORG-9 roared. "I killed your cousin so you could collect the family fortune. You can't turn your back on me now."

"Watch me."

7-JAX raised the spear gun and Zeela cried out, "That... That spear gun!"

"It's just a spear gun," 7-JAX replied, aiming at GORG-9's back.

"You tried to kill me!" Zeela shouted.

"No. Never. An intentional miss. After our time on the boat..."

Before he could finish his sentence, a black-gloved hand slid an electro-razor across his bronze throat. 7-JAX dropped to his knees, releasing a shot from the spear gun on his way down.

The spear penetrated GORG-9's back. His chest plate burst off and his inner cords unraveled. Red and yellow and orange and curled, they poured out from inside of him onto the bathroom floor. There must have been miles of cords stuffed inside, and they all wanted out. The ones torn by the spear sparked and crackled. GORG-9 remained standing though, despite the black oil pouring from his mouth. The humans turned toward their master, confusion and worry in their eyes.

Folding up the electro-razor, the Ambassador said, "If you want something done, you have to do it yourself. I do hate dirtying my hands though."

"Dear?" Zeela said, confused.

"I'm not here to save you, if that's what you're thinking. I hired these reprobots to end your run. I'm glad I only paid twenty-five percent up front to take care of my cheating wifebot. I fear they were both too enamored with you to do the job. Amazing what a pair of spread legs and an open port can accomplish."

The Ambassador stepped forward, pressing one fist into the other.

"You don't have to do this," Zeela said. "I love you."

"No you don't."

At that moment, GORG-9 collapsed. Smoke gushed out of his seams. His hands loosened on the leashes and the humans broke free. Their primitive minds were not so dense as to not understand murder. They knew exactly who had taken their master from them. Wailing with rage, they dove at the Ambassador, tearing at his flexi-steel face with their bloody nubs. Within seconds, they had disassembled it. One of the humans climbed onto the Ambassador's shoulders and tore into the bot's head circuits. The savage must have hit the power source, because a burst of flame filled the room and the beast fell to the floor, blackened to a crisp.

Zeela used the opportunity to splash out of the oil bath and run, but she wasn't fast enough. One of the beasts latched onto her and pried her back panel off with its teeth. It tore at her wiring. This did not feel good. No pleasure accompanied this pain. The human's wild strikes carried not the faintest hint of sensuality.

The savage got her back panel and some wiring, but couldn't get a grip on her oiled silver surface. She broke free. She ran as fast and as far as she could to escape the vengeful howls of the humans as they tore her husbot to pieces. She still heard those howls when her wounds got the best of her and she collapsed in the dusty streets of the resort town, where the residents rushed to her aid.

***

Zeela led policebots to the bungalow. She waited outside as they swarmed, killing the humans that ran amok. The mechano-doc who had repaired her stood at her side, watching her cautiously for any further signs of damage. She held her head in her flexi-steel hands, still trying to comprehend what had happened. Not one, not two, but three of her lovers had conspired against her, and brilliantly too.

Perhaps not as brilliantly as they had hoped. She had made it out alive. They hadn't, and neither would their pets. Even so, she felt no relief, nothing of the sort.

In fact, she felt nothing at all. She reeled and the mechano-doc caught her.

"Doctor, I thank you for bringing me back to life," Zeela said in a hoarse whisper, "but perhaps you can tell me, why do I still feel dead?"

SENSORIA

ANYA MARTIN

"Not only is it the last show, but it is the last show I will ever do."
—David Bowie as Ziggy Stardust,
Hammersmith Odeon, London, 1973

The smoky hole of church-turned-club pulsates—vibrating sweat-drenched bodies getting off on themselves and each other packed within the pews of a gigantic granite womb. Sasha fanned her chest with a show flyer, the heat of tightly packed bodies tempered only mildly by her rain-soaked, but quickly drying hair and the removal of her lightweight white shawl, which she had wound around her purse strap so as not to lose it. Sober unlike most of the throng, she imagined the audience a great gyrating beast, arms rising up like tentacles, legs scurrying side to side like centipedes to the throbbing industrial drone that the DJ was spinning until the band came on. The "pit" crowd pushed into her and she shifted with it, reactivating her punk rock instincts to navigate her way towards the chancel-turned-stage. She staked her territory, leaned her chest onto its lip. Wasn't she too old to be packed in with the horror hipsters, Goth groupies and neo-punks who had bought their way in to use him as their dildo? Why did she come out in a pouring thunderstorm, pay for an expensive taxi so as not to be late? And yet here she was waiting to experience Dorian Cain LIVE for the first time.

The music halted, and the crowd applauded. Mist tinted scarlet by spotlights spewed onto the stage and out into the audience. The crowd quieted, the pounding rain outside momentarily audible on the stained glass windows above the pulpit. The keyboardist took his place first, a tall black man with a purple mohawk in a fringed leopard print jacket. His fingers initiated a jangly lullaby-like melody. The rest of the band came on stage, one by one, the volume building as each instrument joined in. A red-haired female cellist in a netty purple gown seated herself. A shaved-head guitarist in shiny silver shirt, red pants and cowboy boots took his station by a standing mic. The Iggy-skinny bass player with spiky hair and goatee in a Wolf Man T-shirt and tight jeans slouched towards another mic stand. A pudgy guy with teased big white hair slipped in last behind the drums at the rear. From above the stained glass windows, a large screen descended, on it a flickering image of a dark-haired woman with big eyes lined in black. She closed her eyelids, reopened them and had no eyes, blood dripping down her deeply chiseled cheeks like tears.

Stretch Limo to the Dimension of Darkness

Sasha looked up to see Dorian Cain towering above her, all black leather, licorice tongue lapping tense circles within his lips—curving in, breaking out.

Better Hide Your Soul

He swung his long dark hair in a wide loop, then his eyes exploded open gazing down at her, black onyx rimmed with a corona of sea-green.

Guard Your Passion

His pointy black shoes literally grazed her nipples through her stretch velvet sleeveless white minidress. She felt a wet dribble of Dorian's sweat fall on her cheek.

Thieves everywhere

Then he danced away, all thunder and tease.

A granite ripple of bass guitar wove down, down.

Crash.

Pale and Salty.

Dorian sang now from the other end of the stage.

Salt Milk.

He swiveled his pelvis like Jim Morrison…no, Nick Cave.

Be Your Daddy. Teach You.

The music softened back to a cello tingle, followed by frenzied strumming.

Rose up again, drums pounding, the chancel vibrating and her body shaking with it.

A shatter of cymbal.

Now center stage, Dorian leaned into his crotch, his jeans ripping across his knees. He dropped his black leather jacket onto one shoulder flashing black T-shirt, sleeves ripped off, and the tattoo she'd seen in photos—the horned skull, the black rose.

Rock 'n' roll stays the same. Rock changes.

Dorian was more dynamic musically and exuding more goddamned sexuality and stage presence than Sasha had heard—and she had heard all of that. She reminded herself she was supposed to be a rock journalist, here just to watch and document.

As Dorian thrashed at the far left end of the stage, Sasha's view of him was blocked by the bouncing heads of a gaggle of big-haired groupies. Left-right, left-right they swayed, the old in-out played out in the rhythmic throttle of teased manes—the kind sprayed with so much Ultra Hold Aqua Net that not even a follicle strayed from place. One blonde like lemon meringue pie filling in a sleeveless zebra print mini-dress. Another strawberry redhead with brushstrokes of metallic gold in neon purple. But mostly Goth chicks in spidery black.

Behind them Sasha noticed a man with short-cropped dark hair and black sunglasses in a trench coat. The coat made sense for the rain outside, but considering how hot it was inside, she couldn't imagine anyone keeping it on. Was he a flasher? She couldn't tell if he had pants on, his legs lost in the throng of the crowd. Mr. Trenchcoat was staring intently at the blonde, then his gaze wandered to other women in the crowd, lingering on each for several seconds and then moving on to the next. Mechanical. She forgot the concert for a moment, caught up in the weirdness of his ritual.

As if he sensed someone was watching, he shifted—a stiff jerk compared to what had been a slow ritual—towards her. He lifted a black-gloved hand to adjust his sunglasses and grinned, full and toothy—gray heavy metal braces.

Sasha averted her eyes back to the stage. A new song had started and the volume spiked abruptly. The big screen now projected a woman with shortly cropped white hair in a long black gown running through a cemetery, hands reaching up from the graves and grabbing at her ankles. An ornate crypt loomed ahead with a weeping angel at its door. The angel's eyes moved.

Angels and devils call to her.

On the screen a black-gloved hand brandished a large hunting knife. Slashed into the woman's back. Blood spewed like a fountain from her wounds. Every horror movie cliché and yet the cinematography was stunning, Sasha thought.

She won't give them her number.

"Slip it in, baby," a male voice said next to her—Sid Vicious clone, pale with black spiky hair, white ripped T reassembled with safety-pins, and Levis.

The Sid twisted his tongue in spiral eights around the lobe of his Nancy, lapping along the edges of her mass of curly blonde perm curls up the rim of her ear. With his other hand, he pulled a black box out of his pocket, opened it delicately and removed a red and black beetle. It scrambled in his fingers, legs flailing, wings fluttering, eager for escape. What the fuck?!

But the Sid gripped it firmly, the creature exuding a loud squeaky objection that reverberated above the music which had now eased back to cello and keyboards.

Nancy opened her mouth, he popped the insect into it, and she closed, crunched down and swallowed. Sasha could see in the chick's eyes how quickly it kicked in. Her pupils went from tipsy and glazed to dilated, irises rolling up.

Eyes flicked onscreen. Blinking.

Eyes of the ages...

Sid pulled out another box. This beetle didn't struggle as much, allowed him to gently stroke its back, a low hum more like a cat's purr before he popped it in his own mouth and his eyes now glazed over into white empty ovals. Empty to the outside anyway. The two were still grooving to the music but at a slower pace.

Watching her, touching her...

A masculine hand traced the curve of a nude female body above the band as reverb rose, the beat quickened to near hardcore speed.

A conga line of thrashers bumped into the center, feeling their way blind to all but the music, hopping in their combat boots, feet together. They smashed into the Sid, but he was gone—lost in the beetle's whatever effect.

Beyond.

Sasha felt a tap on her shoulder. Behind her stood an albino man with red contact lenses and cat-eye pupils beneath a mane of dreads, smiling perfect white teeth. He curled a hand under her arm and opened his palm in front of her face to reveal a black box similar to Sid and Nancy's.

"Try?" he whispered in her ear, accent Island via Queens. "Only fifty, madam."

Sasha shook her head. She hadn't even had a drink in two years, no drugs in a decade—and then just the most mundane—marijuana, cocaine, one dance with LSD.

"Milady, I saw the way you watched the others experience the wonders of the sensor-scarab, how you are transfixed on Dorian Cain," the man said in caramel tones, his other arm now caressing her waist. Why didn't she brush him away? He could be a date rapist, for all she knew.

"I'm a journalist, just here to watch," Sasha protested.

Another cascade of cello, Dorian Cain towered above her again, swinging his hair. The images on the screen now all blood. Dripping like curtains. Pulling back to reveal a giant beetle, red and black like the one she saw the Sid and Nancy consume.

Hide and seek, till death is all.

"I don't drink, don't do drugs," she said, wondering how they could even hear each other in the loud music.

The scarab dealer lifted up Sasha's left hand with his own left, then flipped open the box with his right. The beetle inside was on its back, legs fidgeting as he lifted it out. He turned it over to reveal the same red markings.

"What is it?" Sasha says. She had to admit she was curious. After all, a journalist always should observe every detail. That is, if she had an assignment. If this concert wasn't an attempt to resurrect a career that had fallen away as she missed deadline after deadline to care for a guy who when he could walk again after being hit by a speeding van made it clear he didn't care for her. A memory flashed of coming home to find all his stuff packed up and gone, no note.

"Sensor-scarab, milady, they call her."

"Scarab, like ancient Egyptian?"

"This lady hails from Guatemala, She will not kill you, just make you reborn."

Sasha imagined his tongue was snakelike.

She glanced up from the insect to the screen to see on it a giant version of the same creature, its shiny crimson back resembling a more rounded version of the black widow hourglass, its legs twitching, its elytra flexing and spreading as it took flight.

She thought back to the little girl who collected cicada skins. How she liked to listen to them sing. How she watched a praying mantis once for an hour. How even spiders always fascinated her, and she would catch one in a jar and take it outside rather than kill it.

Why not try it? While she didn't like the idea of killing an insect, she'd eaten grasshoppers before in China with her parents, and she ate meat. What was different? Sid and Nancy were clearly having a good time. They were holding each other close, their eyes blind but fingers pawing, lightly scratching. She wouldn't have anyone to share the experience with, but right now was all about reclaiming her life, making her own decisions, finding some pleasure. Who knew if she could sell an article anyway, if she had burnt every bridge?

Sasha dug into her purse and pulled out two twenties and two fives. The dealer slipped his right hand off her waist, took the bills from her with the deftness of a magician. Then he placed the scarab in her mouth.

"Bite down, princess, as I let go."

Sasha ground her teeth down on the insect, feeling the crunch of its exoskeleton as a creamy liquid spread into her mouth, swishing in her teeth, under her tongue. The insect must be dead from her bite, but its juice, its lifeblood? Can liquid be alive? She chewed and swallowed, felt the hands of the dealer withdraw from her.

"Salut, darling."

She knew he is gone, dissolved into the throng which presses against her again. Pushing, pulling, vibrating. A low hum, a buzzing drone, like a symphony of cicadas. Are they singing along with Dorian? Has everyone consumed the scarab? She feels herself being carried up like the crowd might take flight. The screen wriggles, full of scarabs, tightly packed, hive-like, crawling over each other in all directions. Their red backs pulsate, flashing bright to dark, bright to dark.

Smoke and mirrors.

Above her, Dorian leans, singing, singing into her mouth.

Your love like a velvet blanket.

His tongue lapping in and out of his own like kisses.

In the rain.

No, like something else, a guitar in his hands, playing the length of the strings, the center hole—her G-spot—like a keyboard, snakelike and amplified.

Down, down, down, down…

Orgasm starts high, shudders, descends into her thighs, her brain condenses to happy jelly. Is this what the beetle-juice does, not a joke like the Tim Burton movie?

She could get used to this. The scarab wasn't a black widow but a love bug. You didn't have to really fuck the star; even the ugliest wallflower in the crowd got off now.

Her euphoria dissolves into rain, her dress soaked and sticky to her body. She's climbing a ladder against a stone wall towards a row of tall arched stained glass windows. Colored lights sparkle against the panes inside. The rungs are slippery so she shakes off her shoes, hears them bounce on the pavement below. She reaches the base of the window and climbs onto the ledge, meets the glass in an embrace. Throbbing amped rumble vibrates through the pane. Enthralled by the light's beauty and the beat, she begins to dance, well, more sway, the space too narrow for anything else. Her hair is wet and heavy. The light, the sound through the window comfort, call. She can see shadows of movement inside.

She glances back to see if he is still watching her from below— the man in the trenchcoat. He is, expressionless, still wearing dark glasses, clutching a wide black umbrella. He pulls the blade from his pocket with his black-gloved left hand, brandishes it with a single slash and nods.

Sasha turns back to the window. She looks down, her dress is zebra-striped. She wants to escape from the rain. She shivers at the cold drenching drops and inside looks so warm. She slams her head into the glass.

Sharp pain in her forehead, through her eye, down her cheek. She propels her body forward, leaps—no, flies. Hundreds of tiny stabs impact her flesh, so sudden, so many.

Like freedom.

Slow-motion and then a heavy slam as her body ricochets. Flash of drums, tuneless brr-ng of cymbal hit too hard. Tumbling, down steps and landing hard on her back onto stone.

Music stops, leaning towards her, a man in black leather with long dark hair—Dorian Cain. Other hazy faces. Screams surround her. Lights bright now—flying buttresses above her. She feels energized, a thousand pinpricks like electric shocks lying in a puddle of warm water. Drowsiness overwhelms, seduces her to sleep, sleep. She thinks of poppies and Dorothy, the Emerald City so close and their deep red color, their scent so sweet.

She turns her head to her left side. The man in the trenchcoat grins his metal mouth under a stone arch. He steps towards her, kneels beside her, next to Dorian—does Dorian even see him? Does anyone else see him? Her arm is weak, but she's able to reach up and pull the glasses off his face. Where his eyes should have been are empty sockets—out of them crawl sensor-scarabs. The scarabs spread their elytra and fly to the left, to the right, each transforming into a poppy—clouds of floating poppies. Then one scarab zooms straight from eye socket towards her. She scrunches her lids to prepare for the impact. None happens so she cracks her left eye and finds herself staring straight into flower.

She shuts it again as sleep comes down.

A scream, shattering of glass.

Sasha snapped her eyes open. No poppies. The music had stopped, house lights on. Dorian was bending down towards the supine form of the blonde hipster-chick in the zebra-striped mini-dress, one of the groupies who'd blocked her view earlier, in the center of the chancel. The stained glass windows were broken, the girl's body stabbed and blanketed in shards of glass, a large frame jabbed right through the center of her face, blood seeping from her many wounds.

"Don't panic," Dorian urged the audience.

Sasha was surprised to hear how Midwestern, ordinary his non-singing voice was. He sounded nervous, vulnerable, a hint of a stutter.

Groupies were screaming now, though to Sasha, their shrieks sounded garbled as if underwater. A residual effect of the sensor-scarab-juice on her hearing? More onlookers just stared, some mumbled to each other, and others made for the doors, including the dreadlocked sensor dealer slipping out to the side. The Sid and Nancy and other random dazed crowd members didn't move

except to sway—other users, though whether from the scarab or
another drug she could not be sure. The man in the trenchcoat
had vanished.

The rest of the band had put away their instruments and en-
circled the body. Two uniformed security guards were climbing on
stage. Bouncers in their usual uniform of black T-shirts and jeans
appeared in the pit.

"You need to leave now," said a heavy-set balding man wearing
a Blue Oyster Cult T-shirt in a booming voice. When Sasha didn't
budge, he glared at her.

"I'm press," she said drowsily, holding up her media hangtag.
There was no way she was leaving now. The concert review wasn't
just a review, a feature any more. It was a news story, an exclusive.

"Ma'am, everybody has to leave," the bouncer said, stepping
forward to push her towards the rear. Despite her hallucinogenic
funk, Sasha outmaneuvered his grasp. She headed stage right in a
warbly conflation of side steps and collided directly into Dorian
himself as he descended the bottom step from the chancel. They
stumbled into a clumsy embrace, their eyes meeting in an uncomfortable lock. Oh fuck, she'd just had a drug-infused sexual fantasy
with this guy. And now she was sure she'd just get tossed out, no
hope of finding out what happened to the girl, much less a quote
from Dorian. No story, and she wasn't in any state to hail a cab.

Sasha felt the bouncer's hand on her arm. Sirens blared outside.

"I'm sorry, Mr. Cain," he said. "I'll escort her out."

"No," Dorian said, not letting go of her. "Don't worry about it.
I'll take care of her."

"But, sir."

"No buts, Hank," Dorian said more firmly.

Hank let go, grumbled. Dorian shifted, putting an arm around
her.

"Are you OK?" he asked. He pulled up her hangtag and read her
name. "Sasha Alexander."

"Yeah, that's me," Sasha nodded, confused by her sudden rescue by the rock star himself.

"Follow me," he said, leading her into the transept and through the arched side door. He nodded at the security guards who'd taken up posts at that exit. She saw the crowd being herded toward the front, just-arrived police officers maneuvering through their throng.

The rain had slowed to a light drizzle but a tent canopy protected them on the short distance to the tour bus. Dorian adjusted his hold, guiding her up the steps in front of him but signaling he could catch her if she fell back. Through her blurry vision, she saw two of the other band members in the front cabin. The drummer by the bar poured what looked to be scotch into a tumbler, throwing a questioning glance towards Dorian. The cellist sat cross-legged, her head in her hands, crying. But Dorian guided Sasha past them into the back towards shadowy bunk beds. He pulled the duvet back on the bottom bed on the right, then lowered her onto the mattress—gently seating her, taking her purse from her hand and placing it behind her, helping her remove her white go-go boots, lifting up her legs. She curled on her side, laid her head on the pillow, and fell asleep instantly.

***

When Sasha's eyes opened again, the room was only dimly lit by fluorescent striping along the center aisle. It took a moment for her to remember why she wasn't in her own bed, where she was. Fully clothed, her underwear on, she noted. No one had taken advantage of her sedated state, but then she was sure Dorian and the band would have no trouble finding willing groupies. A snore. In the bunk across from her, the drummer sprawled belly-down, shirtless, jeans and bare feet on top of the duvet. The upper bunk was empty, looked like it hadn't been touched. Soft breathing told her that the cellist was likely right above her.

Sasha reached for her purse, unwound the white shawl and wrapped it across her shoulders, stood up. She scanned and quickly found the bathroom. In the mirror, the eyeliner on her upper lids amazingly had not run. She splashed some water on her face, did a quick touch-up, and then ventured back into the hall, opening the door into the front cabin.

The shades were lowered so she couldn't tell if it was morning or still night. Dorian was sitting alone.

"Come in, sit down, Sasha," he said. "I don't bite. Well, not on first meeting."

He chuckled softly, adding, "I suppose we could get some light in here."

He stood up, headed for the bar. She expected him to flip a switch, but instead he struck a match and started lighting tall white candles on a brass menorah. How did it stay standing when the bus was moving? Was it nailed to the bar? Or did he just put it away?

"Do you want some kombucha?" he asked.

"Sure," Sasha said. Weren't rock stars supposed to drink booze? Well, it was late. Or more likely early.

"If you're wondering what time it is, it's about 6 a.m., almost dawn," Dorian said, as he dipped under the bar and opened a small refrigerator. He pulled out a bottle, poured the green liquid into a glass, and handed it to her.

"As you can imagine, what happened is already across the Internet, the cable news, crews camped outside the bus waiting for my statement," he added as he poured himself a glass. "Woman hurls herself through stained glass at Dorian Cain concert at church— apparent suicide. Or was it murder? Or was she under the influence of a dangerous new street drug?"

"Why am I here, Dorian?" Sasha asked.

"Call me James," he said, motioning for her to sit.

"You used to go to Mars back when it was still called Masquerade," he continued once she was seated.

"Yeah," Sasha said. Why was he bringing up an old Atlanta night club?

"The good old days," he nodded, breaking into a sardonic swagger. "When synth and hip-hop ruled the Top 40, there was a rock that still shook in the guts and the groin and the guitar. Before MTV and the record execs killed it all with that alternative crap and then synthetic masturbation gave birth to rave counter culture. So sayeth wankers like *Rolling Stone*."

"That's almost a direct quote. Good little local music rag, that *Stomp and Stammer*. Luckily *Rolling Stone* didn't take it personally and gave me a job for a while. I'd forgotten you were from Atlanta."

"I was that scruffy kid in the corner, sneaking in underage," James said. "Imagine me—shy?!"

"Your first band was Sasquatch, I remember. I never saw them, but early articles talked about your stage presence even then. And then you moved to New York, spent some time in London, ended up in San Francisco."

"You've followed my itinerary."

"What makes you different is that you don't just want to use the crowd. You want to bring back old school performance, flesh and feeling, like Mick Jagger, Roger Daltrey, Jim Morrison, Lou Reed?"

He laughed, rocking on his feet.

"In the words of Jeff Park: 'Cain drains the brain…has the audacity to conceive that fans both want to watch him and to pay attention to his music. This is the OTeens, baby. Like a kick in the soul live to the worldwide web.'

"Sometimes I dream I'm no one," he continued, serious. "I compose notes and words, let them touch the ears of millions of idiots seeking some sort of fleeting gratification they can't pull out of their pitiful jobs or their lovers or from the asshole who happens to be president or the clouds of clear waste that clog their lungs with invisible cancers."

"That's why you played in a small church. All your locations on this tour are small, intimate compared to where you could book.

You want to be a performer in a ratty old club in the '60s or the '70s."

James swigged the rest of his kombucha as if it was whiskey. Then he glanced down, stroked the thin stubble on his chin, looked up again and into her eyes—somewhere in between the stage Dorian Cain and shy scruffy kid from the Atlanta suburbs.

"I thought I had finally made it to where I could do what I wanted—that rock star arrogance, I suppose. Rock is dead, punk is dead, Goth is dead, grunge is dead, Kraut-rock, even funk, all dead. But I had made enough money I could bring it back, take it to the next level. Back to Bowie. Beyond sound. To all five senses."

"The sensor-scarab. Sold at a price not too cheap as to be suspicious as a handout, but affordable enough for free-spirited audience members with, let's say, a sense of adventure."

James raised an eyebrow. "You're quite observant, Miss Alexander."

"You're talking to a journalist."

"A journalist who just took an illegal substance and who hasn't had an article in a major publication beyond her blog in three years."

"Are you blackmailing me?"

"No, you can write anything you want. I'm not a pusher. I don't have anything to do with distribution, so there's no story there. But I have been, let's say, been writing songs with the effect of the sensor-scarab in mind."

"Where did it come from? I mean, how did people even figure out to eat a beetle?"

"Central American tribes figured it out first, who knows when. Anthropologists classify it as an 'entheogen'—generating the divine within—a ritualistic substance used by shamans. They used it to create a communal effect—shared hallucinations like group mythology. That's why the CIA took an interest back in the '80s as a way to calm down mass hysteria. Like the street battles in Ferguson between the cops and locals. Rumor has it that the riots only simmered down after sensor-serum was added to the water supply. Rumor also has it also that it could be weaponized to create unrest, but there's not been a single documented case of anyone dying under the influence."

"Nice. You've done your research. And you want to use something that the CIA is playing around with to create a multisensory experience that ties into a specific song? From what you've just told me and what I experienced, it sounds like it's not that easy to control, and it could have triggered that girl to go kill herself. Or was I the only one on sensor-juice, or whatever you want to call it, who was in that chick's head when she jumped through that window?"

"Umm...what?!"

"I had a vivid vision of being that girl before she crashed through that window."

"Really? What did you see?"

"I was her climbing the ladder, dancing on the ledge. No one pushed her, but on the ground, a man in a trenchcoat with dark glasses was watching her. He had a knife but he didn't stab her, just like he was using it to signal her to jump. I saw him earlier in the crowd, surveying all the groupies, one by one, as if carefully choosing which one was to die."

"Weird. Reporters have been interviewing people who saw the show, but no one has said anything like that on the news. Police didn't mention it either when they interviewed me. Not that they'd necessarily give much credence to a drug trip, but if it was so close to what actually happened...

"Anyway, the long and short is I could use a journalist on my side," he said. "And a reporter who sampled a dangerous new drug might not hurt. I'm also interested in hearing more about that vision of yours."

"But you don't want me to admit any of that in print," Sasha said.

"Probably not."

"Hmmm. What do you have in mind?"

"Exclusive on my reaction to what happened last night. Then you can have whatever you want, an in-depth interview, backstage pass, lodging and transport to the rest of my tour."

"Why do you trust me?"

"Just call it an instinct, and you need a ticket back to the music media. I can hook you up with other musicians, bands—whoever you want."

Sasha didn't need a lot of time to think. Was she compromising her journalistic ethics? If some proof surfaced that tied the sensor-scarab or James/Dorian directly to the girl's death, she could always re-assess. But for now, his offer was exactly what she needed to reboot her career.

"Okay."

She opened her purse and pulled out a small digital recorder.

"Are you ready to start talking?"

James nodded.

"Testing 1-2-3. This is Sasha Alexander interviewing Dorian Cain."

That was the first time she met Dorian Cain. When Dorian Cain was just beginning.

***

Six months later she and Dorian traveled back to Atlanta so she could trace his roots for the book she was now writing. They'd been spending almost every day together doing interviews but also just talking, discovering they shared interests in art and literature, cooking, gardening. At Mars, he asked her to dance when the DJ started spinning nostalgia disks—Velvet Underground, Joy Division, Bowie—"Ziggy Stardust." They swayed like old-timers, moving apart and close, him hard at her lower lips. She'd driven in her decrepit 1989 Camaro, and in the parking lot, he pushed her ass up against the door, grating his fingernails across the chipping red paint, shards crumbling loose onto the pavement, as he deep-kissed her and ground against her. They had rough sex in the backseat before heading back to her apartment and making love again in her bed.

***

Prowling the borders of Oblivion
Reach your hand in
Reach your hard-on in
But the Devil has a stake...

The last time Sasha met Dorian Cain, James did it for her—wore a black suit, pulled his hair back in a ponytail. Her mother served Chicken Kiev, and later they made love in her little girl's room on the canopy bed with its lacy comforter. He teased her stuffed lion with his nose. Two years more famous, two years more determined, two years more loving.

Sasha could feel the frustration draining down his spine. James took reviews personally. He could feel his creative power over his audiences. It made him feel guilty and humble and chosen.

He pressed his lips softly on Sasha's and sucked her tongue.

"I wish I could be there in Miami, baby," Sasha whispered.

"Wish you could, too, but you've seen almost every show I've done over the past two years," James said. "And you're giving me a pretty nice warm-up. See me, hear me, feel me, taste me."

"Warm me," Sasha said.

Curled with her back to his chest, she looked out the window at the big red circular full moon. He cupped her nipple with his left palm, and she closed her eyes.

In the morning, Sasha drove him to the Atlanta airport. She was on deadline for the authorized memoir of the life of Dorian Cain.

She was sitting, her laptop on her knees, on the leopard-print sleeping sofa in the living room of her two-story blue Craftsman

cottage in Grant Park, when the call came around midnight. In
the middle of the Miami show, Dorian had collapsed. He was dead
before the medics even arrived.

In the next eight hours, Sasha went from car to airport to plane
to taxi to hospital morgue to just staring at his ice-cold body,
numb and nauseous. The official cause of death was heart failure.
Dorian/James, the most passionate man she had ever known, his
heart had just stopped. She stroked his tattoo, the memory of her
lover's tongue inside her lips, his arms holding her from behind.
She broke into tears.

He'd promised her not to experiment any more with the sensor-
scarab, but she knew. And if she doubted, it was in the footage. In
the pre-concert interview, he told another reporter what he would
never say to her.

"Tonight I won't give them any choice about what they see, what
they smell, what they touch. They'll get sex all right, but on my
terms. Just one song, and I take it back for the artist. And Jeff Park
can suck my dick."

The camera surveyed the crowd and revealed a familiar figure—a
man in a trench coat with dark hair, dark glasses, dark gloves.

Sasha flew home to Atlanta, stopped at the package store on
the way home from the airport, bought three bottles of Tullamore
Dew. Then she sat on the window seat in her bedroom staring out
at the big sprawling oak whose leaves were starting to turn with
autumn's embrace, drinking whiskey after whiskey after whiskey,
lining up the dead soldiers on the hardwood floor next to the red
marble urn that contained the ashes of Dorian Cain. She left her
perch only to pour the occasional glass of water, use the bathroom,
sleep, turned off her phone after the beeps of condolence texts and
messages became too much. The air was turning chilly at night,
but she kept the window open to listen to the melody of the crickets, the rumble of the train down the end of the street.

On the fourth day, after the third bottle was empty, she opened
James's satchel, the one he always traveled with but had forgotten

on his way to Miami. She found his iPod in the side pocket where he always kept it, the one on which he saved his own recordings. She scrolled through the contents—songs he'd never played for her, promised he'd play when he returned. Titles like "The Maze of Her Own Dreaming." "Man Ray Awakens." "The Devil's Matchbook." "Forever and a Day." The song he'd been playing when he collapsed.

Sasha brewed a pot of coffee. Drank it all day until she felt the alcohol's effects purged fully from her body. Showered and washed her hair. Pulled on jeans and a Dorian Cain T-shirt. She made the call and waited.

***

About an hour later, three stiff pounds on the knocker. She hadn't made an order in nearly a year, but the code hadn't changed. She glanced out from the bathroom window and saw a purple Volkswagen Beetle parked in the driveway. She opened the door to find a girl in a knit cap and red braids, fringed brown jacket.

"Where's Lucio?"

"He's busy," she said. "But I have what you ordered."

"Busy, uh-huh, doesn't want to show his face after what happened to Dorian," Sasha said. "So honey, what's your name?"

"Susie." She fumbled in her backpack and pulled out a black box.

Sasha picked up her purse from a table by the door.

"You don't need to get any money," Susie said, looking down. "It's on the house."

"Really?" Sasha said, putting her purse back down. "And why is that? Is that Lucio's way of saying he's sorry?"

"I don't know, ma'am. That's what he said," the girl answered, still no eye contact.

"Anything I should know about this batch?"

"It's what you asked for, the same as Dorian Cain."

"So Lucio is admitting that Dorian was on sensor when he died?" Susie handed the box to Sasha, gave a half-smile.

"Can I go now?"

"Sure, but tell Lucio if anything happens that gives me concern, I might pay him a visit …down at the lab."

"OK," Susie stepped back. "Night."

The girl gave a jittery wave and headed back to the VW.

Sasha closed the door, sat on the fainting couch. She leaned back, raised her legs and cradled the box in her hand. In the beginning, she and James had consumed the scarabs together. Their juices enhanced his music, and later their lovemaking. But then things changed. She started seeing odd things at the corners of her vision—curtains blowing, beetles scampering or fluttering, blinking eyes watching, a gloved hand with a knife. She asked James but he denied any similar anomalies. And yet she detected a shakiness in his voice, saw a twitch in his hand after sessions. Still, she didn't push. What was it when a woman got close to a man that sometimes made her not speak up even when she was worried? Was it because with her last lover she did speak and warn and then he left her? She hated the thought of being that woman, even though James gave no sign of even thinking of leaving her. And yet now he had left her. If she had pushed him more, even gently, instead of giving into her own fears of being abandoned again, would he still be here?

She had suspected that James had continued to partake in the scarab. He would disappear for hours, telling her he was at the studio. She hadn't minded. More time for her to write his bio, and she valued her time alone, too, knew from past experience that too much time together can be strangling. She thought of that moment when her last lover had left and how "I Wanna Be Free" by Davy Jones came on the radio, and she realized she was happy he was gone, remembered that the only child in her could entertain herself quite well. But oh, it was nice to be held at night.

Sasha opened the box. The scarab inside began to buzz softly, flutter. She couldn't let it fly away so she grabbed it quickly and firmly. It twitched, but then fell still as if zen with its fate. The creature was big, four inches long, and almost all red, not just the smudge on the back of the ones she had before. The jewel-toned scarlet shimmered in the light from the Peter Pan lamp beside her, a bit of 1940s kitsch with an Erte-esque femme fatale in green tunic and cap holding up the bulb.

She hesitated, considered letting the scarab fly away instead. But she needed to figure out what Dorian had seen, even if she had to admit she was scared of what she might discover.

"Sorry, little guy."

Sasha popped the scarab in her mouth, crunched down, felt the entheogen spew into her cheeks as she chewed, then swim down her throat. She picked up the iPod from the coffee table and selected the first song in the sequence.

A rough wiry bass-line slashed across her eardrum, like hot lava coursing down the ear canal. Then the music curved, reconfigured.

The splash of water, foamy waves flowing onto an empty beach. Sand sea-green. Palm trees curved like archways. Walking through the sand in her bare toes. Shells sparkle in the twilight, setting sun on the pink horizon. A monkey with white-framed features scampers out from the trees, pauses, startled to see a companion on the beach, then runs along.

Do angels believe in ghosts?

Dorian's voice, like a pendulum's swing muffled by water. Ambient rather than hard.

Do angels, do angels, do angels believe in ghosts?

Dorian's voice mysterious over the tide.

An army of mermen, sensuous with long, thick green seaweed hair and piercing blue eyes—pure sex—their fins flip up and down in the waves. They tease her, testing her celibacy after Dorian's death. She walks to the water's edge, feels clammy sea-stained sand against the soles of her feet.

Follow me to the other side.

A slippery fall of cello. The mermen are gone.

Sky now periwinkle darkens into blackness, starless night. Out in the ocean, the waves rage rough as a drum solo gathers force, strike the shore, splashing her until she is soaked.

Follow the tide.

Theremin edge.

She feels a tickling, scratching on her toes, looks down to see sensor-scarabs scampering across them. The water isn't water, but an army of insects. They flood across her feet and onto the beach until there is no beach, just a seething horde and more coming, an incoming tide of bugs.

Forever and a day, we'll be together forever and a day.

The music recedes again into chittering as the scarab wave reaches the line of palm trees and up the creatures climb until they reach the leaves and the coconuts. Only the coconuts aren't coconuts. They are giant eyes and they are watching her.

Never tear us apart.

Guitar riffs cut like a chainsaw. Sasha opens her eyes. How time passes when under the influence of the sensor. She stretches, yawning loudly. She curls into a ball—content, secure, inexplicably filled with happiness. The chittering is gone, and Dorian's voice sings deep in her head like a lullaby.

Even love won't tear us apart again.

"It's true you know, baby."

Sasha rolls over and sees Dorian on his knees by the bedside. Only it's her bed from her house—the black wrought-iron canopy bed with red-velvet curtains—but not her floor. Instead a checkerboard of granite tiles and behind a row of tall arched stained glass windows. Scarlet concert smoke swirls around them, its smell cloying. They're in the church where she first heard him play.

A ripple of keyboards.

She is lost in the maze of her own dreaming.

"I loved you, James," Sasha whispers, knowing she's found what she was looking for. "I loved you."

His hair folds around his cheekbones like a rock barbarian, his chest bare like a romance novel cover. He reaches out a hand and strokes her cheek. She expects his touch to be cool but finds it unexpectedly warm.

"You think I'm a dream, pussycat. Don't you?"

"Of course you are, some fuckin' dream I'll regret in the morning."

Sasha sighs and reaches her head up to kiss his cheek.

"Do I feel like a dream?"

"No, but that's the nature of dreams. They feel real, inexplicably real."

Sasha can't resist his lips, the opportunity to kiss him again long and full in the illusion.

The bass cuts in again like a razor.

Screaming, fuck you. I'll fuck you baby, too.

"I've been waiting for you to play the music, Sasha," Dorian says, running his tongue up her neck.

Fuck me.

In the dreamtime.

And don't let me wake up until I've come.

Sasha gives in to his hands, his lips, lets him touch her and lick her all over. Run his fingers across her chest, pinch her nipples, suck them, probe her insides.

Any moment it'll be over.

Dorian rolls onto his side, caresses her cheek, smiles into her eyes. She turns over and he wraps himself around her back.

"You've got to get me back into my real body, so we can be together," he continues.

"What do you mean?" Sasha asks, fighting the urge just to relax, remain safe in her lover's arms. Does she need answers or would it be okay just to give in? Except she knows it isn't really safe—that safety is part of the illusion.

Sasha rolls back over to look at him.

"Don't you see what's happened?"

His eyes twitch, his hands twitch.

"When I played in Miami, Sasha, it was just too much. Something went wrong. Went bad. One moment I'm on stage, the next I'm part of the songs. I can't escape by myself. The scarabs won't let me."

"What?"

"I'm sorry I didn't tell you but I know you know I'd been experimenting with the sensor-scarabs. Just think of the concept artistically—if we could transmit the same message, transport them to the same place. Like acid, baby, a shared acid trip without getting fucked up."

"That's crazy, James," Sasha says. "The sensor-scarab is just an insect that has some kind of life-blood that taps into the brain and plays with our subconscious."

"No, you don't get it. When I play for the scarabs, they listen, and if I concentrate on the senses I want to express, they absorb what's in my head, memorize it, recreate it. But something went wrong, and my mind became severed from my body, melded into the music. I don't fuckin' understand it myself. You've got to go see Lucio. He knows what I was doing. He can bring me back."

"I saw your dead body. Then I had you cremated, just like you wanted. Your ashes are in an urn at my house."

James's eyes stare at Sasha blankly. He loosens his grip and slips out from their embrace, spreads his arms wide.

"No. That's not right. There's been some mistake. Can't you fuckin' see, Sasha. I'm alive."

James rolls away from her, turns his head towards the window, his hair hiding his face. Sasha reaches her hand up to stroke his shoulder. Can Dorian Cain—the late great, her lover—be alive, trapped by insects inside the song he composed? The whole experience—see, hear, touch, smell, taste—does seem far too vivid to be merely a dream. Can this be James?

Drums build in the periphery of her hearing. Behind him, through the window, a shadow and then as if walking out from the wall, a familiar figure with dark glasses raising a knife. The glass shatters inward behind the man in the trenchcoat, curving around him, not affecting his pace—slow, deliberate. The wind of the impact knocks her and James off the bed onto the floor into a pool of blood.

The red liquid ripples outward, thousands of tiny bumps scurrying, swimming—sensor-scarabs everywhere. Sasha reaches to grab James's hand, but it's icy cold, limp. The man in the trenchcoat is turning to come around the bed, knife in his black-gloved hand ready to strike. He opens his mouth—the metal grin.

Sasha closes her eyes, wills herself awake.

When she re-opens them she is back on the fainting couch, her heart beating rapidly, the crickets humming outside.

For the first time since James was gone, she gets up and shuts the windows, room to room, all through the house. She crawls into bed, not sure if she can sleep but knowing she needs time to think, time before she goes to see Lucio.

***

The following night, Sasha put on the white dress and shawl she wore when she first met James/Dorian, emptied his satchel and repacked it with his urn. In it, she'd found a notebook, a map and a postcard—Atlanta Undead Apocalypse. The AUA was an annual homegrown Halloween attraction "labor of blood" created by local horror SFX artists and staffed by the city's hordes of horror fans. Every October, the Southern metropolis transformed into Halloween-Town, not that anyone would know it from any of the official tourist brochures. It was all very grassroots, word of mouth. Lucio was the AUA's benign benefactor, its executive producer. The old motel complex with its woods out back not only was big enough for an expansive paintball zombie warzone, but also a perfect front to hide a breeding laboratory for entire hives of sensor-scarabs and launder all that hard cash.

The AUA was south of the Starlight Drive-in, its vintage neon sign and the line of cars outside a vestige of a past the city mostly had neglected to preserve. Beyond the Starlight, Moreland Avenue faded into a dark industrial wasteland. Sasha passed one other oasis of light, a mega-pump gas station as she came up on I-285, the perimeter highway that looped around Atlanta. On the other side, the shadow of a giant landfill loomed to the left like an ancient burial mound. A block later she eased the old Camaro onto a right-fork ramp which merged into a streetlight-less stretch of road, turned the bend and pulled into the AUA's chain-link gates. Spotlights illuminated the camouflage-painted façade of the former two-story motel, a design which made sense when one considered that most of the year the place was a paintball weaponry course, popular with the Second Amendment and survivalist crowd.

A shaggy-haired kid in a Metallica shirt waved her down. She rolled down her window.

"Parking's five bucks."

"I'm here to see Lucio."

The kid threw her a squinty look.

"The word?"

"Osiris."

He shrugged, backed away, waved her along. Heavy metal music blasted in her windows as she drove past the motel's front, a long loud line of haunt-goers, mostly in T-shirts and jeans, trailing along its edifice. She parked at the less-lit far end. A lone zombie, face airbrushed green with latex scarring, terrycloth white bathrobe slathered in blood, sat in a lawnchair before a door covered in black paper. As she stepped out of the car, the satchel slung over one shoulder, he looked up from his iPhone.

"Tell Lucio it's Sasha," she said.

"The word?" he asked.

"Anubis."

The zombie texted into his phone.

A few seconds later, it rumbled back that a return message had been received.

The zombie rose, beckoned for her to follow him through a glass door that had been taped over with rows of black electric tape. Once inside he pulled out a pin-flashlight. In its far-from-sufficient light, she could see a stairwell, but he quickly guided her through another glass door into a hallway. The rank smell of moldy carpet assailed her. She pinched her nose as he led her past a row of doors, some shut with rusty numbers, others cracked open and dark inside. With that tiny light, she couldn't see much. Screams and bursts of paintball AK-47 rounds drifted up from the far end of the hall.

About halfway down, the zombie turned again, the flashlight's thin beam flashing briefly against a dark cracked Coke machine and an ice maker. The sticky floor caught at her boot soles momentarily, and then they were outside again, emerging onto the cracked concrete patio of a tarp-covered swimming pool, its only visible feature a gray paint-chipped diving board on this end. She heard a faint insect hum as they circled past decrepit metal chairs and round tables with posts in the center but no umbrellas. Groaning, gunfire and screaming erupted on the far side of the adjoining courtyard as a pack of faux-zombies converged on about a dozen AUA patrons being herded by a couple of full-geared commandos.

The bath house couldn't look more deserted, more derelict, even though it was clearly the only part of the motel complex that had ever had any real style. Some owner must've thought they could cash in on *Gone With the Wind* fans if they gave it a plantation theme with white columns and green double doors. The paint was badly peeling like everywhere at the AUA that hadn't been rehabbed with faux graffiti and horror-themed murals, but Sasha guessed that Lucio had adopted it as his HQ since the antebellum look didn't really fit with the modern zombie world-coming-to-an-end theme.

Her zombie escort did the triple knock. A few minutes passed before one of the doors opened wide and a giggling Susie popped out.

The zombie kid hesitated, but she quickly shooed him away with her hand, shutting the door as soon as Sasha was inside.

The foyer was round with an about 10-foot circumference, two narrow sofas, a few metal chairs. At the far end was a window where an attendant once would have sat, handing out towels and selling snacks and sodas. A small table lamp was lit in the booth, a magazine spread open. But what Sasha noticed first was not the sight but the sound. The humming, chittering, the music of the scarabs. They weren't here but they were near.

She didn't see Lucio enter, but he must have come in through the black curtain from the left. He looked the same as when she first met him—his long yellow dreads, vampire-pale skin, red contact lenses, long fingers with manicured nails. He was dressed in a silver smoking jacket with black pants, tall biker boots. He clearly fancied himself a rock star of his own ilk.

"Bonjour, dearest Sasha," Lucio said, stretching out a hand.

She lifted hers, but he didn't shake. Instead he turned it over and kissed it.

"My deepest condolences. Dorian was an exceptional man, you know he was dear to me, too."

"Dear to you because he was your meal ticket," Sasha said.

"Now, now, Sasha, that isn't very polite when you haven't seen someone in a long time and I have provided you with so much...," he paused, stretching wide open his mouth, smiling with his perfect straight teeth "...pleasure."

"What happened to Dorian? What were the two of you up to? What did he attempt in Miami? Some super-sensor-scarab? He went on about the five senses. And then last night he told me to come see you. That you could bring him back."

"Last night? But Dorian Cain is dead, my love. Oh, sweet girl, did he speak to you from beyond the grave?"

Lucio threw his head back and laughed. Susie twittered again, too.

"Can you?"

"I am not God," Lucio said, his face turning somber. Susie stopped laughing as well. "The elders in Guatemala, they say they cannot say what the scarab can do and not do, so how can I?

He stretched out his palms towards her, revealing on each a sensor scarab, the largest she had seen, bright red like the one she had consumed last night. They fluttered their elytra but did not fly away.

"But there is a legend they tell that if a man—or a woman—takes last breath with the sensor serum inside then he—or she—lives forever. Are you here to find out if it is more than legend?"

Smooth Lucio, she knew he would never answer questions in any kind of straight fashion. From the notebook in Dorian's satchel, she'd learned that he was a retired SEAL, then CIA. Hard to imagine him in a crew cut and fatigues, harder in a suit. He'd discovered the sensor-scarab on a mission; he'd brought the first batch back, headed the experiments. How did someone retire after all that? Then he took what he learned and used it to set up a booming business as a drug lord.

James believed Lucio was a friend, that he could be trusted, that they were collaborating in a grand experiment that would change the face of rock music. Among his notes were references to the FDA and a big pharma company called NECO. Just think of the net profits if sensor were legal, by prescription. But the resurrection part, was it more than ironic that she was talking about life after death at a zombie Halloween attraction?! Or was it just part of the sensor-fantasy, the seduction to lure her back? Make her forget the bad sides of her trips?

The scarabs in Lucio's palms had ceased fluttering, but they hummed loudly like lead vocalists over the general orchestra of buzzing, the chitterers and occasional squealers providing the equivalent of bass, drums, and intermittent Nina Hagen shrieks.

"I assure you, princess, we would never let anyone, much less the great Dorian Cain, consume the sensor-scarab if it had not been tested thoroughly," Lucio said, shifting his tone as if trying another tactic. "Are you sure, lovely Sasha, that you weren't experiencing the combined effect of it and some other hallucinogenic substance? Raza, jetsam, old-fashioned LSD perhaps? We don't recommend that you use the sensor while under the effects of any other drug, you know, except perhaps common alcoholic beverages."

Susie chirped again.

"Cut the bullshit, Lucio, and you know I don't even drink," Sasha said, impatient.

"Bullshit, that isn't kind, precious," Lucio said. "But I know what you want. You want to know what James and I were doing together during all those days when he left you home alone."

Was it some instinct honed in his intelligence training to cut right to her deepest vulnerability? Sasha forced herself not to give him the satisfaction of showing he'd touched a deep wound.

"Yes, show me."

"Then follow me, my dear," he said closing his hands again around the scarabs. They both squealed, objecting to the sudden pressure of his fingers. Then he swept his left fist towards the black curtain. "Ladies first."

Susie reached down under the shelf in the service booth and pulled out a large stocky flashlight. She snapped it on, revealing a beam considerably wider and brighter than the one the zombie kid had brandished. Sasha stepped through the doorway and into a changing room. Lucio and Susie followed behind her, letting the curtain fall back after they had passed.

In the room's center was a wooden trapdoor. Lucio stepped forward and grasped the metal handle, pulled it up to reveal a ladder. The insect hum rose up from below, louder, closer. The three descended and Lucio pushed open a metal door that took them into a large tiled chamber, the symphony of the scarabs now so loud and shrill that Sasha almost stuck her fingers in her ears. Lucio and Susie flanked her, the beam revealing what she had suspected.

They were in the pool, and they were not alone. Sensor-scarabs everywhere—crawling on the floors, the walls, buzzing through the air all around them. Not like the ones she had first sampled with James but like the one Susie brought her last night, the ones in Lucio's fists—bigger, redder, shinier.

"My dear, I should not have teased you upstairs," Lucio said. "You've had a highly vivid dream. Believe me, it would be quite fascinating if our little scarab could resurrect the dead. We know that it has an ability to remember images, scents, even touch sensations. What James and I discovered was that if you play a specific piece of music to the scarab, it memorizes it. But not just that, they have a hive mind. So if you play a song and you partake of the sensor at the same time, whatever is in your subconscious gets transmitted to all the scarabs within the hive. James was right, for at least one generation of scarab, anyone who listened to his new album would have a shared, similar if not exact sensor-fantasy. So in a way, yes, your lover is still alive, at least as long as these scarabs are."

Susie giggled again, or was it more of a chitter?

Then she lunged at Sasha, her arms surprisingly strong for a girl that size. Lucio raised his right fist and then the other to Sasha's mouth, prying it open and stuffing first one, then the other scarab inside. She tried to struggle but could already feel the entheogen kicking in. With Lucio's hand over her mouth, chewing became a reflex to prevent her from choking, suffocating, the liquid flowing out with each bite, the taste sweet and bitter on her tongue like eating dreams.

Sasha felt Lucio's hand fall away, her mouth fall open, oxygen flowing in. Through blurry vision, she saw him reach to the side and flip some kind of switch. The music began. First softly, then faster, faster, louder, louder, the scarabs more and more frenzied, the room itself shaking. Sasha couldn't make out individual beetles any more. Just swirling clouds of scarlet.

The last drop of sensor slid down her throat, rushed to her head.

The satchel slipped from her shoulder, a thud as the urn hit the floor. Then she followed it.

She feels a hand on her pulse.

"She's very cold." Susie's voice tingles faintly, from far away.

"Bring up her body heat," Lucio replies. "I want to see what happens."

Sasha feels her shawl being removed, pokes across her chest, around her heart and on her forehead as if buttons are being attached.

Then scarabs stream across her, no, a blanket. She wraps herself tightly, curling fetal into a sand-pocket, and stares out into a jet-black ocean. The waves glide gently against the shore, calm with the lack of wind. The air almost unearthly still.

Do demons believe in ghosts?

Dorian's voice quivers in the breeze. If he was trying to create a consistent experience that would run through every play of the same song, this is remarkably close. Though different. No mermen this time. Different enough.

Do the devils, do the devils believe in ghosts?

Sasha turns away from the sea towards the sparkling green sand, sees her blue two-story Craftsman cottage behind a wrought-iron fence. The sand is soft, not grainy, and moist under her step as she walks towards the door. She opens it and steps inside.

How relaxing to be home. She can't remember how she got there.

And then he's standing in front of her—James naked and smiling.

"I knew you'd come back," he says. "Now darling, just tell me how I can get back into my body. Have you got it ready?"

"I dropped the urn," Sasha says, looking around her feet on the floor. "When Lucio fed me the scarabs."

She has never seen him cry, but tears well up in his eyes and run down his face. His skin seems to be falling with them, slipping down and gliding back in place.

"There's been a mistake," he says, shaking his head again and again, faster and faster, grabbing her by the shoulders. "Sasha, I'm alive. Can't you fucking see I'm alive?"

Sasha pulls him close to her and runs her fingers lightly through his hair.

"I'm sorry, baby," she whispers. "I'm so sorry."

James pulls back. His eyes upon hers, with one hand he reaches up and caresses her cheek.

"We can be together, baby. Don't you see? You can stay here with me. We might even live forever. Who knows? I mean, hell, how could we die? We're in some other dimension. We'll be immortal—no bullshit, no fuckers."

"What are you talking about? Stay where? I don't even know where I am. Inside the sensor-scarab's psyche? Lucio said that when the herd dies, so will the memory."

"No, Sasha," he shakes his head, his hair falling across his left eye. "Not in the scarab, inside the song. Playing my songs opens the door; come through, and your mind accesses me. Like you type in the password and the contents spill onto the screen. Except they're spilling into your brain, baby. Just the right combination of notes to recreate all the happiness I feel with you, here in your house. The problem was, I fucked up, baby. I felt too strongly. I got so involved as I played the music that my mind couldn't pull out. So here I am, all alone, here, in the place where I loved you with no you."

He kisses her forehead.

"But you're here now," he says. "The music brought you here. And you can stay forever."

"Forever," she repeats. "Forever and a day."

Forever and a day alone with Dorian. Forever and a day, Dorian alone.

"Please say yes, Sasha, yes, Dorian, I'll stay. Sasha, I love you."

He kisses her on the cheek, on the mouth, curling his tongue into a thick snaky loop down her throat and out again. He licks down her neck, traces her breasts slowly in a figure-eight, her stomach, bellybutton, abdomen, pulls up her skirt, touches her beneath. She feels a sharp tinge of pleasure, of memory, of how he knows every inch of her body, every nook, every crevice.

Then he is just licking and she is standing still, her eyes locked on the whiteness of the ceiling, the familiar—the fainting couch, the Peter Pan lamp, the photo of them together in the little red and green Italian frame.

The words echo in her head now on permanent repeat like a scratched record.

Forever. Forever and a day. Forever. Forever and a day. Forever. Forever and a day.

She pulls away. She stares into his eyes and sees something she has missed or hasn't wanted to see so clearly.

A simple child's game—a pinball shot and a roll. The pupils are dilated, the whites wide and hungry—as if at any moment they can open like a white hole and suck, a gaping mouth not with a hunger but with an inevitability that extends like a tunnel into infinity. Into nothing.

She walks over to the small bookcase. The books still sit there on the shelves. The covers are even colored, but they have no titles. She pulls a green one off the shelf and cracks it open. The pages shine white, no words, just blank. She turns back. James is watching her every move.

"James, what do you do when I'm not here?"

He stares at her.

"I mean, what do you do? How do you pass the time? Do you watch TV? Surf the Net? Listen to music?"

But he says nothing, just looks at her—just marbles. He walks over to her, takes the book from her hands, and lays it down on the shelf.

"I've been waiting for you, Sasha. Isn't that enough? Isn't forever enough?"

Dorian Cain was larger than life, but neither Dorian nor James would have been content to be shut inside an illusion with her. He would go ape-shit in one day. She'd never wanted to be trapped in a cage either. She needed to have two lives—one to share, one to keep. He did, too. He did.

"Tell me, James, that book you really loved, the one about the two brothers. What was it called?"

"Who gives a fuck. Come to bed, baby."

"Your sister? What's her name?"

"Come, baby, come."

"Your father? What's his name?"

"I missed you so much."

Sasha pulls her hands from his grasp and slaps him hard across his cheek.

Dorian looks back at her as if staring through a haze. He squints his eyes. Then he reaches his head forward as if to kiss her again.

"No, James," Sasha pulls back further. "You don't know, James. Do you?"

"Kiss me, Sasha," he begs. "Why won't you kiss me?"

"No, James."

Sasha says it even louder, almost shouting it. He keeps groping for her.

"Sasha, I love you. I love you. I'll love you forever, forever and a day."

She trips backwards towards the door. His voice is a dull whine, and then behind him she sees a familiar figure in dark glasses approaching from the kitchen.

"I'll love you, Sasha, forever, forever and a day."

A black-gloved hand lifts a butcher knife.

An old warped LP spins round and round and round and round. James is moving towards her like a slow motion video-blip, arms outstretched, a visual to an easy-listening love song, droning on:

"Forever, forever and a day. I love you."

Sasha tries to reach out and save him, but invisible hands pull her back, yank her into the front door. The man in the trenchcoat plunges the knife into James's back. Blood explodes everywhere as the knife descends again and again, and James crumples to the floor.

Dying forever for the third time.

The man in the trenchcoat is now stepping across the body towards her. Sasha scratches at the pressure on her chest, on her forehead, feels small weights fall away. No longer tethered, she swings around and pulls the door open, leaps into darkness.

The beach is gone, replaced by pitch black, pouring rain, a flash of lightning? The deafening hum. The rain isn't rain. Scarabs. Everywhere. Falling from the sky.

The scarabs land on her dress, circling it in wide bands, a tingling sensation as they crawl on her body, dripping thick black liquid icy cold through the fabric to her skin.

A hand grabs at her arm as she starts up the steps, but she shakes it off. Or maybe the clouds of scarabs around her protect her. She keeps running until she is outside, throwing open the doors, a wave of scarabs flooding out behind her flying up into the night sky.

She circles the covered pool and dashes into the courtyard, scarabs trailing her, swarming everywhere and away. On the other side of the lawn, she hears heavy music, a band playing somewhere ahead, remembers vaguely from the flyer about concerts after the AUA's closing. She's not sure where she's going, just keep moving, get away, get to the music, find people. Most of the scarabs have left her now, flying to wherever, free. But a few linger, buzz. Her dress is striped with their inky residue.

As she rounds the side of the motel, the music is louder and she sees its source, the back side of a curved stone building with tall stained glass windows, colored lights reflecting against the panes from inside. If she can just get to it, get inside. A ladder leans against the wall. She climbs it. The rungs are slippery so she shakes off her shoes, hears them bounce on the pavement below. She reaches the base of the window and climbs onto the ledge, meets the glass in an embrace. Throbbing amped rumble vibrates through the pane. Enthralled by the light's beauty and the beat, she begins to dance, well, more sway, the space too narrow for anything else. Her hair is wet and heavy. The light, the sound through the window comfort, call. She can see shadows of movement inside.

She glances back to see if he is still watching her from below—the man in the trenchcoat. He is, expressionless, still wearing dark glasses, clutching a wide black umbrella. He pulls the blade from his pocket with his gloved left hand, brandishes it with a single slash and nods.

Sasha turns back to the window. She looks down, her dress is zebra-striped from the inky stains of insect trespass. She wants to get out of the rain. She shivers at the cold drenching drops and inside looks so warm. She slams her head into the glass.

Sharp pain in her forehead, through her eye, down her cheek. She propels her body forward, leaps—no, flies. Hundreds of tiny stabs impact her flesh, so sudden, so many.

Like freedom.

THE RED CHURCH

ORRIN GREY

At first, Yvonne was happy to get the assignment. She'd been working for *The Current* for two months now, and hadn't gotten anything even remotely interesting. Art walks, First Fridays, gallery openings. Nothing juicy.

Wade Gorman was, if nothing else, juicy. He was a brilliant underground sculptor, or so the word went. He'd had a chance to go mainstream when the Sprint Center went up, was supposed to do something to commemorate the spot where the Union Prison Collapse had killed four women and injured dozens of others back in 1863, precipitating the Lawrence Massacre. The designs he turned in got him kicked off the commission. Yvonne couldn't find any good pictures of them online, but the blurry cellphone photos she did turn up looked like a sort of tower made of piled bodies, though whether those bodies were wrapped together in death or pleasure, she couldn't tell.

"Why would you even commission someone like Gorman for something like that?" she asked Dale one evening, spinning her laptop around on the kitchen counter to show him one of Gorman's sculptures, a variant on Saint Sebastian; bald, gray, and sunken-eyed, looking like a corpse from a plague pit, and impaled with dozens of lengths of rebar.

"The people who put that stuff together don't even know what he does," Dale said, leaning down to slide a pan of vegetables into the oven. "They just tell their assistant, 'Give me someone hip, someone edgy,' and then when their assistant brings them a guy who sculpts stacked corpses, they chew his ass."

There was surprisingly little about Gorman on the Internet. She was able to find a few pictures of his early work, but nothing for at least the last six years. Her editor said he was still working, though, churning away in this building that he owned outright, that was his apartment and studio all in one. "New projects," her editor said. "Nobody's ever even seen them. It'll be an exclusive."

In more ways than one, she found, because Gorman had never, ever agreed to an interview before. Even when he got the commission and lost it, when the *Star* was hounding him for a piece, when even the national news syndicates had come down to try to talk to him, he'd turned everyone away with short, terse replies and "No comments."

Yvonne didn't ask her editor why now. She assumed that Gorman was planning some kind of comeback, and hoped to use the interview as a catapult. But more than that, she didn't actually care why. She was so damn sick of fluff pieces, so happy to get something she could at least sink her teeth into, that she didn't want to look too closely at the mouths of any gift horses.

Gorman didn't live in one of the nice lofts in the Crossroads, like most of the artists she knew. His building was farther downtown, and farther east. A brick two-story with a thick iron door and an electrical substation across the street, an old envelope factory next to that. There was nothing else on the block where Gorman's building sat, and the weeds in the vacant lots on either side grew taller than Yvonne, sporting unlikely purple flowers.

Her editor told her that Gorman didn't have a phone. She just had to go. "He's always there," her editor said. "Where the hell else would he be?" But the first time she went, she banged on the metal door for fifteen minutes to no avail. Upon first driving down, she'd assumed that the factory across the street was closed, maybe turned into lofts like all the others, but there were workers standing out on the loading dock smoking cigarettes. They watched her, and talked amongst themselves in quick, quiet bursts, but thankfully they didn't cross the street, didn't hoot or yell or whistle, even though she was wearing the black skirt that she knew showed off her ass. Eventually, she drove home and left a message on her editor's voicemail that Gorman hadn't been in.

She got a text message back saying, "Try again."

***

The next time she went by Gorman's building it was spitting rain out of a gray sky. She went on a Saturday, because maybe Gorman would be more likely to be home then. Maybe he secretly had to get a day job to support himself, since he wasn't selling any sculptures these days. Maybe he was even working across the street at the envelope factory.

She also figured that, on a Saturday, there wouldn't be anyone at the factory to watch her. But as she stood in the damp air and pounded the heel of her hand against the door, stepping from foot to foot because of the cold that bit with each gust of wind, she found herself wishing that they were back, because their stares and whispers were better than the barrenness that filled the place now.

Though she was constantly *aware* of the danger, she'd never felt unsafe in the city. She was always conscious of the proximity of so many other people, and it comforted her. The country was the place she couldn't abide, where emptiness stretched out around her like the cold vacuum of space. Here, though, standing outside of Gorman's building, she felt that same loneliness, felt cut off from all the souls that she knew inhabited the city in which she lived.

As she was thinking of that, the door suddenly disappeared from beneath her hand. She made a startled sound, a squeak, and was instantly annoyed with herself. It was, of course, just Gorman, towering in the now-open doorway. She took him in with a glance. There'd been the occasional picture in the papers, but they didn't capture him. Didn't capture his height, the distinctness of his moon-shaped head, his forehead and chin so prominent as to be called jutting, his eyes dark and small, like beads set in his face. His hands were big and strong-looking. *Sculptor's hands,* she wanted to think, but *strangler's hands* is what her mind supplied instead.

"The paper sent you?" he asked before she could speak. She nodded, then fumbled her notepad and held out her hand to shake.

He ignored her proffered hand, appraised her obviously with his gaze; not in a sexual way, she didn't think, not at all the way she was used to being appraised by men, but like he'd just been asked to judge the value of an antique clock, or the health of a stranger's horse.

"Watch your step," he said, disappearing back into the dark.

Just inside the metal door was a concrete hallway, bare and unlit except for what illumination straggled in from outside, and what fell down the metal stairs that Gorman was already halfway up by the time her eyes adjusted to the dimness. His footfalls were surprisingly quiet on the stairs, and she winced at each clang her own shoes made as she followed him.

The entire top floor was the studio. It was dark, drenched in shadow. Though the back wall was all windows, drapes were pulled closed across them, letting in only a shaft of gray light. Bare bulbs hung from the ceiling, but they seemed small and insignificant in the gloom of the place. Yvonne wondered how Gorman managed to work there at all.

But work he must, because the room was filled with pieces. She counted quickly as her eyes skimmed over them. She couldn't be sure, but she knew there had to be more than a dozen, all covered in white sheets, like the furniture in an old castle in some movie.

"Are these all recent works?" she asked, but he didn't respond. "What's your medium?" she tried again, but he simply waved his hand, as though her questions were of no importance. Yvonne shook her head, thinking that she was wasting her time, that this was going to be a very disappointing assignment after all. Then Gorman pulled the sheet off one of the figures in the middle of the studio.

In the red forest there is a red church

After that first meeting with Gorman, she had a dream. She was walking through what looked like a forest at night, only it also *didn't* look like a forest. The ground beneath her feet was as white and featureless as a sheet of paper, the night solid black and bereft of any star or cloud. The trees that grew up everywhere around her were red from trunk to tip. They appeared to be denuded of leaves, but their red branches split and split again until they became too small to see, until they became like a red cloud filling the air above her head.

***

She woke up in bed, Dale breathing easily beside her, and she realized that she couldn't remember the sculpture that Gorman had shown her. She tried to call it back to memory, but her mind kept playing tricks on her, replacing it with constellations of glowing light or masses of moving feathers. After he'd shown it to her she'd made her mumbled apologies, to which he had seemed almost pleased, as though this was the reaction he'd intended, and then she'd stumbled down the metal steps and, with their clangor still resounding in her ears, had been sick next to her Malibu.

When she'd looked up, there'd been two men standing across the street, next to the concrete wall around the substation, their hoods pulled up against the spattering rain, staring at her. They'd stood there, unmoving, until she'd wiped off her mouth and driven away.

It scared her that she couldn't remember the sculpture. The next morning, she drove down to the offices of *The Current* and sat at the curb with her engine running for twenty minutes, trying to work up the nerve to go in and tell her editor that, no, she wasn't going to be able to do this Gorman story. Or even a lie, that Gorman had refused the interview. In the end, she didn't do either, just drove away.

She didn't go back to Gorman's that day. She went out to lunch, even though it was barely ten, and then drove all the way down to the Plaza and walked around looking in windows until one o'clock. She kept telling herself that she was *going* to go to Gorman's, that she was just putting it off because he was an artist and they kept weird hours, that he probably wasn't even going to be awake before noon anyway. That excuse worked for awhile, and then she went to a movie, some light, romantic comedy that she barely remembered, something that was supposed to be funny but that she couldn't laugh at, and then she went back to the apartment before Dale got home. She ordered Chinese for dinner, and then was startled when the doorbell rang.

When Dale got home from work and asked how her day had gone, she found herself lying and telling him that Gorman hadn't been in when she went by. "He's probably trying to make himself seem mysterious," Dale said, and she just nodded.

Whatever she may have dreamed that night, she couldn't remember it upon waking.

***

The next day, she felt stupid about dodging work the day before. She drove first thing down to *The Current*, and made a big show about rooting around in her desk, picking up files, letting anyone who saw her know that she was on the job. Then she drove back over to Gorman's.

The factory was open again. It was a cold day, not raining this time, but windy enough that she clutched her notebook to her chest when she got out of the car. There was no one out on the loading dock smoking in the wind, but she felt eyes on her from the dark doorways, though she told herself that she was just being paranoid.

She beat her palm against Gorman's door and waited. At first there was no sound from the other side, just the dull echoes of her own poundings, and she worried that maybe she had pissed him off by not coming the day before. Had she said she would? She couldn't remember.

Then she heard a sound from the other side of the door. A far-off moaning, or a scraping, like something being dragged. The kind of sound a ghost might make in an old story. She leaned forward to press her ear to the door, just as it came open and Gorman was standing there. He reminded her, she realized as she whipped her head back, a little bit of Frankenstein's monster, with his jutting features and imposing height.

"You came back," he said, as though genuinely surprised to see her. "Good."

And then he was leading her up the stairs again, just walking away into the dark interior of the building, expecting her to follow.

The studio was different, she realized as soon as she crested the stairs. Everything had been moved around, and the pieces were no longer draped in their ghostly sheets. Her eyes skimmed them, skipping across each piece and waiting to take them in later, looking for the one she had seen on Saturday, the one she still couldn't remember, but none of them looked familiar.

"Are these…" she started to ask, but Gorman shook his head, gesturing around.

"Look at them first," he said. "Take your time."

So she did, walking from piece to piece, letting her gaze soak up all the details. Though they seemed natural extensions of Gorman's earlier work, still she'd never really seen anything like them. She'd gone to that Bodies Revealed exhibit with Dale when it came to Union Station, but these weren't like those.

She couldn't tell what they were made of, but they looked real. Human bodies, stripped of skin and exploded, so that their anatomies seemed to be bursting apart. Here was a head, the side flying off, one eye leaping forward, and a glowing lightbulb in the place where the brain should have been. There was a man whose ribcage swung open to reveal organs suspended on wires, like a macabre orrery. Each of them affixed all over with careful little paper squares bearing letters and numbers, figures from the Greek alphabet, and symbols she'd never seen before.

Of course they couldn't be real, she knew that, but they *looked* real. She reached out to touch one, but her hand paused, hovering just over a suspended heart. "What are they?" she asked, without looking over her shoulder to where Gorman stood.

"Saints," Gorman replied. "Angels. Apostles. Boddhisatvas. They come to bring us the word, the light. They go before, to show us the way."

That wasn't really what she'd been asking. Not *What do they represent?* but *What are they made of?* Still, it made her remember that she was supposed to be interviewing, made her pull her hand back, fumble out her notepad, her pen.

Saints, she wrote on the otherwise blank yellow page. *Angels.*

In the red church there is a red altar

The next time she had the dream, she saw a building through the trees. It seemed strange to her, even in the dream, because the building and the trees were the same color, so how could she see it?

It was a wood-plank church, like the one they had in the town where she grew up, where she couldn't wait to move away. It had a little steeple and everything, except all the planks were as red as red could be. Maybe, she thought, they were cut from all these red trees, all sawed up.

In her dream, she walked up to the door of the church. It was black, not a door at all but a hole into the night sky, maybe, and as she stepped through it she felt so cold.

***

Dale woke up that time, followed her to the door of the bathroom where he stood rubbing his eyes while she let the water in the shower heat up. She wanted it hot enough to broil her, to bake her skin red.

"I'm worried about these dreams," he said, even though she hadn't told him about the dreams, not really. "You're not sleeping."

"I'm sleeping," she said as she stepped into the shower, but even as she said it she didn't know if it was true. She couldn't really remember how much sleep she *had* actually been getting.

When she'd gotten home from her second attempt at interviewing Gorman, Dale had asked her what his stuff was like. "Do you remember in *House on Haunted Hill*—the new one—when they go down into the basement? You remember those bodies in the glass cases? They're sort of like that," she'd said, even though, as time passed, she thought less and less that even *that* was quite right.

"Creepy," Dale had said, and she'd realized that, yeah, she guessed they were, but the sculptures weren't what scared her, not after that first session, anyway. What scared her was what she couldn't remember. She kept her notes carefully hidden from Dale, something that she'd never done before, because they scared her, too. They weren't like any interview notes she'd ever taken, and she couldn't remember writing them down. Couldn't remember what questions, if any, they were in answer to. Couldn't remember Gorman saying them at all.

They were just scrawls, the kind of notes she'd write if she were running out to catch a bus, and they said things like *Men of science turn their eyes toward the stars in the hopes of finding there the invisible gears that turn the universe, but you can't see the truth in the largest of things* and *The human body is a temple, it's true, but when we go to the temple, we don't worship out in the street, do we?*

***

When she went back the last time and pounded on Gorman's door, the clouds had gone away and the day was sunny, though a chilly breeze still scudded along the ground, blowing bits of trash and making the tall purple flowers in the vacant lot bob their heads. The men at the factory were standing out on the loading docks again, but this time she welcomed them, welcomed their tenuous connection to the life of the city she usually felt all around her, but from which she felt strangely severed here.

She struck the door three times, and on the third blow it simply swung open, like the front door of some haunted manor in a bad movie. She stepped inside and called Gorman's name up the stairs, but he didn't answer. She stood at the bottom, uncertain, and for a moment she considered walking down the cinderblock hallway, seeing what was on the bottom floor of the building. *Probably nothing,* she had always told herself before. *Boarded up storefronts or whatever.* But today, standing there without a guide, she was suddenly curious.

She strained her ears, listening for any hint of movement, any indication that Gorman was waiting for her at the top of the stairs, that he might descend at any moment and catch her in her trespass. All she heard was a low, distant hum, coming from down the dark hallway.

She didn't follow it. She took a step in that direction, two, and then she looked up at the top of the stairs again, at the doorway there. She could imagine Gorman standing silently in it, watching her with his moon-face, and she shook her head and ascended the stairs instead.

Gorman wasn't there. She looked in every corner, behind every sculpture. She pushed aside the drapes that blocked off his cot, and peered into the bathroom, but he wasn't anywhere to be found.

On her second visit, she'd pulled out a camera and tried to snap some photos, but Gorman had stopped her, held his hand in front of the lens and shaken his big head slowly back and forth, as though he was disappointed in her. "These aren't ready to be shown," he'd said.

But he wasn't there now, and she pulled the camera out of her bag and began taking pictures of the sculptures, hurriedly, furtively. The lighting was bad so she had to use the flash, and every time she raised her face from the viewfinder, every time her eyes adjusted to the light, she expected to see him standing there, ready to admonish her, to snatch the camera from her and smash it on the concrete floor, she wasn't sure what. But he never appeared.

Her illicit photography made her feel giddy, and when she ran out of space on her memory card she stumbled to the stairs and down them, her shoes clattering on the metal steps. As she reached the bottom, a sound came from down the dark hall at her back that stopped her in place, froze her blood. A moan. Not ghostly this time, not the sound of an unused door, but a gurgling, pleading sound. A sound that had blood in it, and pain.

She ran.

Outside, the day was still blustery, still sunny, but the men at the factory had disappeared. There was nothing anywhere that told her that the city she stood in the middle of was inhabited at all, anything but a carcass now, bereft of whatever life it had once possessed. Far off in the distance she could track what she thought was a single car moving along an overpass, but it might have been her imagination, or a trick of the light. For the first time in her life the idea struck her that maybe the city was empty, that all the windows looked in onto cobwebs and dust.

She got in her car and drove until she saw people.

Later on, she explained the moan she'd heard a million ways. Guilty conscience, overactive imagination, the wind. And even if it had been a human voice, as some tiny, inside part of her knew it had, then there were a hundred reasons for it, reasons that were none of her business, that she was better off leaving unexplored.

She went to the office late, after she was sure that her editor and anyone who knew her would be gone, and pulled up the photos on her computer. As she scrolled through them she expected, as each new image materialized, to see Gorman there, hidden by shadows, just the edge of his profile illuminated by the camera's flash. But he never appeared. Just his sculptures, their details painted in exquisite relief, every vein, every ridge of muscle preserved, captured. *They're so real*, she found herself thinking as she printed off the best of the pictures.

But they couldn't be real, could they?

And upon the red altar there is a red knife

Inside, the church was bigger than it had appeared from without. The walls were vaulted, and they alternated stripes of black and red. It was, she decided, like being in the belly of a whale, like in *Pinocchio*, as she watched the walls expand and contract, expand and contract, as though with breath.

There were scattered pews on either side of her, and ahead, where the altar and the cross would have been in the church back home, there hung a huge heart, suspended in the air and connected to the walls and ceiling by a network of branches, all beating in time to the expansion and contraction of the walls.

***

When she woke up, she slipped out of bed as slowly as she could, so as not to wake Dale, then locked herself in the bathroom and looked through the photos again. She'd taped one to her notepad, a picture of a torso with its chest removed, its innards spilling out, its organs floating up from it on wires. Beneath it she had written—in dark, repeated strokes—*This is a map of the universe.*

Of course, she couldn't remember writing it.

The next day, after she kissed Dale goodbye when he left for work, she sat at the computer and read about Gunther von Hagens and his plastination method, which had yielded up the Bodies Revealed exhibit that she and Dale had attended, and others all over the world. She looked at picture after picture of human bodies, plasticized and exploded, and she held the photos she'd taken in Gorman's studio up next to the screen. Gorman's were different, yes. Different in tone, different in style. But in detail, in execution?

She shook her head. No way. No way he'd been plasticizing real people, real bodies, and no one had heard about it.

There was a lot to read about von Hagens, and her searches also led her to the wax anatomical sculptures of Gaetano Giulio Zumbo and to images from the vaults of the Hunterian museum, with circulatory systems shellacked to wooden doors. Before she knew it, darkness had fallen outside the apartment and rain was slashing against the windows. Thunder boomed and rattled the glass, and she looked up to see that her phone showed that she'd missed a call. It was set on vibrate, but she'd been so absorbed in the macabre images she hadn't seen it light up, hadn't noticed it moving.

She picked it up, clicked over. It was Dale's number, but the voicemail, when she listened to it, wasn't any words at all, just a rasping, choking sound, and then terrible silence.

As little as two days earlier, and she would have called the police. It would have been her first thought. She would have tried Dale back and, when he didn't answer, dialed his work, and then the police. But not that night. That night she just ran, leaving the computer open to a picture of a flayed man on a flayed horse, leaving her notebook open to the last page where she'd written *Where is the red church?* Ran out into the rain to her car, and from there drove to where she knew, knew in her guts and in her bones, the call had come from.

***

She tried to call Dale three times on the way over, but the phone just rang and rang until voicemail picked it up. Each time she heard his voice telling her to leave a message, her heart jumped, thinking she was wrong, thinking he was OK after all, and then it sank again, deeper each time.

When she parked in front of Gorman's building, the phone still pressed to her ear, ringing once more, Dale's voice telling her again to leave a message and he'd get back to her, she slammed the door and stood in the rain for a minute. Her hair was soaked, spilling water down her back. She stared at the metal door, wondered if it would open this time, wondered what she'd do if it didn't.

But it did, it pushed open under her silent touch, just as it had before; as if the building was abandoned, no one home. But as she stepped inside, above the thunder of the rain pounding against the walls and the roof, she could hear a distant sound. The ringing of the phone against her ear, and the answering chime, the song they'd danced to at the Drum Room on their second anniversary, coming tinnily from down the dark hall ahead of her.

No light filtered down from upstairs, none worth mentioning came in through the door that hung half-open at her back. The hallway was dark as pitch. She hung up, and held her phone up in front of her, lighting her way.

The door at the other end was painted red, something she'd never noticed before as it had always been lost in shadows. It was metal, like the front door, and when she rested her hand against it she found it warm to the touch, as though the heater was on full blast on the other side. There was a smell, too, not like blood, or not like what she thought of as being like blood, but a hot, moist smell, like the reptile house at the zoo.

The door had a place for a padlock, but it was gone. Just a metal latch held it closed now, and she knew, somewhere in the back of her mind, in the part that remembered watching scary movies, that she shouldn't go in there, that it was a trap, that something terrible and irrevocable was waiting on the other side of that door for her and that all she had to do to survive was to run, run now, run away, and everything would be fine.

But of course it wouldn't be fine. She was too far into the movie for that. Leaving now, she was just delaying it, making it worse. What was behind that door, whatever it was, it was her fault, somehow. She knew that now. It was her bed, she'd made it, and now all that was left was to step inside and lie in it.

She opened the door.

Take the red knife and cut red bread!

Yvonne had never been in a slaughterhouse, so she couldn't compare the smell of the room to one. It smelled like snakes to her, like terrariums and like the red, watery blood that used to pool in the bottoms of the Styrofoam containers of meat that her mother brought home from the grocery store.

The room was lit by old-fashioned fixtures set in the wall. They made a low buzzing, and at first she thought that's what she'd heard when she almost went down the hall earlier. But no. Not them. Flies.

There weren't that many of them, the ones that slipped in when the doors opened, the ones that crept in through tiny cracks in the building, but there were enough. They buzzed from place to place, settling on the black streaks of dried blood, settling on the bodies that hung from the wall in front of her.

What had she imagined she would find? Mad science labs from old movies? A surgical suite, laid out for plasticizing bodies like the ones upstairs? No, those weren't the bodies. Those were just sculptures, expertly done. Just practice. Gorman's voice, "These aren't ready to be shown." Here was the real thing. Bodies laid open, organs pulled out. Hearts still beating, lungs still pumping. Heads looking from side to side, eyes blank, gray. Breath whispering in and out in soft little moans and gasps. How did he do it? How were they still alive?

She scanned their faces, willing herself not to count them, willing herself not to feel guilty when she breathed just that much easier when she saw that Dale's face wasn't among them. Then, her phone buzzing in her hand, Dale's number flashing up on her display, and from the shadows a movement, tall and moon-faced, and the flash of a knife.

Ten years in the city, and she'd always felt safe. But her father felt safe in the country, in the small towns where they'd lived, and he still kept a gun under the front seat of his truck. She'd taken self-defense courses for six of those ten years, and while they had mostly taught her how to avoid bad situations, how to look confident, to keep her cellphone handy, they'd also taught her how to use an attacker's superior weight against him, how to turn a knife blade, how to break a wrist.

The knife clattered to the concrete floor as Gorman stumbled past her, nearly colliding with his own pieces, his own sacred relics. By the time he turned around the knife was already in her hand, and then it was in his stomach, turning, sliding up, and he was choking on blood.

If it had happened even a week earlier, it probably would have ended there. As it was, she carved and carved until Dale went on a break at work and noticed his cellphone missing. Until he called her to see if he'd left it at the apartment and got no answer. Until he drove home and found her gone, found her notes beside the computer. Until he called her editor and her editor called the police, who found her, bloodied and smiling, in the midst of the sculpture that had once been Wade Gorman. "He's a saint," she kept repeating as they dragged her away. "An angel."

BALCH CREEK

CAMERON PIERCE

The dog licked his face and whined. Charles Ellis rolled over in bed and checked the alarm clock. 5:37. Out of habit, he reached a hand out for Teresa's side of the bed, but all he felt were cold sheets. She was in Germany, thousands of miles from here.

Charles fumbled out of bed in the dark and nearly tripped over unwrapped Christmas presents stacked at the foot of the bed. He dressed in thermals and wool socks as the dog panted heavily.

Architeuthis, who they called Archie, unless he annoyed them, then simply *the dog*, was part Border Collie and part Australian Shepherd. He panted, gazed up at Charles with a pleading look in his eyes.

Charles retrieved his coat and Archie's leash from the coat rack by the front door and slipped into muddy tennis shoes. With Archie leashed, he stepped outside into the frigid forest air.

It took most of his strength to restrain Archie as they hiked up into the woods behind their condo.

Thick fog had descended over the forest, lowering visibility to what was immediately in front of him. Charles stumbled over tree roots and avoided ice patches as he led Archie to an out-of-the-way plot of grass for the dog to do his business.

When the dog finished, instead of heading straight indoors Charles turned, toward the hiking trail that curved along Balch Creek. A semi-truck rattled by on the green bridge above.

For two weeks, Charles had put off starting his latest commissioned cover painting. Over the weekend he told himself it could wait no longer. *First thing Monday morning, I'm knocking that thing out*, he'd said to Teresa when they last spoke on the phone.

A walk through the woods will clear my mind, he thought now. *Or let me procrastinate a while longer.*

As he and Archie approached the trailhead, the roar of the creek grew louder, until it eventually drowned out all other noise.

Danford Balch, the creek's namesake, was the first person ever legally hanged in Oregon. When his oldest daughter eloped with a man called Mortimer Stump, one of the Balch's hired hands, Danford Balch was enraged. Balch intercepted Mortimer in what was then downtown Portland, as the newlyweds were boarding the ferry across the Willamette River. Balch shot Stump point-blank in the face, ending the man's life and launching one of the most famous tales of tragic love in Portland history. Afterward, Balch had returned to his homestead, drenched in his son-in-law's blood. These woods, the former homestead of Danford Balch, were now considered one of the most haunted sites in the city, and people who dared wander into the forest after nightfall claimed to witness the ghosts of the Balch and Stump families, still at war with one another after all these years.

Although he did not believe in an afterlife, the legend of Danford Balch was enough to keep Charles out of the forest before sunrise and after dark. Once you fell under the canopy of Douglas firs and western hemlock, darkness became that much darker. Half the year, a plethora of mushrooms—some edible, some poisonous, some psychoactive—burst forth from everything. The other half of the year, icicles formed along the steep bank of the creek and ice coated the trail, rendering it slick and treacherous. Whether coated in ice or fungi, something about the forest unsettled Charles enough to keep him out except for daylight hours, but this morning, he preferred the dark woods to the work that awaited him.

Charles slipped on a patch of ice and momentarily considered turning back. The cold ate through his parka and thermals like a horde of starved piranhas. Archie panted happily, staring up at him. Charles patted the dog on the head. "Okay, to the waterfall and back," he said to the dog.

He took off jogging and Archie bounded ahead, pulling the leash taut and choking himself. The dog worked his muscular legs to quicken their pace. Charles sped up, but the frigid air hurt to breathe. It caught in his chest and made him light-headed. He pushed himself, letting the dog pull him, as they ascended the steep, rocky trail.

The further they went, the steeper the drop-off to their right became. The creek was now fifteen feet down. The mountainside to their left was a wall of ferns, icicles, moss, and trees that had found a way to grow vertically out of the bank. Slipping off the edge here would result in serious injury for either of them.

The fog roiled just above the white-capped water, swirling in spirals that seemed almost unnatural.

When he'd caught his breath, he and the dog continued along the trail through the darkness.

Another few curves in the trail and they arrived at the footbridge that led across the largest waterfall on the creek. Charles stood with Archie on the wooden bridge and stared down into the deep pool beneath the waterfall. Sometimes he spotted cutthroats here as they waited to pick off insects that got swept over the falls. This morning the water ran the color of mud. Charles raised his eyes to the trail ahead, where a felled Douglas fir blocked the way. Icicles hung from the fallen tree.

There in the floodwater lay a man.

Charles could just make out his form in the fog. He thought he was mistaken at first. In the forest, especially in the dark and fog, trees looked like people, rocks had faces, and the rustle of every shrub suggested a predator on the prowl.

Charles studied the man from a distance, watching for a sign of life—or for him to reveal himself to be a tree stump or some other natural thing. But the man remained a man, unmoving.

Charles felt his pocket for his cellphone, only to remember he'd left it on the kitchen counter.

Archie whined and sniffed at the air as if something troubled him.

"Come on, buddy," Charles said. "Let's see what's what."

He choked up on the dog's leash and approached. The man had fallen face-up, and the water lapped at his sides. Then Charles was standing over him, and Archie began to growl. Someone or something had torn out the man's throat. Charles had painted scenes just like it for countless lurid magazines and book covers. All he could think was *It's gone, his throat is gone.* The man's head was nearly severed, attached to his body only by frozen tendrils of blood and sinew and bone. Yet his eyes betrayed a sense of warmth and love, as if he'd died happy. Beside him lay a fishing pole.

Archie lunged for the dead man and barked. Charles restrained him, taking a firm grip on the dog's collar. His knees felt weak. Despite the freezing temperature, he broke out in a sweat. His heart thudded and fuzzy black dots crowded his vision. He was going to be sick.

What could do this to a man? he wondered. And then something occurred to him. *It might still be out here.*

He spun around in circles, inadvertently lifting Archie off his front legs as he spun, and searched for any hint of a threat, unsure what to expect. A sinister face amongst the trees? A psycho charging him with a bowie knife? The ghost of Danford Balch?

He was growing dizzy from spinning.

He was definitely going to be sick.

He bowed in half and hurled.

He wiped his mouth on his sleeve and Archie licked his leg. Such a good dog. Always trying to soothe. Charles lowered his hand to the dog and let him lick it, forgetting for the moment that they stood beside a dead body in the woods where the killer maybe lurked, maybe watched them. Only one option remained: run like hell out of the forest and call 911 as soon as they returned.

He breathed deeply, bracing himself for the long, excruciating run. He closed his eyes and tried to centralize his core, some meditation shit he remembered from his time in art school. Centralize his core. More like try not to piss himself from fear or keel over from a heart attack while overextending his out-of-shape ass.

He rearranged his grip on Archie's leash and stood on his toes, popping up and down, stretching his ankles. He stared down the trail that led to home and began a silent countdown.

10.

9.

8.

7.

6.

5.

4.

3.

Movement to his right caused him to cease counting. Amidst the trees, something moved, scaling the incline, moving at a rapid pace away from him, further into the forest.

The thing seemed moss-covered, like a tree, but with the face of a man, a face filled with razor teeth like a shark's. In its right hand, the thing wielded a shotgun. Its moss-like flesh glowed.

Somehow, the glow was the worst.

Archie cowered against Charles, whining. The dog had seen the thing too.

Without another second's hesitation, they took off running down the trail.

*** *

He couldn't get the creature off his mind, and because of it, the conference call had been a blur. He'd known the meeting was going to be bad, but that it would go as poorly as it had, damn. He'd had no idea. He shifted uncomfortably in his chair, recalling that moss-like flesh.

Jill, an old college friend and art director of a genre imprint at a New York publishing house who not infrequently found work for Charles, was on the other end of the line. Charles felt sick inside. He'd fucked up the latest commission pretty bad. His income was already dwindling, had been for several years, as digital art replaced oil and acrylic on the covers of horror and science fiction books. He couldn't afford to fuck up.

Nobody said anything for a long while, until Jill spoke up. "Charlie," she said, using the name nobody called him anymore, "can you turn in something else, something more appropriate, by next Friday?"

It was Monday. That gave him under two weeks.

"Yeah, I can do that," he said. "No problem."

And he could, if he allowed himself to fall behind on the other two covers that were due to other publishers.

"We commission work from you because you're cheap and easy to work with. What happened?"

What happened?

"That wasn't rhetorical," Jill said. "I want to know what's wrong."

Charles squeezed his eyes shut, seeing the dead man. "Yesterday morning, I came across a dead man in the woods behind our place. He'd been mauled by something."

He omitted what else he'd seen.

The moss man.

The shotgun.

The glow.

"Oh my god, that's terrible," Jill said. "You called the police, right?"

"They brought out a canine team to sniff around for bears. Guess that's what they think did it, but I don't know."

"You don't think it's a bear or…"

"I don't know what I think, Jill."

"What's Teresa think?"

"I haven't told her. She's in Germany."

"You remember that time we went to the county fair and you won that goldfish? You called me up hysterical a week later when the goldfish died. I decided not to date you after that."

"Was that how it ended? I remember things differently."

"The point is, maybe you do have an unhealthy fear of death. I mean, you destroyed your apartment over a goldfish that was half-dead to begin with, a fish you had no emotional attachment to."

"So what do you suggest?"

"Get it out of your system. Paint it out, if you have to."

"You're not going to hire me for more covers, are you?"

There was a long pause.

"It's not you," Jill said. "The industry is changing. Book buyers, our distributor…they want digital covers, photorealistic covers. I'm sure it'll swing back the other way eventually, but right now, this is what readers respond to. Paintings just aren't in vogue."

"I'm not in vogue."

"It's not you, Charlie, I promise you that. I have another phone conference. Call me if you need anything, and please do get better."

"Better in my work, or better at life?"

"Has there ever really been a difference with you?"

Charles hardly managed to say goodbye before she hung up the phone.

What's the difference?

He sprung up from the chair and left his office. He put on his hiking boots as Archie wagged his tail, knowing that the boots meant a hike. Charles pocketed a sketchpad and left home, Archie dodging around him to piss on trees and chase scents. Already Charles could hear the roar of Balch Creek, thundering more loudly than usual due to the recent heavy rain.

At the head of the trail, a bouquet of red, waxy-looking parrot tulips lay on the ground, smashed by the footfall of many people. He knew this was not what he came for, but he knelt anyway, sketched the tattered flowers. Maybe all he wanted was a little time before returning not just to the place where he'd discovered the dead man, but also to a world where his art no longer paid the bills. A Giant Pacific Salamander stared at him from the shadow of a mossy tree stump.

He made several quick sketches of the creek and the scene of the murder before the sunlight turned murky and vanished as rainclouds descended from the mountains and a fine spring rain misted down. The raindrops beaded on his thick-framed glasses and he realized that Archie was no longer at his side.

"Archie!" he called.

He heard barking in the distance.

The dog came bounding down the mountainside, trampling ferns and careening between the tall pines.

Archie skidded to a stop in the mud and looked up at Charles. The dog was so goddamn muddy, but Charles couldn't help smiling. The dog's brown irises were visible, his eyebrows expressive. They lent Archie an uncanny range of facial expressions for a dog. Right now, he was smiling, the happiest creature on the earth, and the best friend Charles ever had ever known. He patted the dog on the head and gestured toward home. Archie trotted along beside him as they turned away from the cold green wet of the woods for the warmth of home.

What's the difference?

The difference, for him, was death.

***

That evening, Charles got into his truck and drove to Portland International Airport. Teresa's flight was due in at eight.

He parked the truck and ducked out into the rain. Inside the terminal, he checked the time. He'd arrived an hour early. He walked by the gate where she'd be arriving. The plane was still scheduled to arrive at eight. He entered the nearest hotel bar and ordered a lager.

As he drank his beer, he searched for images of throat wounds on his smartphone's browser. The search results yielded images of red streaks blossomed across human necks. Knife wounds, bite wounds, hockey stick atrocities, and worse. Inexplicably, there were also numerous Nike advertisements for crimson sneakers. In one ad, the sneakers lay in a shallow creek that ran red with blood. Charles could not stifle the feeling that someone was fucking with him.

He put his phone away and watched the Trailblazers game, which played on the flat-screen television on the wall behind the bar. He ordered another beer, something darker this time.

Eventually, eight rolled around and he settled his tab and left the airport bar. He stood around with other people awaiting the arrival of their loved ones as people stepped off the plane from Germany. Around him people hugged and he felt glad to be a little buzzed. He felt uncomfortable around the intimacy of strangers. Even kissing Teresa in public made him feel self-conscious. But then she emerged from the tunnel and she looked so beautiful. She ran toward him and she looked so good in her black midi dress. He opened his arms wide, embraced her, squeezed her too tight, put his cheek to hers and felt whole again, felt like himself. He kissed her and then kissed her again. She laughed a little, obviously surprised by his show of affection. But he'd missed her. He'd missed her badly. She didn't know how badly he'd missed her.

"I brought you a present," she said. "Close your eyes and hold out your hands."

He closed his eyes and held out his hands.

She laid a heavy, stone-like object in his palms.

"Okay, open your eyes," she said.

In his hands: rubble.

A piece of a broken wall.

"It's a piece of Max Ernst's childhood home. I visited the museum in Cologne, but it was such a beautiful day, I didn't feel like being cooped up inside. So I asked the concierge if she knew where Ernst grew up and she drew me a map."

"And you happened to have a hammer on you to steal a piece of the property?"

She had a mischievous look on her face. She leaned against him, kissed his cheek. "You like it?"

"It's the best thing anyone's ever given me."

"I thought about getting you a souvenir from the museum gift shop, but everything seemed so tacky."

"I love you," he said, but for some reason it came out desperate and forced.

She looked at him quizzically. "Either you missed me more than usual or something happened while I was gone."

He focused on the heft in his hand, a piece of the childhood home of a man he never knew but had studied and worshiped for half his life. Then he recalled Sartre's *Nausea*, poor Antoine Roquentin holding the stone on the beach and becoming inexplicably sick with himself.

"I missed you is all," he said, thinking maybe he'd tell her about the dead man later, thinking maybe he'd better not. "We've got a dinner reservation at Wildwood."

"How come you missed me so much?" she asked.

"I miss you this much all the time."

She smiled as if she wanted to believe him.

"Let's go get my bags," she said, and in silence they walked to baggage claim.

In the pocket of his overcoat, Max Ernst's home felt heavy.

***

They decided to blow off their dinner reservation and on the drive home they stopped and picked up takeout Thai. Green curry and Pad Thai and shrimp rolls. Archie greeted them when they opened the door and leapt on Teresa, happy to see her home. The dog spun in circles.

They ate their food at the kitchen table in relative silence as the rain picked up outside and became a constant roar.

They opened a bottle of a cabernet they'd been saving and Charles broke out the box of truffles he'd purchased as a welcome-home present. They talked about watching a movie as they sat on the couch, drinking wine and eating chocolate, but they never decided on anything, and they never put anything on. After weeks apart, sitting together was enough. Archie lay at their feet, playing with his stuffed platypus. The stuffed animal had a hollow belly that could be stuffed with plush squeaky eggs. The dog spent many hours gnawing delicately at the belly of the platypus, attempting to remove the eggs.

The dead man seemed so far away.

After finishing the bottle of wine and eating too many truffles, they went to bed. Teresa drifted off almost right away. Charles lay awake and listened to the rain until eventually he too fell asleep.

Sometime in the night, Teresa shook him awake. She was sitting up in bed next to him. He looked at her with half-closed eyes, feeling irritated and confused, and asked, "What is it?"

"Someone's knocking on the door," she said.

Charles sighed. Teresa woke often from nightmares, had ever since she cut herself off from sleeping pills. He wondered if she'd started taking them again in Germany and quitting again had brought back the nightmares more intensely.

But then the door erupted under heavy fists. The pounding of a pissed-off man. Charles was surprised the door's glass panes hadn't shattered. Five consecutive knocks, then a brief pause before another five knocks.

"*It's glass*," Teresa said, the fear in her voice telling Charles everything she meant by those two words.

Underneath the pounding, Charles heard Archie's guttural growl. The dog's presence calmed him, and when he sprang out of bed, he felt alert and focused.

At the end of the hall, he paused and looked around the corner to the entryway, where Archie stood, hair bristling, at the door.

The panes were frosted glass, preventing Charles from seeing who stood out there pounding, but the glow of the porch light washed over someone.

Someone was there.

From this side of the door, all he could make out was a man-shaped shadow.

Charles looked about the living room and entryway, wondering how he might see who was out there without drawing attention to himself. If they knew he was here, he might be at a disadvantage.

The pounding increased now to a near-constant barrage. No pauses. Certainly, the glass should have shattered. Archie's growling lent him little confidence now.

Teresa came up behind him. "Should we call the police?" she said.

Charles shook his head, dismissing the idea.

He wondered if he could still throw a punch. He'd spent some time in boxing gyms. He used to throw a nose-breaking jab. Now his arms felt like toothpicks stuck in a bloody steak. The fear of what was out there overloaded him. He seriously debated suggesting they sneak out the back door, but a thought occurred.

We're trapped.

He did not know what it meant or why he thought it, and yet in his gut he knew it to be true. They were trapped.

The pounding on the door intensified, as if the person on the other side had many fists.

"Charles, please…" Teresa said.

She was crying now. He couldn't blame her. He was almost crying too.

Man up, mofo.

He stormed out of the hall, marching straight up to the front door, standing tall. Archie gazed up at him as if this act of courage surprised even the dog.

"Who is it?" Charles shouted.

The pounding ceased.

"What do you want?"

The shadow on the other side loomed, remaining still in a way that also suggested movement, its edges crawling.

"We've called the police," Charles said, even though they hadn't.

The shadow increased in size, smothering the porch light. Either that or the shadow began to glow.

The door handle jiggled.

They were trying the door.

They were trying the fucking door.

"Look, I don't know who you are or what you want, but—"

The pounding returned so loud that it drowned out Charles, and this time the glass did crack.

A pane of frosted glass shattered inward, shards falling down around Charles's bare feet.

Another pane shattered beneath the blow of a fist and this time Archie yelped and scampered away to cower behind the sofa, but Charles did not know if the dog was hurt or just afraid.

From behind, Teresa came up, tears streaming down her cheeks, and said, "Leave us alone! Leave us alone! Leave us alone!"

Silence.

The pitter-patter of the rain returned. The shadow dispersed.

Charles stood, listening to the rain, wanting to throw open the door and discover some meth-head asshole or something, beat the fuck out of him and go back to bed with the assurance that when the darkness of the world encroached, you could always beat it back with your fists.

Instead, he went to the phone and the phone was dead.

He pretended to speak to the police anyway. He did it for Teresa's sake.

Already he'd decided for himself that what had visited them was less than human—or more.

He and Teresa sat on the couch, holding each other, waiting for the sun to rise.

The torrent of rain was deafening. The lights of their home were all on. It almost felt like they were waiting for guests to arrive for a party. The only thing missing was everything.

HELLO, HANDSOME

GARRETT COOK

ur sisters and us we whisper beneath the glass. There are so many of them, in and out, stopping to look at the case, shaking their heads and walking. Some of them hear. Some of them bend an ear or take a closer look. Some of them we reject. We are perfect and thus, we are vain. A gangly thing with a pockmarked face wants to touch us, wants to bring us home, but we hiss and I know he hears us hiss. So he keeps walking. The girl behind the counter, she looks sad, robbed of her commission. Callous bitch.

Then we see him, then we smell him, the right one. We coo to him inaudibly soft but we know that he can hear it. His face is weathered some but not displeasing, unblemished, not browned by the sun but age and a great deal of smiling. He looks smart in his grey hat and his raincoat, so very smart. The sort of man who would shop at a store like this one, where the finest is sold to the finest. The finest, that's the sort. We cannot help but notice his hands. It is in our nature to notice someone's hands of course.

The hands are strong, the fingers slim and exquisite. His wrists are slender, the bones of his knuckles hard. These are not the beaten hands of a man his age. These are not the hands of a working man but nonetheless hands with purpose. I barely need to let him know I'm here or to talk over our sisters. He is deep but is wonderfully legible. Wonderfully, wonderfully legible. He approaches the salesgirl and points into the case.

"I'd like to see that pair."

Oh, yes, oh yes, you would. You would like to get to know us and let us know you. You would like to take us home. There are stories we read in the people that come and go about the things that happen when we're taken home, the exquisite warm sensations, the adventure and delight. Some of his secrets are legible but there is so much more to know.

She opens the case. Our sisters, our envious sisters, say "PICK us PICK us" but they know how this works. I'd say they should be ashamed of themselves but we've often shown the same lack of refinement ourselves. And looking at those hands of his, they'd all be fools not to want him or not to want him to want them. The salesgirl gingerly presents him with us.

He slides one hand in and we know that there's part of him that can hear us moaning. He extends those long and lovely fingers out, spreads them, wriggles around, filling all us secret places and crevices. We sigh in him. We know him. Angelo Sardi. A jazz pianist, he must be careful with his fingers. Oooh, those fingers…you can feel the care he takes. And we can feel that he'll take very good care of us and us of him.

We are one, the fit is perfect and it's destiny. He was made to have us forever, long as we live, long as he lives. He was made, this man, to have us forever. He fills us, we fill each other, with each other. We whisper "you are ours now, we will keep you warm. Not just your precious hands. We will keep you warm."

"I'll take them," he says. Why wouldn't he? We are in him as his hands are in us. He is slow to remove himself from us to reach for his wallet and pay. His pearly hands, his soft and skillful hands must feel cold as death now. Poor darling. Even this short separation must hurt him so. Why would it not? We are kind to him, devoted and pliant already in our moments of service and loving. The girl wraps us in tissue paper, the bitch. She places us in a small box, in the dark.

It is only moments before he has opened up this box again, freed us from our crackling tomb, freed us from suffocation and raised us to the light. Again, the ecstasies of those fine hands inside us, again, more knowledge soaking in of everything he is, of his music of his memory of his heart and hopes and fears. His father was stern and beat him with a belt. His mother was a thing chiseled out of ice, a modish untouchable mannequin who would be as much at home posing in the store as she would be shopping in it. His childhood was spent with books and records and a tyrant grand piano. This black and white beast would own his every moment.

He had one of his own now and we know it right away to be our enemy. It is his slave driver and the source of his bread all at once and when his fingers are on those keys they aren't in us and we're apart. He makes us sit on a glass table in his parlor to look at the red velvet couch and the chairs that match it. Those hands make such music rolling across our rival's spine. Those hands make it spring to life. We have not heard such music often though I'd heard snippets in the frontbrains of some of the shoppers. He is a famous man, Signor Sardi. Famous and talented and lovely. We scream for him to touch us.

He approaches cautiously, confused. Hello, handsome. It's alright. He picks us up, runs his fingers up our five fingers, feeling our exquisite black leather flesh. We tingle some. He is being cautious and being coy and driving us to sighing and desperation. You want us, Angelo Sardi, you need us, Angelo Sardi, we're one now, Angelo Sardi, come and touch us. Come and touch us, come and know us, Signor Sardi.

He doesn't know why he needs us but he does. We were in him, he was in us, he must know. He slides those perfect fingers in again and stretches them out. There is something in him that fills us with wicked notions. We think he and our wicked notions can be good friends and us with his. Sometimes he sits at the window in his living room, shades drawn, so that he can look out to the

building next door. His great, secret shame is that he does this. He
tries each day not to do this but sometimes he succumbs. As his
fingers rest inside us, he considers it. And we whisper our agree-
ment into him.

He goes to the living room and he draws the shades. Across the
street is the blonde, the great white thing. A Swede. He watches
her every time he can't not watch her. He wants her golden hair to
brush across his chest. He wants his teeth on her throat and on her
shoulders. He wants his mouth on the pink tips of her pale peaks
and those hands, those perfect hands grasping her buttocks. We
like the taste of his arousal but the thought of separation hurts us.
But somehow he knows that he wants to satisfy us.

Hands still firmly in us, he unzips his pants and pops his man-
hood out. We had seen them in people's dreams before but never
one in person. We like the firmness and smoothness of it as he
grabs it, we like the length and textures of it, the myriad different
textures and contradictions. We thirst for all his textures and contradictions. He lets out a sigh as he watches her and we clasp him
tight. She is naked at her window, all her geometries on display, all
her textures, her repulsive bubbles of texture not firm like his body
and hands not firm like…ooh.

She shimmies back and forth in place at her window, not at all
concerned about who might be watching. She actually turns and
looks right at him and she smiles a gigantic smile. She squeezes her
breasts, she leans toward him, showing her big, full, woman's body
to him, the whore. We like the hardness and firmness, we like that
he is springing to life but I hate what he feels toward her, we hate
the excitement that should belong to us, even as it belongs to us
since he is in us and we in him.

She backs out of the room and we're relieved. He is breathing,
heavy, he's confused, he doesn't get up or look away, he waits for
and he longs for and he hopes for her again. And the whore, the
tease, the subject of his worst impulse doesn't disappoint. She returns with a chair, sitting in it and facing the window as he is.

She spreads her legs wide and taunts us with her pink complexity, taunts us with the wandering of her hands which he echoes with his own, squeezing tighter, yes, tighter, yes please...squeezing tighter, pumping harder, eyes rolling back in excitement almost falling back in his skull please please please don't please don't you mustn't you mustn't let go I need this you mustn't let go we need this forget the whore we need this forget the whore we love you forget the whore we need you this look at her filth. Does that filth, does it...

That hurts. He squeezes so tight it hurts, and suddenly bubbling out, salt sweet and life dripping down the shaft and onto us where we drink it through our fingers thank you MORE...

He is finished. He breathes heavy. He's delighted in our touch on him even as his eyes delighted in her. But who should he be faithful to, his eyes or his hands? We can see in him that this has always been a difficult decision and that is really no right answer for some men. He wipes his gift, his seed from us. He just bought us, after all, and doesn't want it to crust. We want it to crust, we want it soaking through and on our every surface.

He realizes what he's doing all of a sudden. He places us once again on the glass table. Alone with a red velvet couch, alone with the red velvet chair, alone with the pedantic piano. And without him. We are without him. It isn't fair. We have only one purpose. We are here to keep him warm and why begrudge us that? We whisper at first and then we scream for him, to let him know that without him, this is a nightmare. We want only to keep him warm.

He trembles, this man of music and discipline and austerity and he lifts us up and he kisses our knuckles and he presses us to his heart. We are here to keep you warm and keep your hands clean and to touch what you don't need to judge and to absolve those hands from anything that they would need to be absolved from. Anything, our darling, we mean anything. Somehow, not feeling foolish, he takes us to bed. He sleeps with us pressed against his bare chest, feeling the beat of his heart. We stay awake in the dark full of hope and ecstasy. We are tempted to see if we can creep into his dreams and make him bring us back down to the big juicy gift between his legs to tenderly kiss and caress it and drink what it has for us to drink. But we let him sleep. We know he needs to sleep to stay so sharp and so good at what he does.

He awakens, looks down at his hands and he casts us off. He skips morning coffee and opts for whiskey instead. He sits with his shot and he looks at us there on the kitchen table, unceremoniously cast off, ungrateful bastard. After all we've given you and all we can give you! Go to your piano and your whore, you monstrous ingrate! You make us sick!

Oh, darling, we didn't mean it, oh, darling, don't be mad...

He examines us as if he expects us to move of our own volition.

"I know you can hear me," he says, scared that he is saying it, "I don't know who you are but I can feel what you're doing to us. I don't understand this."

He downs the shot and gets up and paces the room before returning to us. We coo for him coyly. We whisper his name and he feels a stirring in his stomach. He sits down with us.

"You're just a pair of gloves, I'm going crazy."

No, darling, we swear it, you're not. No, darling, it will be fine. No, darling, we're here to help you.

He picks us up and he presses us to his face, swimming in the feel of our leather, sharing skin again with us. So intimate, what we have. So perfect. Are you afraid now? You're not afraid.

He places us down again, mouthing an apology, and he goes to the tyrant piano and he starts to play, listening to a recording, following the metronome. Such discipline. We hate the piano but we love the man who plays it. We admire his discipline here but we miss his hands.

We always miss his hands. We have to keep his hands warm, we have to keep him warm. How can we do this resting on a glass table?

He finishes playing and puts his hands in us and we go for a long,

long walk through lovely Roma. He shows us how the bronze of the statues feels and tortures with the chill of gelato. He strokes the wiry fur of dogs and sneaks a pinch at a dark-haired woman's buttocks. We savor the texture, we savor the pinch and we savor his surrender but we admonish him over the whores. We are tired of the whores. He doesn't want to seem crazy so he waits until he is someplace private before saying that he is sorry. We want to say that we accept his apology and take enough pleasure from the symphony of touch he has provided but we are not content.

We lead him again to the living room and make him hurt and film him with shame. We want him to do the wrong thing. We want him now to be filled with shame and maybe we want another taste of him as he watches the whore in the building next door undressing and working her fingers and dancing for his pleasure. Again, he does this, again he feels himself as she works in and out. He feels something amid the disgust. It is just a blip, a passing fancy of a man whose mind is under duress. Loved as he is and confused as he is, he is mind is under duress.

He wants this temptation gone. He wants to be free of this. We can be free of this. We can all be alone. We know how this can be done. He shakes his head, though his body is fluttering and responding. He tries to tell us "no" as the whore at the window says yes not knowing what she had said yes to. Yes, darling, you will be fine. We will keep your hands warm. We will keep them dry and we will keep them pure. You don't need to worry anymore.

He walks off to the kitchen and finds the knife. Hello, handsome. Mmm I love the contours of its handle and the idea of the sharpness of it, the idea that it can mean the end of the whore. He holds it in his hand and begs us not to let him. It's fine darling it's fine we'll help you with this. Your hands are warm and protected. Your hands are safe from this. He hides it in the pocket of his coat. He returns to the window and he waves hello to her. She waves "hello" back. He motions for her to wait and she smiles and nods.

He walks to the front door of the ancient white building next door. He pushes the buzzer and she buzzes him up. He ascends the stairs to her apartment and he knocks, gently he knocks to spare us the impact of it. He loves us like that, he loves us so very much. We will return his affection again. We will serve our purpose and free him from this obsession. She answers the door and lets him in. She is still undressed, clad only in a big, ignorant smile.

"Sit down," she says to him and he sits down.

"Can I get you a drink?"

He nods.

He sits, breathing heavily, eager, anticipating. We tell him over and over this is a good idea. It is something that he wants. He wants to be free of this, of the nerves and the shame and the anticipation.

He places us against his heart so we can feel the beat going fast. It's alright, darling, we are here for you, darling, we are here. He stands up, whispers his love and knows this will be okay.

She enters, carrying drinks and he charges, thrusting the knife into her doughy stomach. He places a hand over her mouth as he stabs her again and again, splattering us with thick, red burbling sweetness, a wellspring of thick, red burbling sweetness, splattering us with whore and she tastes so good, so right, soaking into us, she feels so good. More fluids, more delight. We beg him for more and he complies, making a long horizontal slash and tearing into the wound that he's created, ripping a great jagged hole.

She gasps her last and he lets us into the cut, to feel around, to splash and swim and soak up heart and soul. We know her now, just a bit, as we knew him. We feel even less alone, we four now that we have that knowledge. Though ecstatic and excited, he withdraws us. We must be going, out the fire escape and elsewhere. His hands are warm, his hands are clean but we are dirty and joyous. There is so much more to touch.

WE CAN ONLY BECOME MONSTERS

ENNIS DRAKE

Philip Winthrop: "Is there no end to your horrors?"
Roderick Usher: "No. None whatever."

—House of Usher (1960)

"It's ironic, but until you can free those final monsters within the jungle of yourself, your life, your soul is up for grabs."

—Rona Barrett

his is my story. If it abode by its own rules it wouldn't exist. But what is a story if it isn't told? And what is my story if I don't confess my doubts?

I doubt everything. My work—my ability as a writer. My worth. Even my humanity. But what is self-worth, really? The value of Self? And how do you measure it?

For much of my life I've measured mine in restless nights and jumbled bedclothes; by the depth of hollowed eyes searching out

---

1. Can you approach the self critically? "…the distinction between the self as *I*, the subjective knower, and the self as *Me*, the object that is known." James,W. (1890). *The Principles of Psychology,* Vol.1. Cambridge, MA: Harvard University Press. Or is it all just meaningless words?

faces in the popcorn ceiling by the blue light of a monitor at 4:00 in the morning; in the beats of a blinking cursor on a white page; always the page; larger and whiter, obscuring every thought like an expanding aerial shot of some blighted arctic waste; I measured it by the mocking wall of plaques, awards, and citations[2] arranged cruciform above my desk—drowned in the same blue light as the ceiling (that color, like brain death); I measured it in sweat, tossing and turning, hopeless and angry and sleepless in twisted sheets...

I used to want things. I used to want this story (*I*, the objective chronicler). At some point that in itself had mattered.

And so, from there to here: What is the purpose of a life (you and me, me and you, the objects that are known)? And who gets to determine it?

***

I met Paul Toombes[3] for the first time in 1977 at the Coastal Vista

---

2. The MA from Stanford, The Hillman Prize, my Pulitzer nomination for *Cielo Pigs*.

a) *Cielo Pigs*, 1971, W. W. Norton & Company, Deena Katz and Robert Gantry. Arguably the most successful American true-crime book since Truman Capote's *In Cold Blood*, *Cielo Pigs* recounts the investigation, arrest, and prosecution of the so-called Mason Family (aka The Tribe of Udug) for the brutal 1965 slayings of actress Shannon Toombes, Cynthia Bergren, Terrence Day, and coffee magnate Patricia Folger.

3. Born Paulus Valfid Urbanczyck, May 27th, 1933, in Zurich, Switzerland, Paul Toombes is a naturalized-British film director, producer, writer, and actor. Toombes' films have inspired generations of directors, from the Coen brothers, and David Fincher, to Darren Aronofsky, Abel Ferrara, and Wes Craven.

A Holocaust survivor, Toombes was returned to Switzerland in 1946, and after completing his primary schooling began working at a local radio station owned by his grandfather. From 1951 until the summer of '54 Toombes performed in dozens of live commercials and radio dramas, and regularly assisted with the

Institue in L.A. In my socks, beltless, I was led by an enormous woman (her back like a white canvas wall; a sail curved with wind; her back her totality) into a modest cafeteria with high grated windows. The room was full of long folding tables—the kind you can find in almost any elementary school—but empty of people, save Toombes and a tall thin black man in the same starched scrubs as my escort. It was late afternoon, the light slanting from the west, illuminating little but the eastern wall, and though everything is remarkable to a woman who "remarks" for a living, the thing I remember most distinctly was the smell of meat (in the loosest sense of the word; meat quote-unquote) cooking from somewhere

---

production of sound effects, voice overs and voice acting, recording, writing, and even direction. In 1954 he enrolled at the Polish National Film Academy in Lodz where he produced the Złota Kaczka award-winning short film, *Morderstwo*. However, Toombes was expelled from the Academy the following year amid rumors of an assault, though the alleged victim was never identified and no charges were ever filed with the voivodeship or the Policja. To escape the scandal, Toombes moved first to Paris in 1956, then to London in 1958. In London, he produced a number of art house and commercial films, and in 1959 directed and starred in his first feature-length film, *Animus,* which won an Academy Award for Best Foreign Language Film. In 1961 he moved to Hollywood, California, securing his eminence by directing the horror film *All of Them Witches* (1963), followed in 1965 by *War for Water*, starring Tom Nicholston. *War for Water* was a critical success and was nominated for eleven Academy Awards. He has since received three Oscar nominations, a Bafta, two Césars, a Golden Globe and the Palme d'Or of the Cannes Film Festival.

Two months before the release of *War for Water,* Toombes' wife, Shannon Willit, who was nine months pregnant, was murdered by members of the Tribe of Udug (the self-proclaimed Mason Family) at the couple's Benedict Canyon home overlooking Los Angeles. Following Shannon's death, Toombes removed himself from public life and would not act or direct until producer Roger Castle encouraged him to helm an adaptation of the Italian giallo, *Dis.*

behind the serving counter[4]. Toombes sat sidesaddle at a table they'd set up for us, smoking one of the Hamlet cigarillos he was famous for choking rooms with. If he was aware of my arrival, he made no sign; he stared east at nothing/at the pale beige cinder blocks, lost in some middle-distance of memory.

"Mr. Toombes?" I set my cassette recorder on the tabletop along with the composition book and black marker they'd provided me.[5] "It's Deena, Mr. Toombes. Deena Katz." I waited for recognition, but when it didn't come I found myself unable to say the words *Cielo Pigs*.[6] "I'm from the *Times*," I said instead.

"Ah," he said absently, coughing on his cigar/cigarette.

I sat down and lit a Marlboro of my own; slid the dime-store

---

4. Is there anything more evocative of the institutional than a cafeteria serving line? Everything sorted in modular stainless steel, perfectly compartmentalized, perfectly segregated. Vegetables here, powdered starches there, meat-product piled up like stacks of outdated magazines in a waiting room (with a taste and texture to match); food reduced to absolute necessity (cattle at the trough), served and serviced by women and men in stiff colorless uniforms, gloved and capped, and indifferent as the softly careening universe.

5. Name. Address. Telephone #. Copy of your California driver's license. Turn out your pockets. Everything into the cardboard box—its ABBOTT LABORATO-RIES labels half torn away, the word VISITOR written across the front in the bold black strokes of a marker. Purse with wallet, change, keys. Notepad. Pens—lethal, the mountainous woman on the other side of the counter assures with a nod that might not require three chins to fully express its gravitas, but that's how many she used. Lose the belt. Lose the shoes. The blazer. The…what is that? It's a tape recorder…it's not dangerous. She doesn't believe it. Skepticism is the central tenet of her life here at Coastal Vista. I'm here for an interview with Paul Toombes, an interview he very much needs to give if he hopes to still have a career. For which I need the recorder. If you need to get Dr. Ljong, I'll wait, but not for very long.

6. While he'd refused on multiple occasions to be interviewed for the book, de-spite a short conversation on the phone he'd allowed me to record, I had co-written the definitive account of his wife's murder.

reading glasses from the top of my head onto the ridge of my nose and made an exaggerated effort of arranging my things on the table.

He closed his eyes, took a long drag from his Hamlet, let it out; an improbable mushroom cloud of electric blue smoke that completely obfuscated his face. "Which?" he asked just when I thought he wasn't going to speak again without prompting.

"Come again?"

"You said you were from the *Times*. Which?"

"L.A.," I said, tapping my laminate, which I'd re-clipped to my blouse for effect. It wasn't an overt lie. It was my position at the *Times* that'd gotten me the interview, though I'd already pitched whatever came of the interview as a sort of "gonzo serial" to Ben Fong at *Rolling Stone*.

"Ah. Not the London, I didn't think," Toombes said and chuckled: that endearingly-maniacal affectation that'd gained him millions of fans and international stardom. "Katz?" he said, rolling my name around. *Katz, Katz, Katz*, like an incantation and each time he said it he seemed to awaken a little more. "Jewish?" he asked, but didn't wait for me to answer. "*Germanic* Jewish…a genuine daughter of Zardok," he mused.

He pulled up his sleeve, showing me the tattoo on his forearm: a six-pointed star and a five-digit number too faded to read. "My father was a Child of Zardok. Like me," he said, touching his chest. "Like *you*," arm extended toward me. My stomach rolled. It felt like an accusation. An acknowledgment of a more vile link between us[7].

---

7. Perhaps he sensed it—our true sameness. While my conscious self violently resisted this perception, the id knew better. Just as Toombes knew better (or at least suspected). In hindsight, it's obvious what we were in that first meeting: monsters in masks that looked like human faces; monsters in ball dress—legs crossed, silver smoke rising from our cigarettes—sniffing each other out over aged whiskey, biding out the civilities (an act, just an act), dancing the dance of humanity till it was time for (the curtain to close) teeth and nails and blood.

"We were held at Stutthof for much of the war. My family and I. 'Political prisoners', you see. Though we were Swiss citizens, my father and his brother were born Poles. And they were Jews. It was an outrage, of course, our being imprisoned...not that anyone did a damned thing about it. But you know this, I'm sure. Boring. Exhaustively documented.[8]

"*You*...you're here to inquire of the allegations," he said. I watched as the smoke enveloping him sailed upward—curling, thinning, drifting and dissipating—and as it cleared I saw he'd set

8. In 1936 Toombes' father, Miroslaw Urbanczyk, was appointed Consul-General to Poland, and the family moved to Warsaw, where they lived until the invasion of Nazi Germany in September of 1939. Arrested and held as political prisoners early in the war, Toombes and his family were sent to the Stutthof prison camp in Danzig. In January of 1940, Toombes' maternal grandfather, Halvard Lindahl, heir to the Lindahl Chocolate empire, sued for the release of his daughter, Madelaine. Surviving documentation from the office of the Außenpolitische Amt der NSDAP showed a "donation" to the party in the amount of 100,000 Deutsche Marks. There was also documentation, supplied by Halvard to the office of Reich Commissar Alfred Rosenburg, proving Madelaine was of non-Jewish descent. Madelaine was released into Halvard's custody on February 14th, 1940. Toombes, his father, his uncle, and his cousin remained at Stutthof (Toombes' uncle, Bratomił, had served as one of Miroslaw's Deputy Consuls, living in Warsaw with his daughter, Gisella, until the occupation). In January of 1945, Stutthof was evacuated. Toombes, his father, Bratomił and Gisella, along with five hundred other prisoners (mostly women) were marched up the Danzig-Elbing highway to Krynica Morska, where they were forced into the waters of the Baltic and machine-gunned. Toombes and Gisella survived by hiding beneath the bodies of their fathers. Miraculously, the pair evaded recapture, making their way as far as Torgau, Germany, where they were rescued by Allied forces and returned to Switzerland on Christmas Day, 1946.

But Toombes' return was not a joyous one. In February of 1947 Toombes' mother, Madelaine Urbanczyk-Lindahl, committed suicide, leaving Paul in the care of his indifferent, if not hostile, grandfather.

his eyes[9] on me for the first time since I'd entered the room. He was "awake". Engaged. I had the totality of his attention and it was orders of magnitude more terrifying than I wanted to admit.

Toombes, starting with his lion's eyes: carnal, predatory, penetrating; slight frame, but tall—well over six feet, I'd guess; hair a perfect salted pompadour; beige ward-tunic and stockings like religious vestments where they shewed beneath his silk robe; hard Caesarian face; imperious mien.[10]

"We—" I began, trying to redirect the interview (I needed to gain control), but Toombes cut me off.

"My proclivities have never been anything more than a 'Hollywood secret', which I don't have to tell you, Ms. Katz, is no kind of secret at all. The drugs, the parties, the women, the men..." and to *men* he gave special emphasis, raising his brows comically.[11]

"Do you mind?" I asked, gesturing to the recorder with my cigarette.

---

9. Gaze. He'd set his gaze on me. That's what I'd originally written: purple, overwrought, even for me and I'd made my name on the bruised nature of my creative non-fiction. Despite the editorial change, I note it here simply for the fact it was the fact: the truth of both the action and the moment. It reminded me of a photo I'd seen in one of my father's *National Geographic* magazines: I'd been around nine or ten, just flipping pages and there was this black and white spread of a lion mounting a lioness: I'll never forget its eyes: hatred and pleasure in perfect alchemy.

10. This was not the face that had so many times graced the pages of the London *Times*, *Newsweek*, *Apparel Arts*, and *Esquire*. This was not the face of the self-assured playboy-auteur Toombes' adoring public was so familiar with.

11. Hollywood has always been a rumor mill, pounding the chaff from the wheat in reverse, and supermarket rags like the *Enquirer* and *Vader's Midnight* had moved tens of thousands of copies speculating on the sexual orientation of Paul Toombes; speculation Toombes himself encouraged, and in more than one case (if rumors were to be believed) fostered—particularly those suppositions that dwelt on the nature of his relationship with longtime valet, Reynard Deniau. And why not? What better distraction from the more vile rumors that Toombes' taste was for young girls?

"If you insist, my child." Toombes smiled. His teeth were perfect (if many and slightly yellowed), the gums the same color as the sooty end of his diminishing Hamlet. His Dali-esque mustache raised like antennae with the corners of his mouth and he stroked one side in careful exhibition. Outwardly, the man seemed to be little more than a series of carefully constructed affectations—the subsumptions of a lifetime's worth of *dramatis personae*.

"Yes, well…" I took my eyes from him reluctantly[12] and fumbled the recorder on. "There we are."

"Here we are," Toombes exclaimed merrily, arms opened like Christ.

It struck me then that Toombes was not (as I'd previously supposed) an addict of any flavor: not sexual, not chemical: he was not still caught in the receding wave of "free love" of the sixties, neither was he homosexual, nor bisexual: Toombes was, quite clearly, a psychopath of tremendous appetite.

My hand shook, dashing ash across the laminated table top.

"There are certain moral, certain social, and thereby legal—should we say *standards*?—under which I have done terrible things," Toombes said and, once more, smiled; an expression of joyful self-satisfaction that transformed even his predatory eyes into something beatific. "I'm curious, Ms. Katz, have you never found pleasure in pain? Have *you* never done 'terrible things'?"

My skin crept, but my anger rose, crawling up from the dark pit at the center of me. The silence between us unwound like meat from bone.[13]

---

12. Toombes commanded attention (and that he expected and received loyalty and obedience, I do not doubt). He was vital in ways ordinary men were not; more ALIVE than anyone I'd ever met. I knew and assumed many things before meeting Paul Toombes, but the reality of the man was now obvious and I didn't know if it was because he was letting me glimpse that reality, or if the accusations and the ensuing ordeal had left telling cracks in his veneer.

13. Toombes, of course, enjoyed (and read more from) my silence than any lame answer I might have given; it was in my head where we shared our moment of

Toombes took a final pull from his cigarello and dropped it in the cup of water between us. "Shall we talk about the young Miss Gellery, now? We should, don't you think?"

"Yes," I said, low, through my teeth; breathy and breathless; an unwitting lover's *Yes* that I hated myself for, but could not sublimate.

---

consanguinity—the details of which were blessedly secreted from him—the details of which were irrelevant; it was only to incite the moment itself, some memory, any memory, that he sought: He's 17, you're 14, and he's brought you to his house—his family's house—and you know exactly what he wants to do, you've known all day, you've known since yesterday, since he drove you home from school. It was the hottest May anyone could remember—you knew that because it was all anyone was talking about—the sweat on your neck shining like oil, like its own skin, second skin, and his hand is on your thigh, and your thigh's sheathed in sweat too, slick and pliable, and your cotton shorts are too short, and your hand is fighting his as it moves inside your shorts, your lips open in a laugh and he kisses you and his fingers are against your clit and when you go home, you masturbate for the first time, and now, now is tomorrow and you're in his car and you're pulling into the driveway, and he's kissing you hard all the way to the bunk beds he's outgrown, his brother long since gone off to UCLA, and you're both breathless, and your skirt's coming up and he talks you out of your pantyhose, the panties themselves damp and slack and they move away like the thin non-barrier they are and you moan into his kiss and his cock is hard and out of his shorts and you're scooting away from him (but he's moving with you) till your heads are bumping against the wall behind the bed and you're interjecting little No's between kisses as he presses (forces) his cock against the lips of your pussy, and you're wet, so wet (your body betraying you), and you don't think he even hears the No's anymore, doesn't feel your hands against his chest because he's stronger and he's sliding inside you (overcoming you) and it feels like everything you knew it would feel like—pain and fullness, pleasure and shame—and then he's dropping you outside of the school, dress tucked into your pantyhose, eyes red-rimmed and swollen (red and swollen as...), and you're ashamed and angry and he never talks to you again and something inside you is forever broken, but what has been broken down has also been banked like coals...

State Attorney's examination of Angelina Gellery from "People of the State of California vs. Paulus Valfrid Urbanczyk, aka Paulus 'Paul' Toombes, June 27th, 1977":
Excerpt 1

PROSECUTOR: Please state your name.

ANGELINA GELLERY: Angelina Gellery. I...I don't have a middle name.

PR: How did you first meet Paul Toombes?

AG: It was after an audition. He invited me and my mom to a party.

PR: And did you you and your mother attend the party?

AG: Yes.

PR: Can you tell us about the party, please...

AG: Um, it was in Beverly Hills, I think...um...the place where his wife was killed...

PR: 10066 Cielo Drive. For the record, Miss Gellery is referring to the murders of Shannon Toombes (née Willit), Cynthia Bergren, Terrence Day, and Patricia Folger. Is that correct, Miss Gellery, you are referring to the home at Cielo Drive?

AG: Yeah.

PR: Yes or No, please.

AG: What?

PR: You must give clear Yes or No answers, Miss Gellery.

AG: Oh, um, yes.

PR: At this party, Mr. Toombes indicated some interest in photographing you?

AG: Yes. He told my mother he thought I was very beautiful and that he was disappointed I didn't get the role I'd auditioned for. He said that he'd like to take some shots of me for his personal files... that he'd like to use me in the future. It scared me a little. The way he looked at me when he said it.

PR: Did he take pictures of you the night of the party?

AG: Yes. A few.

PR: Was your mother present?

AG: ...

PR: Miss Gellery?

AG: No.

PR: Where was your mother?

AG: I...I don't know. I told her I had to go to the bathroom. I'd had a couple glasses of champagne and my stomach felt bad...and...and she took me to a bathroom upstairs. I got sick and...and when I came out she wasn't there.

PR: You were alone?

AG: No.

PR: Someone else was upstairs?

AG: Yes. When I came out of the bathroom he was standing there.

PR: Paul Toombes?

AG: Yes.

PR: How many glasses of champagne did you have that night?

AG: Two, I think. Maybe three. My mom gave them to me.

PR: Were there other young people there drinking? Others, like yourself, well under age?

AG: Yeah. I mean: Yes.

PR: Did you feel as though you were drunk?

AG: No. Yes. I don't know. Yes, a little, I guess.

PR: Did Mr. Toombes say anything to you when you came out of the bathroom?

AG: He showed me a camera—he had it on a strap around his neck—and said, like, "Why don't you come here and let me take some pictures of you?"

PR: Did you agree?

AG: No. I asked him where my mom was and went to walk downstairs, but he put his hand like here...

PR: On the back of your neck?

AG: Yeah. I mean: Yes. He put his hand on the back of my neck and sorta steered me to the door across from the bathroom. He went, like, "Mommy's downstairs fetching us some drinks, dear. Come here, don't be shy, we'll take some pictures while we wait for her." I was afraid to say no. And I really wanted to be in movies and I knew, you know, I needed him to like me. I did want him to like me.

PR: What happened next?

AG: We went into the room. He called it a withdrawing room. It looked kind of like a living room. He told me to sit on one of the couches and started taking pictures of me. I was a little nervous, I guess, but the champagne helped, and he started like giving me direction, telling me to move my head this way, and to smile, or to look serious. It was kinda fun.

PR: How long were you alone?

AG: I don't know. Maybe fifteen minutes. Probably fifteen minutes.

PR: How many pictures would you say Mr. Toombes took of you?

AG: I don't know. He took a whole roll and maybe part of another one. I know he changed the film because it was after he changed it that he started trying to get me to pose with, you know, with my top down and...

PR: You said in the initial interview that at this point he tried to kiss you. Did he kiss you?

AG: No. He tried but I turned my head and said my mom was coming.

PR: How did he respond?

AG: He laughed. He said he was sorry, but he couldn't help it, that I was so beautiful. Then he said how much he liked my dress and he slid one of the straps down over my shoulder and took a picture of me. He told me to lean back and he slid the other strap down and we took a few more pictures. I started pulling the straps up but he stopped me and said just a few more and he pulled one of the straps down kind of hard. I mean, not real hard. Hard enough that...that I knew he was going to get what he wanted. [crying]

PR: Take your time.

AG: ...

AG: He grabbed me by the hips and pulled me toward him. I asked him what he was doing and he told me to trust him, and he pushed my dress up a little and put his hands on my knees and...and spread my legs…and he took a couple of pictures, but I sat up and fixed my dress. I told him that was enough.

PR: And how did Mr. Toombes respond, then?

AG: By then we both realized my mom was standing in the doorway.

PR: Did he seem alarmed?

AG: No. He laughed and said "Finally," or something like that, and took one of the drinks my mom was holding.

PR: What did your mother say or do at that time?

AG: She…she laughed. She said…I don't know. She told him something and they both laughed.

PR: And what did Mr. Toombes say?

AG: He called me his little Lolita. Then he said something French, I think.

PR: Was it *ménage à trois*?

AG: I think…yes.

PR: What did your mother say?

AG: She was like, "Not this time," and kissed him. Then she told me to go downstairs and be seen.

"But you already know all that, don't you, Ms. Katz?"

"I'm sorry, are you corroborating Angelina Gellery's statements, Mr. Toombes?"

"I'm, legally," Toombes paused, summoning an expression of playful apology, "medically, incapable of corroborating anything, I'm afraid."

"What is the nature of your malady, Mr. Toombes?" I was seething. It was hard to breathe.

"Malady…ah, you mean what is the condition with which I have been diagnosed?"

"Are you willing to discuss it?"

"Have you not spoken with Dr. Ljung?"

"Dr. Ljung has been unwilling to speak with anyone, except when and how he is required to under the law, which is to say: not at all."

"Ah, well," Toombes said, giving a matter-of-fact gesture with his hand. "Shall I continue? In regards to Miss Gellery?"

He was enjoying this.

State Attorney's examination of Angelina Gellery from "People of the State of California vs. Paulus Valfrid Lindahl, aka Paulus 'Paul' Toombes on June 27th, 1977":

Excerpt 2

AG: ...his driver picked me up. I think it was around lunchtime.

PR: This was Reynard Deniau?

AG: Yes.

PR: Did he speak to you?

AG: Not really, no. He just gave me like this really funny look when we got to Tom Nicholston's house. Like...like I was...I don't know how to explain...like he knew something I didn't.

PR: Were you aware of where you were, of whose house you were at?

AG: Yes. Paul [Toombes] told my mom when he called and asked to do another photo shoot with me. She told me. We were both excited about it. I mean, Tom Nicholston! I'd seen *War for Water* with my dad—it was one of his favorites.

PR: Did you ever suspect Paul Toombes had arranged more than a weekend stay at Nicholston's with your parents?

AG: ...

PR: Miss Gellery?

AG: I guess I knew there wasn't much my mother wouldn't do to be a star, or to make me one. And I knew my parents seemed really agitated for a few days before Paul [Toombes] sent for me. I guess I knew *something* was going on.

PR: Tell us again who owned the house Reynard Deniau brought you to...

AG: It was Tom Nicholston's house. Tom Nicholston, the actor.

PR: Did you take a quaalude when you arrived at Nicholston's house?

AG: Yeah. I...Yes.

PR: And who gave it to you?

AG: Reynard [Deniau].

PR: Had you ever taken a quaalude before?

AG: [hesitant] Yes. Half of one. With my boyfriend.

PR: Did you take half of the pill when Reynard Deniau offered it to you?

AG: I started to break it in half, but he reached over the front seat and stopped me. He said, "I'm being your friend right now, girl. Trust what I say. Take all of it. Take all of it right now."

***

What follows is an excerpt from the only article Deena Katz ever published re: the Toombes-Gellery investigation. It was published on May 23rd, 1979—the second anniversary of Angelina Gellery's disappearance—in the *San Francisco Examiner*. By this time, Deena Katz had left the *Times*, and her failure to deliver the promised "gonzo-exposé" to *Rolling Stone* had effectively ended her career as both a journalist and an author.

May 23rd, 1977—three days *before* Angelina Gellery would file charges of rape against him with the Los Angeles County Superior Court—the day *after* the premier of his latest film, *Dr. Dis*, Paul Toombes was admitted to the Coastal Vista Institute in Santa Fe for an unspecified mental illness. Two years later it's still unclear whether the much-beloved star of films like *Animus*, *All of Them Witches*, and *War for Water* was committed to the institute, or sought its protective care voluntarily. The facts are surprisingly few, but this is what we do know: At the Hollywood premiere of *Dr. Dis*, held in typical red carpet style at the iconic Chinese Theater, Paul Toombes left midway through the showing, complaining to Executive Producer, Roger Castle, of acute anxiety. Toombes' departure, at approximately 11:00 PM, has been verified by numerous eyewitnesses, including Toombes' personal valet, Reynard

Deniau. According to Deniau's statement, Toombes requested that he be taken to his residence at Summit's Ridge, where they arrived sometime around midnight. Again, according to Deniau, he and Gerda Karp, Mr. Toombes' estate manager, escorted the actor to his room. Sometime after midnight an ambulance arrived and Toombes was—presumably—whisked away to Coastal Vista. Both Karp and Deniau allege they have not physically seen, nor performed any service for their employer in any capacity aside from the day-to-day maintenance of the estate and the actor's collection of classic cars, as set forth in their respective contracts of employment, since his admittance to Coastal Vista. There are no records or eyewitness accounts of Toombes' whereabouts between the hours of 12:00 AM and 3:01 PM on May the 23rd of 1977. According to one of only two documents released by Coastal Vista Institute during the Toombes-Gellery investigation, Toombes was declared mentally unfit within hours of his admission to the facility. The declaration preemptively precluded Toombes from standing trial for accusations of rape that would not be brought against him for another three days...

***

She's out of the house. There's an unlit pool surrounded by pavers and a low stucco wall. She smells chlorine. She smells the night. She smells metal. She's covered in blood. Some of it is hers. She's naked, her insides torn. Her reality is warped by a fish lens of alcohol and methaqualone.

There are voices coming from the house, but she can't understand them. She tries to run but the most her body can do is stumble. She thinks if she can get over the wall she might have a chance.

Someone's shouting.

Toombes, she thinks.

She's almost there. Almost...

Someone grabs her from behind and her foot slips into the ja-cuzzi. Whoever grabbed her falls away. She hears a splash; hears bone on stone. She yanks her foot out of the jacuzzi and throws herself forward, toward the wall, but it's further than it looks. She's clawing for it, crawling, tearing the skin from the palms of her hands.

Someone says: Get back here you little bitch!

She grabs the lip of the wall. Pulls herself up and over and she's falling...

...she wakes to the faint light that precedes the dawn. Up the cliff face she can see the house lit up. She's in a ravine. She can hear voices, far off, and when she sits up she can see flashlights a hundred yards to the north. She almost calls out, but stops herself. She hears no sirens, sees no flashing emergency lights. Whoever is out there is not there to help her. She makes her way to a culvert a quarter mile to the south and hides. She's in and out of conscious-ness. She stays in the culvert for two days...

..."Help me!" she tries to scream, but she has no voice, and the car—a silver Porsche—only slows enough to get around her, then peels away. "No! Please! Stop! Stop!"

But the next car does stop...

...she's in the police station, dressed in stripes like a criminal, wrapped in a blanket. No one can reach her parents. No one takes a rape kit, and no one takes her statement for another twelve hours. After her examination by the State Attorney's office she is released under her own cognizance, despite her allegations, despite her being a minor, and she is never seen again...

***

On the desk, in the corner of Deena Katz's bedroom, half buried under a stack of magazines and discolored, mis-folded newspa-pers (*The Telegraph*, *The Sun*, *The NY Times*, *The Plain Dealer*, but mostly *The Los Angeles Times*) is a yellow legal pad that reads:

Attempted interview w/Gellery's parents
France—Provence-Alpes—Côte d'Azur, Fréjus
Oct. 11[Th], 1978

Flights were exhausting. Fifteen hours in the air. LAX to JFK[14],
JFK to Nice. An hour and half ride southwest from Nice to Frejus
in a downpour, cramped in the little Puegeot loaner Fong had
arranged for me. Halfway across the world, in one of the most
beautiful parts of the world (and on *Stone*'s dime) and it was fucking dark and fucking cold and fucking storming and I didn't even
know what I was chasing anymore, or why[15].

***

Scrawled after this in a quick, jagged hand (I can almost remember
the thrill that drove that hand):

Townhouse—Cathedral Square
Rue Sieyes and Rue de Fleury

---

14. The layover in NY was short and I was thankful for that. Ben Fong was not
happy about the envelope full of francs he was handing me and I didn't blame
him; if he knew what I knew, he would not be giving it to me at all—a year and
a half after my initial interview with Toombes and with every lead I became more
certain that my comprehensive article, my career-cementing act of journalism, was
never going to make it farther than my desk. To Fong I only said: It'll be worth it.
To which he reflexively replied: It better be.
   But it wouldn't be. Not to him.
15. Oh, Deena…the lies you tell yourself. This was only about the Why. It was
about exposing abuse and challenging power. It didn't need to be about more than
that, did it?
   No, but it was. It was about a life. It was about blood and satiation and retribu-
tion.

58 Rue de Fleury
GELLERYS!!!

It was late. Too late to have an unannounced journalist knocking at the door of the French townhouse no one was supposed to
know you were at, but my time was limited, I had resources to play
with (the envelope in my jacket pocket heavy with promise), and
I was hoping the shock of my presence, particularly at this hour,
would throw the Gellerys off-kilter; give me the advantage. But
there was no advantage here. The faded red door cracked and from
what seemed the infinite blackness of the interior a disembodied
voice said: "I'm only going to say this once, Ms. Katz—leave Frejus." English. Not French. No discernible accent (unless it was
Californian).

"Five minutes, that's—" but I barely got the words loose. I never
saw the blow; but I felt the frame of my glasses bend, twist; felt the
lens fracture, glass teeth biting a shark-jaw-circle around my right
eye, saw the star-strewn red velvet of my eyelids, then the black
of momentary unconsciousness. I came to lying on my ass in the
pouring rain, flagstones digging into my palms, a man in shadow
standing over me, a pistol in his hand—a Luger, I think; dark and
sleek, both ahead and out of its time, thirty years old yet still like
something you might see on *Logan's Run* or *Star Wars*. "Listen!
Would you just fucking listen to me?" I said, trying to ignore the
pain in my eye, in my head, "I'm prepared to offer a significant
sum for—"

Again the man with the gun[16] cut me off: "What I just gave you
is as good as it's going to get. Not another word, Ms. Katz. Leave
Frejus. Leave France."

---

16. I wouldn't realize it till later, till I'd landed safely in the States and was back
in my own bed, but do not doubt: the man with the gun was Reynard Deniau,
personal "valet" to one Paulus "Paul" Toombes.

***

I woke the next morning to a light but persistent knock at my door. I was staying at the *Quai dei Caravello*, in an efficiency not three blocks from the Gellerys' townhouse on *Rue de Fleury*. The knock wasn't much of a surprise. And neither was Derrian Gellery. He was tall. Six-three, six-four, maybe. Thin. With long stringy blonde hair pulled into a loose ponytail. There was an arrogance in the way he held himself, in the hawkish, narrow cut of his nose and face, the tiny black eyes that surreptitiously gauged the potential weakness in all they saw (as the falcon gauges the distance of the dove before it folds its wings and, talons outstretched, plummets). But something changed in his port when he saw my face.[17] A body-wide flicker of fear that touched every nerve. It only lasted an instant, but it was there. I saw it and he knew I saw it. Whatever we were in, it went deeper than a Hollywood sex scandal.[18]

"You have money?" he asked, a first-language-French lilt to his

---

17. I'd spent an hour tweezing shards of glass from round my eye, which was swollen shut and turning the same shade as the Sauvignon I'd been drinking all night to hedge the pain. I was less impressed than Derrian Gellery. It certainly wasn't the first time I'd been assaulted on the job, which shouldn't come as a surprise to you or anyone else. My editors over the years tended to brush these incidents aside as "the nature of the game". Never mind that I'd been hit with twice the regularity of my male counterparts. The fact was: I'd been threatened with physical violence, even rape, my entire career, and not just by the subjects of my reporting, but by my so-called colleagues, sources, even readers. I shut it out, shut parts of myself down. I really had no other choice. In return I was considered "one tough bitch"; a point of pride in my youth. Now, I recognized it for what it was: dehumanization as a system of control.

18. There was a single photo of Toombes in *Cielo Pigs*. Bob Gantry had taken the picture at the crime scene two days after the killings, and I couldn't get it out of my head: Toombes on the front steps of the house, the word NERGAL written in blood on the door.

English.

"Yes," I said, suppressing a flurry of emotions running the gamut from satisfaction to disgust.

"*Cathédrale Saint Léonce. Me recontrer dans le cloîter,*" then: "Meet me in the cloister," repeating himself in English, enunciating every syllable. "*Une heure. Vous comprenez?*"

"Yeah. *Ouais. J'y serai.*"

"Bring the money."

***

Not eight in the morning and it was pouring rain—the storm had taken a deep breath in the night and was blowing again; second wind. Wind under the palm fronds, skidding dead through the cobbled streets; fallen angels' wings. Wind, driving rain at 40mph, so hard it stung, so hard it came in sideways. Cathedral Square was apocalyptic; shades of ash and decomposition. It was Saturday and early enough that there were few lights in the windows of the villas and townhouses; the glass fronts of the "provincial" tourist traps dead faces in the dark. A block northwest, *Saint Léonce* was an iron-gray gauntlet signaling the heavens with the upraised finger of its spire; the Merovingian equivalent of a neon sign: God is there. There is God. God, who art in Heaven, who made man in his own image so that when we look in the mirror and despise ourselves we can take heart because what we loathe is the Divine, and when we look in the mirror and sin because we are proud of our beauty it's not really sin at all because our pride is in our resemblance to Him, and when we are cruel there is little wonder because God, too, is cruel and delights in His works.

I never had much use for God. My mother had practiced Catholicism as devoutly as my father had practiced Judaism, which was as religiously as I practiced safe sex in the sixties[19].

---

19. Stanford, Class of 1968. You do the math. I don't know how many bullets of

The wind picked up, almost snatching the umbrella from my hands. I could see the octagonal baptistry ahead so I let the damn thing go and started running. I was wearing mules with a kitten heel (idiot) so I reached down and broke the stems off, one then the other, so I didn't break my neck on the cobbled streets.

The iron-bound baptistry door was cracked open. It swung in easy enough; and it shut the storm out behind me just as obligingly. The baptistry itself was warm with candlelight, the volcanic rock walls returning both light and warmth in a hazy red spectrum of welcome. In that cozy, holy red space my inner disquiet relented. I wanted to stay there. I wanted to sit and be still and be silent for awhile. I stared at the baptistry well for a long time, wondering what that must be like…to be cleansed and made anew[20].

From the baptistry I made my way to the cloister—eye of my personal apocalypse abandoned for its leading edge; comfort and stillness and light exchanged for chaos and darkness and the company of monsters. Heaven for Hell (*do you think you can tell?*).

Have you never found pleasure in pain, Ms. Katz?

That was the question. A shrewd one aimed at peeling away my mask. The answer didn't need to be spoken: I ONLY found pleasure in pain. I'd chosen this. Everything that'd ever happened to me, that I'd ever done, every action, every inaction shaped who and what I am.

So what am I?

A (hunter of) monster(s).

The cloister ceiling was a hand-painted apocryphal bestiary. An improbable collection of demons and monsters difficult to reconcile with either Torah or Bible. Above me: a woman with the

---

"free love" that is I dodged, but it's probably of a quantity significant enough to make me rethink my belief in miracles. As in: miraculously disease-free. As in: miraculously w/o child.

20. I remember reminding myself then, as I remind myself now: biology is biology and it was always too late under its shadow.

body of a lion, the nipples of her exposed breasts as red and beady as her eyes (as the blood that wept from her fanged mouth). The iconography was Assyrian (if not Sumerian). I knew because Gantry and I'd pored over surviving Assyrian-Babylonian religious imagery when we wrote *Cielo Pigs*. Mason and his following called themselves the Tribe of Udug. The Udug were Sumerian demons. The Assyrians called them Utukku, but they were the same: collectors of sacrifice for the dead god Nergal—a god that'd come down all the way from the Sumerians to the Caananites, among whose gods' council Yahweh kept.

I thought of Toombes. Toombes and his lion's eyes. Toombes in black and white on the steps of 10066 Cielo Drive. Toombes next to the word NERGAL painted in his wife's blood[21].

Derrian Gellery was waiting at the other end of the cloister. I took the manila envelope (damp, now) Fong had given me from inside my jacket and held it out to him.

"That's ten thousand, cash. *Une centaine de nouveau francs,*" I said, shivering. It must have been forty degrees and I was soaked through. I longed for the red baptistry.

Gellery snatched the envelope out of my hand. "*Dix mille balles?*" He laughed at it, at me, but he took it and that was something. He was going to give me *something*. I could feel it.

"Talk to me, Derrian," I said, unable to keep the pleading tone from my voice.

"For this?" He held the envelope up. "All right, OK. Go fuck

---

21. Painted there by the "Tribe of Udug". And what of Willit's unborn child? The boy would have been Toombes' firstborn. It was well known the baby had been cut from Shannon's womb. It—*he*—had been bodily removed, yet the remains were never found.

I have two horrific thoughts (pin the first and stretch red twine from it to the second): 1) The prodigious success of *War for Water* and 2) The Udug were collectors of sacrifice for the god, Nergal. Now, stretch the twine from #2 to Gantry's crime scene photo of Paul Toombes…

yourself! There is your money's worth, huh?" But he was already thumbing the bills, counting.

I waited.

He jammed the envelope into the front of his pants and said: "Do you have any idea who this man *is*?"

I honestly thought I did. I knew what Toombes was worth…but until now I'd underestimated the reach, the influence, that kind of wealth really signified.

I'd underestimated *everything*.

"My God, this is your daughter we're talking about! Your little girl!" I screamed, but it all came together and I understood. I hammered Gellery with my fists until I lost my breath; breathless, I grabbed him by the lapels of his raincoat and shook him, shoved him, backing him from under the cloister and into the courtyard, into the driving rain. "What did you do? What did you *do*, you fuck?" I screamed till I was hoarse. No breath, no strength, nothing to support the rage inside me: smaller, hotter, denser, till I collapsed in on myself and I was on my knees, mouthing a question I knew the answer to, but which I was about to hear anyway.

"I sold the little whore to him! But popping mollys and screwing old men didn't have the same appeal as spreading her legs for all the boys in the neighborhood!"

I uncoiled, a spring, and shoved him. His knees clipped the wall of the well he didn't know was behind him. He tore the sleeve of my blouse, but he couldn't hold on to it. The knife in my pocket was in my hand and I flicked it hard and the blade folded out and snapped into place. I jabbed it just under his belly and shoved again. He was gone. And after a few minutes the rain washed away his blood and my hand was clean. The knife was clean. And the world, too, was a little cleaner.

That was the end of it. Of my "investigation". My career. Of any chance at a normal life.

So what am I?

You know the word(s).

(I'm a) killer.[22]

***

Piled among the legal pads and papers and clippings is a typewritten transcript, again headed by (my) Katz's oblique script:

[1985—Olivia Gellery Telephone Interview]

OLIVIA (LINDY) GELLERY: I...I miss her [crying].
DEENA KATZ: When's the last time you saw her?
OLIVIA: [clears throat] [noise]
DEENA: Mrs. Gellery?
OLIVIA: It's...it's Mrs. Lindy, now.
DEENA: Yes. I'm sorry. You remarried.

---

22. He was my friend. I'd known him my entire life and he betrayed me. He stole my agency and forced me to recognize how powerless I was. It's not something most people have to live with: the knowledge of their own insignificance. It changed me and I hated the person it made me. And when I caught him in the parking lot after baccalaureate, windows fogged, forcing himself on a girl in the backseat of his father's BMW, I did what begged to be done. His father kept a .22 target pistol under the driver's seat. When I opened the door the overhead lights came on and the door chimed; he shouted in surprise, the girl begged for help. The pistol popped three times. I hit him twice in the back and once in the head. I would have kept firing but the gun jammed. The girl ran screaming into the dark reaches of the lot. I could hear other voices rising up in the distance. I reached into the back seat and took his wallet, his money. I wiped the door handle with my dress, looked at myself in the window glass: with one of my stockings over my head I looked like a mannequin that'd been in a fire. My nose misshapen, mouth lopsided and drawn down, eyes only hinted-at depressions above my cheeks.

a) he didn't die, not for another two years, but the damage to his brain and spine was so severe it would have been a blessing if he had. The case was never solved, his victim never found.

[silence]

DEENA: Mrs. Lindy, Olivia, when was the last time you saw your daughter?

OLIVIA: [distressed] The day he sent for her… [sobbing]

DEENA: You didn't see her after she filed the charges against Toombes?

OLIVIA: No.

[silence]

DEENA: Olivia?

[silence]

DEENA: Have you been following Toombes' return from…retirement?

OLIVIA: Retir…? [noise]

DEENA: I—

OLIVIA: [interrupting] He killed her. He killed my girl and you know it. It was supposed to be a weekend. A party! I didn't do anything a hundred other mothers weren't doing! I wanted her to be a star!

[call disconnected]

***

I've been expecting his call for more than a decade. Every time I heard a phone ring, even if it was on the TV, I imagined it was him/that it preceded him.

I tell myself there's nothing Fortean, or predestinate about it, but the timing is more than uncanny: ten years of notes, recordings (magnetic tape yanked from the casings in glittering fistfuls), clippings, interviews, contacts, police reports (few and doctored as they are) piled on my back patio, stinking of lighter fluid. I toss the transcript of my conversation with Olivia Gellery on top of the pile, a box of kitchen matches chattering in my hand. I used to want this (*I*, the subjective knower). This story. I used to have a life that wasn't consumed by (the) rape and death (of Angelina Gellery [the object that was known]).

The phone…

Match head against the striker strip.

…trilling…

Pressure.

…ringing…

Ssssliding. Spark.

And it's burning. It's all burning. Flushed away in fire.

The phone. Beige. Sleek. Hanging in its cradle next to the bare pantry. Dangling its absurdly long pig tail. Jacked into the wall, jacked into itself, snake devouring itself. Full circle.

I pick up the receiver. Tuck it between shoulder and cheek. I'm listening to the silence of miles and time zones, oceans and nations pouring out, pouring in (ocean in itself, sea of stillness, teeming beneath its surface).

"It's time for a second interview, Ms. Katz."

Toombes.

He sounds old. He sounds arrogant and impudent and wholly predatory, all pretense to civility fallen away with the years. There's a long quiet between us; much being said without anything being said.

"I'll send for you," he says and hangs up.

I set the phone in its cradle and watch as my life's work burns on the patio, the stink of it filling the kitchen, my nose, my lungs: clinging and permeating—the plastic reek of it, the senseless waste.

I make a call of my own and pack.

***

Private car with a driver. I don't know him. Don't recognize him from my investigation. LAX. Private plane: a Hawker-Raytheon 700. It isn't even a year old. Gleaming white outside its hangar. LAX to EWR (Newark Liberty International).[23] EWR to ZRH

---

23. While the Hawker sits on the tarmac, refueling in New Jersey, a P.I. who's long

(Flughafen Zürich) in Switzerland. Fourteen hours. A black Mercedes waits at the Hawker's ramp when I disembark at Flughafen. I'm well-acquainted with the man standing in front of it.

Reynard Deniau.

He hasn't aged well. He was an ugly man ten years ago, and he was uglier still, now: as grisly as he was in the *Côte de A'zur*, but thinner, his square face gone soft at the chin, along the jaw, brow that had climbed to a widow's peak now climbing to the crown of his head, a wispy island of hair left behind on its northward trek. Nested in folds of permanently bruised flesh, his eyes (like his jaw) have gone soft.

He opens the door to the back seat, motioning for me to get in. His coat flaps with the gesture and I see can the pistol under his arm.

The airfield is as private as the Hawker and the cars, the drivers...the dead P.I. in my bathroom in Studio City[24], and the

---

been on Toombes' payroll is tossing my house in Studio City. He puzzles first over the charred remains on the lanai, then at the faded geometry on the walls of my bedroom/office, the monitor turned over, smashed, hard drive at the bottom of a tub full of water in the master bath. I've done his work for him and it makes him nervous. He stares at the hard drive. It's a problem. It could be recovered. Even after he sets the house on fire, there's a risk some information might survive. And he's reaching, despite the hair rising on his neck, the plunging sensation in his guts, he's reaching because he doesn't see the extension cord hidden by the shower curtain, its female end cut, wires exposed and sunk in the water...heat...seizing... eyes smoking...tongue cooking...flesh burning...he can't pull his arm free...can't let go of the iron tub...and he's just so much meat stuck to a frying pan.

24. I wonder if it's true. Did I just kill a man I've never met? It seems preposterous; gross and unlikely; unreal, and so easy to dismiss. The mind all too willingly, all too graciously flows around the idea; river around a stone, wearing it smooth; grit turning to a pearl inside an oyster. I know it isn't always this way. There (are) will be moments, dark moments, in whatever future is left to me where the anguish over what I've done, what I'm going to do, will be almost unbearable...but I realize, too, the majority of the rest of my life will not be so. The mind will do its trick:

Toombes Estate—officially the Lindahl Estate—is, as you should expect, serviced by a private road. Two miles of asphalt winding alongside the *Zürichsee* before it turns west and plunges into the forested hills of the *Sihlwald*. The woods are black; primordial and poised; a living thing, whole and sentient and eager to pull the string of road and unravel all these fabrications of modern man.

After ten or fifteen minutes, we turn north, pulling to a stop at a high iron gate. Somewhere beyond the *Sihl* the sun is setting. The light of day is abandoning us. Ornate gas lamps hang from the marble-clad pillars that support the gate, but they remain unlit.

"Are you ready?" I ask Deniau.

His eyes move over my reflection in the rearview mirror. They say everything: confusion (Ready?); realization (I didn't search her); resignation (She has a gun, she has a gun on me); and finally, relief.

"For longer than you can imagine," he answers and I can feel the weight coming off him with every syllable.

A buzzer sounds and the gate swings open.

The drive to the mansion is long and straight, the woods kept at bay on each side by a hundred yards of perfect lawn.

"You loved him," I say.

We roll to a stop in the raked gravel drive in front of the house. Deniau puts the car in PARK and turns it off. Without turning around he says: "There was a time, yes. Love…and power. They are powerful motivators, Ms. Katz."

There's a black van parked in front of Toombes' family estate. We are nose to nose with it. The cloaked figure behind the wheel is surreal; grotesque.

"How many?" I ask huskily. My eyes are swimming, tear-stung. "Do you even know? Does he?"

"How many what? How many girls like Angelina?

---

water round a stone; grit to a pearl…

Is there any greater power humanity possesses? Than the power of the mind to deny, to rewrite its own history, to justify, and so comfort itself?

"It was 1965, I think. Maybe '66. I don't remember the date anymore. You'd think you couldn't forget a thing like that. Anyway. That was *my* first, if you want to call it that. We were in Vegas. Paul had several girls that week, but there was one in particular... very young, very beautiful...and...and Paul, he got a little too excited with a pair of nylons. Choked the poor thing to death."

"How many?" I say again, rage overcoming my woe.

Around the van, figures are gathering. Cloaked (in black satin). Masked (Death's Head). In the growing dark their silhouettes shift and overlap. There might have been five. Or ten. Or twenty.

"Legion," Deniau mouths, almost inaudible. He could have been talking about the women in the Dr. Death costumes, or answering my question. "'...then went the devils out of the man,'" Deniau whispers.

I cock the snubnose .38 in my jacket pocket.

"I buried her out in the desert. Paul, he waited in the car while I dug. I dug deep as I could, but the ground's no good for digging out there.

"These *are* the things you want to know, yes?" Deniau asks.

The cloaked Death's Heads surround the car.

"What was her name?"

"Her name was whore, Ms. Katz. And that's how she died: like a girl that sold pieces of her soul for twenty dollars a cut."

I feel some essential part of my consciousness leave my body; like the essence of me (*I*) has shifted sideways into some neighboring dimension of being, leaving behind nothing but my physical self and my intent. I press the Saturday Night Special into the back of the driver's seat hard and fast enough to punch the leather. The shot comes harder, faster. The report in that closed space perforates both my eardrums. The +P load burrows through the seat, through Deniau, through the dash and into the engine compartment. Blood, like vermillion spittle, flecks the windshield.

"I...I should...have killed you...in Frejus," he wheezes, but I can't hear him. He's dead before I close the car door behind me.

***

"And I saw the woman drunken with the blood of sinners, and with the blood of kings: and when I saw her, I wondered with great admiration," Toombes rasps. He laughs, amused with himself, but one of the Death's Heads yanks on the metal wire looped around his throat, silencing him.

He's bound in friction tape to a wooden chair in the center of the house's opulent, domed foyeur. On the western wall is a 16mm Kodachrome projection of Angelina Gellery's examination with the California State Attorney's office. The clicking and purring of the reel-to-reel are louder than the audio, and you can only hear snatches of Angie's testimony:

PROSECUTOR: Did you get in the jacuzzi without your panties on?
ANGELINA: Yes.
PROSECUTOR: What happened when you got in the jacuzzi?
ANGELINA: He gave me some more champagne.

"Do you think you will get away with this? Do you think *they* will let you get away with this?" Toombes spits blood on the marble floor.

"They already have."

A clutch of Death's Heads have gathered at my back, but they part like a sea when the front doors open behind them. I, too, step aside.

A figure, cloaked in black silk and wearing a mask fashioned from the head of an elk, enters. Unhurried, the elk's dead eyes regard us each in turn; the head inclines toward the projection of Angelina, watching for several minutes.

PROSECUTOR: What did you do when he said, "Let's go in the other room"?
ANGELINA: I went, "No, I better go home. You should take

me home". But I just went and sat on the couch. Because I was afraid.

PROSECUTOR: And what were you afraid of?

ANGELINA: Him.

Elk's Head turns to Toombes.

"Tom?" Toombes asks Elk's Head. "Tom? Is that you?"

The Death's Heads draw their knives.

"What is this? Tom? Tom! TOM!"

THE THRESHOLD OF WAKING LIGHT

E. CATHERINE TOBLER

In the vast and unending gray of the world, there spilled a stain of crimson, rushing like a swelling sea wave over the threshold of a door that should not, could not, would not exist, but did so in the here and now, existing so forcibly that Kasper Mack could only stare at the scarlet-wet boundary filling what should have been the end of the alley behind the busy automat. Where once there had been a Dumpster, shedding rusted paint as more trash was packed into its gaping maw, there was now a door, a door that contained a sanguine sea that tongued itself into the gray ground and bid Kasper closer.

He stepped closer, his heart constricting in his chest like a warning he would never acknowledge. This literal spill of color was wrong and backwards and thick like blood as it continued to pool from the doorway, the illusion of the sea sloughing off the closer he stepped as the alley lights moved across its oily surface.

Kasper knew the color's name the way he knew the true horrors of this world, having seen its bright mark against the faces of those who had committed crimes and lived to tell the tale. Those marked—those *colored*—were paraded about as warnings to others; misstep, betray your gang, and see where it got you. It got you colored by a shine girl was what, marked for eternity. Kasper

lifted his hand now, to regard and confirm the shades of gray that
defined his fingers, knuckles, palm. As gray as the sky and he liked
it that way, because it was normal, and this crimson was— Not.

The door had not been there the night before. Kasper knew because he'd taken a piss beside the Dumpster, but now the Dumpster was gone, and here this door, iron once coated black but now
flaking its coat to the street, to the puddle that spread across its
threshold. Before he realized, Kasper found himself reaching for
the edge of the door and it was cold under his fingers, sharp as
any blade his boys carried. It opened his skin without a hint of
pain and Kasper didn't even realize he was bleeding until his shoes
trespassed into the crimson flood (tacky, spreading) and he felt the
same wetness between his fingers and looked to see the oil-dark
blood sliding down fingers, into his palm. He drew a handkerchief
from his pocket, wrapped his fingers tight, and then saw the woman. His chest constricted again, a sterner warning also ignored.

If ravens could be ivory, the woman was a raven, standing within
the room that the door enclosed. Her face was sharp, her body
fluid as if wrapped with feathered wings, and she looked expected
to take flight in any second. The room should have been dark,
Kasper told himself, but a soft and wonderful light filled it to the
brim, this light exposing every color his own world did not nor-
mally possess. The woman's hair was the red of a hundred dreamed
sunsets, knotted in a braid that reached to her toes. The tips of her
high breasts were shaded in deep pink, a realization so startling
that Kasper took a step backward; that he could see through the
glacial gossamer that enfolded her was arresting. He felt a fist in
his throat.

"Kasper."

She knew his name and under those two syllables the fist opened
and then closed harder to steal his breath. Circles of absolute
void—no color, no light—blossomed across his vision, gobbling
pieces of this colored realm, and then she, oh she, stood before
him, with her hand around his neck. Her fingers, or were they

talons, were strangely warm when he thought they would be cold; he could feel the press of sharp claws into his skin, the threat of spilled blood.

"Alethea."

He knew her name? He knew her *name* and from her fingers spilled more than blood; the color of her and her realm seeped from every whorl in her skin, straight into Kasper. His suit did not change; the fabric maintained its somber blacks and perfect whites while his skin rioted in color and pain. His entire body flushed with rose and gold, and he believed for one raw moment his body had turned inside out, that she had tucked his skin inside, to leave a long length of aching muscle, vein, and bone exposed to the chilled air. His nails gleamed chalk white where he clung to her without remembering how he had come to cling. He tried to pull free, but his fingers streamed with a black liquid like ink, corrupt against the flawless edge of her feathered arms, and he could not be moved. Something cold slithered within his pocket.

"Bring the girl," she said, and her voice was a gleaming silver awl plunged by a hard palm into the base of his skull. Kasper felt himself press to his tiptoes in an effort to escape the needle of pain, in an effort to let her go, but he could not do either. The warmth of fresh blood pooled in his collar. "Bring the girl."

"Kasper?"

He took a breath and it felt like the first breath of all the breaths that were to come. The tension pooled from his body and he stood, only breathing in the gloom of the world he knew best. The door was gone and so too its crimson threshold, and there was only the brimming Dumpster, him standing near its corner, on his tiptoes, his hands raised as if he had been holding something. Had he been holding something? He looked down to find only the wet oily sheen of the alley as if after rain. His collar was dry.

The man who had called his name, Miles, stood a few steps away, his forehead creased with a frown. He was shaped like a granite mountain and rarely given to expressions of glee, but this frown was more extreme than any Kasper had witnessed before. Kasper lowered his arms and pretended to fasten his trousers before turning to face Miles. At the familiar motions, Miles's expression eased, but there was still no smile.

"Axel's inside," Miles said.

Kasper, refusing to glance behind him, followed Miles down the length of damp alley and around the corner, to the automat, same as it ever was, filled with people changing their nickels into food via the countless glass slots that lined the walls. Only they weren't countless, because Kasper always counted; had to know, had to be sure, especially after the alley (the doorway (the crimson) the doorway) that everything *here* was normal. Kasper counted, his thumb moving against his fingers as he counted and multiplied and came up with three different answers by the time he reached Axel's table.

The table sat so that Axel could see the whole of the room, from front doors to kitchen doors and every stretch of wall between. Axel liked to say he didn't need no ambushes in here, liked to eat his meals in peace, and Kasper never blamed him. Only glanced at his fingers as he joined Axel at the table, to make sure they were gray and not the rosy warmth they'd been in the alley with—

Crimson, crimson, and a drape of white feathers. The memory was like a bird trapped in his chest.

"Nearly one," Axel said and tapped his wristwatch as he leaned into the table to stack French fries into a neat bundle. He folded the fries into his mouth, licking salt from his fingers. "You forget the girl, Kas?"

Bring the girl.

Kasper blinked, fingers still moving against fingers as he counted the automat's vendors.

"T-the girl? N-no, boss." Kasper couldn't strip the warble from his voice, his heart still jumping around like a bird in a half-open cage. He pressed one hand against his chest, expecting to find his ribs curved beyond the confines of his shirt, steaming warm like an offering at the automat. But his shirt buttons were fastened, his ribs tucked away, and he drew a breath.

"Nora, right?"

Axel leaned back and the chair's white vinyl creaked beneath him. He narrowed his eyes and said nothing for a long time, so long that Kasper could count the vendors twice more, to finally come up with the proper count. There was always and ever twelve in each category, and eight categories down each wall, save for the beverage station, which—

"That's right," Axel said. "You're a strange one, Kas. Don't know where you are half the time. We need that girl, right?"

"Every—" Kasper pulled his eyes from the vendors, wondering why he felt uneasy about the girl. He had done this before, gone to collect a girl who wanted to work for Axel. Axel, slicker than ice in December. "Everyone needs a shine girl, boss. Keep the boys in line."

Bring the girl.

Axel's eyes narrowed a little more and his chin came up. "She's on the one-thirty train. Miles saw you in the alley, followed you back there...but the train ain't in the alley, is it, Kas?"

Kasper abruptly stood from the table, metal chair clattering on the checkerboard floor with a sound of scattering rocks. "No, boss. That's where I was headed—the train—but then I..." He trailed off because he couldn't remember and gripped the chair to make it stop rocking. Everything before the alley was cloaked in haze and he wouldn't make an excuse that was a lie. "On my way, unless you needed something?"

"Just for you to bring Nora back here, Kas. For a slice."

Twelve windows with twelve flavors of pie, Kasper knew. He bolted from the automat, glancing briefly at Miles before he went. Miles had been in the alley? Maybe he remembered, but Kasper didn't stop to ask. Not if the girl was on the one-thirty.

The worn train platforms tangled up in the heart of the city. Kasper didn't know where this train was coming from, and didn't care, not until he saw her through the windows, gathering her bags, pulling her long gloves over her hands, all the way up over her elbows. Shine girls and their gloves, he thought, and for a moment, saw her under a cloak of white feathers that spilled crimson over the threshold of the train's doorway when she stepped onto the platform.

It was only steam from the train and she stepped out of it easily enough, a slim shadow among all the other passengers. Her suitcase didn't appear large enough to hold any clothing, but Kasper couldn't stop looking at her gloves, at the way the satin caught the daylight and made every ripple in the fabric run like shining water.

"Mister Mack?"

She walked right up to him and asked him, and Kasper didn't know or care what she had been told to look for when it came to the person who would collect her. He wanted to see the color of her eyes beyond the threshold, wanted to know the color of her soft mouth, and what color her wrist would bleed when cut open. He wanted to strip her gloves off and see colors spill from her fingers the way it had from Alethea's. Alethea's? He could not place the name.

"Mister Mack, this is my associate, Bowie," she

(Nora, he told himself (Nora), her name was Nora and not Alethea (the doorway (the crimson) the doorway where she)

gestured to the man who toddled up beside her, a dwarf no taller than her elbow. Kasper stared at the diminutive man, an uncomfortable feeling pricking down his spine. The dwarf's eyes floated like pools of milk within a frame of lashes, pearls that reflected nothing. The dwarf's cheeks shuddered as a train passed the platform and much like Miles, no smile crossed his lips.

"Meester Kasper." Bowie curtseyed and Kasper could not tell if the dwarf saw him or not. Not knowing how much those milky eyes could discern, Kasper only nodded, did not offer a hand for shaking, for none was offered to him.

"Axel know you brought someone with you? S-shine girls don't usually…"

The dwarf was a complication, though Kasper didn't understand how even as the thought came to mind. He had to take Nora somewhere, and that word, *somewhere*, spilled crimson and ivory in his memory. He felt drunk at the mere idea of doorways and thresholds, and knew he could not take the dwarf over them, knew the dwarf would be dead before they reached *somewhere*, his small body folded in on itself like a crushed can, those pearled eyes seeing nothing of whatever it was they saw now.

"No, they don't," Nora agreed, but she didn't explain about Bowie and Kasper didn't ask, knowing what he knew.

Before Bowie could, Kasper took the small bag Nora carried and tucked it under his arm. Bowie's mouth opened and closed on words unsaid, telling Kasper he saw plenty. They walked from the train platform back to the Chrysler and from there it was a slow drive to the threshold.

Kasper would have liked to say he didn't remember each and every step across and into the crimson spill, but he remembered each with such clarity they were like knives in his gut. He remembered how Bowie's body crumpled as if it contained no bones whatsoever even as Kasper heard them snap in his own hands; even as he intimately knew the break of arm and leg beneath quivering muscle. Bowie's body, small and stunted as it was, proved a good container, for it spilled nothing, holding the wreckage of itself carefully inside as Kasper made every bit of it cease. What was one more bundle in the heaps of trash that clotted the Dumpster? Nothing.

And Nora—

Bring the girl.

Frozen Nora who did not move until Kasper advanced on her. She shrieked and Kasper belted her across the mouth, not wanting to break her the way he had broken Bowie. Not wanting it, but doing it all the same, because her scream was like candy in his mouth, bright yellow and lemon, and he wanted it until he could no longer feel his tongue. Nora dropped to her knees, the pavement clawing long ladders into her stockings, and he advanced on her, pulling a knife from his pocket—a knife he did not recall until he remembered the cold weight from beyond the crimson threshold. He drew the knife, thumbed the blade out of its mother-of-pearl sheath, and—

Kasper reeled back with a scream as Nora's bare hands fell to his face. Her gloves pooled like snakeskins in the wet alley, and her fingers, her *bare* fingers, injected him with fiery pain. He managed to push her away once, long enough to see strands of color spill from her fingertips like living threads. They surged out of her with intent, hemorrhaging color into the gray air around them, and then she was upon him again, injecting the color into his gray skin.

It was overwhelming, a heady rush that was part alcohol, part tobacco. His mind spun, but even then he felt the hook of her—

Bring the girl.

—into his heart, his heart beating bright red in the gray alley wet. With a wrenched sob, Kasper pulled Nora into his arms, knife blade carelessly pressed under the curve of her breast. Heart's blood soaked her dress, streaking the gray fabric black as Kasper lifted her from the ground and carried her toward the door—the door that should not be there, but was there, falling open to allow him delicious entry. He did not slip in the crimson wet, but rather felt guided by its strange course; as if it held him the way he held Nora and they were all part of something larger than he could ever explain.

Alethea's face was as sharp as he remembered, cold and ice and her maw stood ready to pluck Nora straight from his arms. Nora came loose with a sucking sound, blood and sea foam and things stranger trailing from her. There were planets and stars in the strings that bound them, and Kasper found himself trying to catch each and every one before they fell into the oblivion of the sanguine sea. The stars slid between his fingers, while pieces of shell shattered amid the harsh sunlight bouncing off fresh snow; his fingers hooked the rings of a heavy planet, but it was lost to him, the crimson liquid parting to swallow the orb like a molten mouth. Its rings shattered and Kasper dropped to his knees, watching Alethea with Nora even as fresh color still clawed its way into his cheeks and chin. He shuddered, pinned to the ground as butterfly to foam.

His eyes found Nora's. In this place hers were no longer gray, but the endless violet and topaz of a flower he had once dreamed, the promise of blue hidden somewhere around the next curve. It was then he knew, what Nora could unlock in this space but more than that, outside this space, in the gray world he knew—she could topple the world, and Alethea—

She could suck Alethea dry if she wanted. Any shine girl could. Was that where they drew their powers, marking flesh with Alethea's own colors? But Alethea wanted more.

Kasper came to with a violent jolt, sitting upright in the bed he had always believed to be his own. Nora was gone and Alethea could not exist, and he told himself these things were both true even if they rang false in his liar's heart.

The sweat-drenched sheets clung to him even as he made to get up. At some point in the night, he had stripped himself naked, and as he staggered across the room, he saw slivers of himself in the mirror's cracked glass and within these slivers... Within these slivers stood a patchwork man, a man who had been touched by a shine girl's bare fingers

everyone needs a shine girl

and now bore the mark of her touch forever. Unnaturally pink skin striped itself diagonally across Kasper's gray face, but more than that, his eyes—

His eyes.

His right eye was the slate it had always been, flat and unremarkable, but his left rose out of the shadows as a startling orb of emerald, winking with facets of gold and deeper down, blue. He had never seen such a thing, and felt himself falling into the pupil, which was not entirely black—not the black of his right eye, but somehow deeper, richer, surrounded by all that green. Kasper sucked in a breath, tracing the bands of color upon his flesh, a long spiral that trailed from hairline over cheeks, and shoulders, belly, and thighs. Tattooed by Nora's touch, marked in a way only criminals were marked.

He fell to his knees before the mirror and smashed his fists into the already-cracked glass. Silver glittered across his arms, his thighs, and onto the wood floor where it burned with a crimson heat. In the smallest bits of glass he saw Alethea's face, and in the shower, after he managed to pick himself up and walk to the bathroom, it was ivory feathers that fell from his hair. He washed them loose, but they clung in the drain, refusing to spiral down.

The crackle of broken glass on his hands complicated dressing. He could not tie his tie without small pricks of pain, though he could not see any glass to wash away. The pain was simply there, much as Alethea lingering in the corner of his emerald eye. Kasper stood at the mouth of the automat's alley, daring the door to appear, but no door did come. Only Axel, asking questions that Kasper had no way of answering.

"Shine girls been vanishing all month," Axel said.

The relief that washed through Kasper was surprising, but then, another prick of pain, of fear. "W-what?" Did Axel believe him responsible for them all? And was he? Kasper didn't know that he wasn't.

"Dix lost his, and even as far west as Oak Park—girls not where they're supposed to be." Axel's forehead creased with a frown, and then, "Then there was the sunrise. You see it?"

Kasper shook his head, but Axel didn't exactly explain. Only told Kasper to go home, sleep, and wake early enough to see what the coming dawn brought. And what it brought—

Kasper crawled out of the window and stood barefoot on the iron fire escape. Beyond the rising buildings still cloaked in night, the sun had begun to pierce the darkness of the world. But it came not with the white light Kasper had always known, but with a golden glow. The gold coated everything it touched, dripping like liquid over buildings, filling up streets like a river might. Within the clouds that clung to the horizon was a riot—gold and scarlet and deepest orange—and every color imprinted itself deep within Kasper's eye, his gleaming emerald eye, until these colors were all he could see, and he felt himself drowning.

He raised his hands to the color as if he might hold on to the edge of the abyss, but found himself startled by light and shadow. The light coated him too, a trembling effigy in gold flowing down fingers and wrists, over arms and into the hollows of elbows. Everywhere Nora had already colored him ignited with heat and he burned like a thousand stars in the blackest nights, and only then did he realize he was screaming—screaming like dozens of others in the street going mad from the rush of colors. He lurched inside and latched the window, pulling the curtains as tight as they would go, but even then a thin line of gold light burned itself upon the floor, frolicking within the shattered mirror's dust.

Kasper didn't rouse until evening, when the sun had tucked itself away, but everywhere he looked, he still saw color. Color streaked the walls and splattered his floors, as if flung by a tremendous force. When touched, the color would not smudge and could not be chipped away. It was part of the walls and floors themselves; just as his skin and eye had been transformed, so too the world, and he quailed at the sight of it, his guts churning.

When he finally willed himself to open the curtains, it became evident the same was true of the world beyond his room: color splattered everything, dripping over gray awnings turned orange and trees speckled spring green. Farther out, where the streets ringed the park, color splotched the lake, cool gray swirling with the violet of Nora's eyes. Within the lake's very heart, Alethea stood in the fountaining water, spawning a storm of color that whirled outward into the gray world on every droplet.

Unnatural, his mind whispered.

Hideous, the world echoed and it shuddered, a motion so deep

Kasper knew it within his own bones.

Kasper pressed the curtains between his trembling hands and wished that he might crawl out of his own skin to escape both the color and the sensation that the world was falling through fathomless space. The awl that Alethea had jammed into his brain hummed, a live wire coated in ice, and he vomited himself empty within his room before he found the steadiness by which to leave it.

In the halls and the streets, his neighbors shrieked at the colors they saw. Some sprawled on sidewalks and streets, clutching manhole covers as if they feared falling in. Others lay twitching, unable to comprehend anything they looked upon. Even the sky above was not the flat black star field Kasper remembered, but something deeper, with the texture of cat fur stroked backwards and the scent of peeled grapefruit. Kasper staggered under its weight, keeping one hand above his head so the universe—oh gods, the universe!—would not fall upon him.

He had brought Alethea the girl, he had done this, but how he might undo it was yet beyond him. He only knew that he wanted his world back, the world of monochrome and monotone. In the city's distance, he heard piano keys being struck in a rhythm never called music, but he did not care; he found a solace in their repetition, in the memory of their simple black and whiteness.

He staggered past doorways (the doorway (the crimson) the doorway), but none of them called to him the way she did, Alethea wet and overflowing the park, so it was to her he crawled. Nora deserved better, she deserved—

The lake had begun to flood the park, lapping over the color-saturated grass and into Kasper's trousers; the water was cold and felt like the dwarf's eyes, all pearls and milk and things he could not see through, but it was Nora breathing underwater and moving like a fish he *did* see beneath the violet torrent. Given the violet water, her eyes were lost to him, but she saw him and floundered away.

Within the water, he saw shadows of the other shine girls brought to Alethea, bound into her service, inundating the world with their colors. With the doorway open and the threshold crossed, Alethea cracked each shine girl open and from their breasts and bellies, forced life and light into the gray world. Every globule of falling color brought with it the sensation that the world was plummeting faster through the universe.

Kasper tried to reach Nora, but could not. He came up with a handful of dark brown hair tangled around his arm. The shine girl stared at him with sightless eyes, her mouth gaping as she struggled to breathe above the surface of the violet lake. Her skin was puckered, color running from her the way water should have; she spilled blue in waves that felt like fish scales and Kasper dropped her. She vanished under the rising surface and swam away, into deeper waters where he could not see her.

The world responded to Alethea who was no longer confined behind the threshold she had once known. And when she saw Kasper wading toward her in the high water, her tender mouth (her beak, her hideous beak) split in a grin that welcomed him. He shuddered, but helpless, he strode toward her, begging mercy, begging that she undo what she had done. But Alethea only laughed and doused Kasper in a downpour of leaf green water.

Kasper raised his hands, to stem the tide, but he could not. The water cascaded where it would and until Kasper felt his fingers open, he knew of nothing that might stop it. But his fingers—

Where the door had sliced him open, where the door had taken a taste of his flesh and blood, his skin parted anew. Though this doorway was far distant, Kasper felt and knew its edge as an old friend. He reached his cut fingers into the bloody wetness that obscured the threshold and pushed it back, just to see if he could. It retreated and Alethea shrieked.

For an instant, Kasper felt as though he had his hand inside her body, fingers spreading in the warmth that was not water, but her body's own blood; that he held within his sliced fingers the jewel of her heart, beating, but slowing at his whim. But when it slowed even more, it was the shine girls in the water that began to screech, as they were cut off from their source. Nora, tangling around his knees, pulled at him, in an effort to dislodge his hand, but Kasper would not be moved.

He pushed both sides, shine girls to the left of him, Alethea to the right, until the colors pouring from Alethea began to dim as they were condensed behind the black doorway she had always known. She howled, an unearthly sound that rattled Kasper's bones as her talons lodged deep within his forearm. He was captivated by the color of his own blood, so bright as it washed over his skin and into the rising lake. He released his hold on Nora, so that he might find the blade Alethea had given him, the blade that now cut her fingers free of him and sent her spiraling in a funnel of colored water back into the realm she knew best.

She drowned before his eyes, water siphoning past the door's rim, and she had no fingers with which to cling to the edge. Alethea's voice was small then, calling his name, but the frozen awl of her within his mind had gone. She fell helpless, into the water that grew black the deeper it went.

Everything faded to black in this place, Kasper knew as he came back to himself, spread upon the wet park lawn, a dozen shine girls flopping like fish nearby. They sputtered and sat up and blinked in wonder at the gray world around them. At the gray, still world that spread as it ever had and calmed Kasper's rioting heart.

Nora did not touch him when she crawled closer, her hands lacking gloves, but Kasper dared touch her, his door-cut fingers spreading blood across the gray of her cheek. This scarlet smear faded to black as the world righted itself. His hand slipped down, to where he had stabbed her, where her blood had run to fill the world.

"I killed you," he said and his skin burned everywhere she had marked him with color.

Nora pushed the sodden mess of her hair away from her face and looked him in the eyes, colored and slate both. She touched him then, pressing a single finger against the skin she had already transformed and his bones burned; his skin turned itself inside out to escape the fire of her, even as it could not. There were things worse than death, he understood now; he had saved the world from Alethea, but the shine girls still had access to her colors.

"Only for a little while, and then not much at all," Nora said, and pushed herself to standing. Water cascaded from her dress, pattering down upon him. "Maybe you'll do better next time."

But, savoring the colors she had burned into him, Kasper knew he would not.

THE COMMUNION OF SAINTS

JOHN LANGAN

1. *Cannibale* (Lecter)

To start with, Calasso lets Alter handle the questioning. His partner begins where Calasso supposes he would, too: "So Anthony Hopkins—sorry, *Sir* Anthony Hopkins took your son." He succeeds in making the statement sound more reasonable than Calasso thinks he could.

The woman seated across the table from them is enormous, obesity and diabetes egging one another on. Mrs. Madeleine Connolly wheezed all the way into the room, and after she lowered herself into her chair, needed a full five minutes to catch her breath. Her style of dress is what Calasso thinks of as lower-class-defiant. From a T-shirt that would do most women he knows as a dress, Elvis Presley delivers a heavy-lidded black and white sneer. Pink and yellow floral-print leggings hug thick legs that descend into short black boots with chunky heels. She accessorizes with dangling black and white earrings that remind Calasso of miniature chandeliers, and a tiny hot pink purse that looks barely big enough to contain a cell phone. Yet her short, grey hair has been cut in a contemporary fashion, and her face has been made up in an understated way that accentuates its underlying kindliness. It's difficult to imagine her being responsible for anything happening to her eighteen-year-old

son, any kind of violence—but people will surprise you. She fur-
rows her brow at Alter's words and says, "Not him—the one he
played. In the movies. The doctor, you know, the cannibal."

"Hannibal Lecter?"

"That's right," she nods. "He's the one who took my boy."

"But he's a character in a film. If you saw him, you would've
been seeing the actor who played him."

"Or someone who strongly resembles him," Calasso adds.

"Uh-uh. It was him, the cannibal doctor. He was dressed the
same as in that movie with the lambs, one of those orange prison
jumpsuits."

"All right," Alter says. He consults his notepad. "You said the,
uh, doctor was living in the apartment across from the one you
and your son share."

"Had to be," Madeleine Connolly says. "I thought the place was
empty. Had been for six months, since Mrs. Lindstrom died in it.
She was a sweet lady. Died in her sleep. None of us knew about it
for days, until she started to smell. Super hasn't been able to get
the stink out of it. Too cheap to pay for a professional cleaning.
No one who's come to look at the apartment has come back."

"When did you notice Dr. Lecter living there?"

"I didn't. I didn't think Richard did, either, but could be, I was
wrong. He's a deep one, my Richard. Could be, he saw that horrible man opening the door to that place and didn't want to worry
me. He's always looking out for me. It makes sense, though. I
mean, it's the perfect place for a man like that to live, isn't it? A
place that smells like death."

Calasso considers disagreeing. The way the character's portrayed
on screen, at least, he seems more of an aesthete. But that's hardly
relevant to the matter at hand, so he keeps his peace.

Alter says, "Can you think of any reason why the doctor would
have wanted to abduct your son? Did they spend any time together?
Did they disagree or argue about anything? Had Richard borrowed
any money from him? Had he borrowed any money from Richard?"

The woman shakes her head. "Richard didn't have anything to do with that man. Why would he? He'd seen his movies. He knew what he'd be dealing with."

"Okay," Alter says. "And you're certain Dr. Lecter didn't say anything when he took your son?"

"Not a word. It's like I told the other officers. Richard and I were watching TV. *Wheel of Fortune.* I heard the front door open, which was strange, because I always keep it locked, bolted, with the chain on. I said to Richard, 'Did you forget to lock the door when you came in?' No, he said, he hadn't. Then *he* came racing into the living room. He had on that orange jumpsuit, and his hair was all slicked back against his head, and his mouth was open and awful. He ran right in front of me, over to where Richard was on the couch. He grabbed Richard's hair, and hauled him onto the floor. 'Hey!' I said, 'You leave him alone!' I was so shocked. I fumbled with the remote, tried to turn the TV off. But I hit the wrong button, and put the sound way up. All I could hear was a commercial for Burger King. Richard struggled, grabbed at the man's hand, but I don't think the doctor even noticed. He dragged Richard down the hall, out the front door, and over to that apartment I'd thought was empty. I don't move too fast, on account of my size, but I was up from my chair and at that door in time to hear it being locked. I pounded on it, and shouted for the man to open it, but the only thing happened was, my neighbors stuck their heads out of their doors and yelled at me to be quiet. Can you believe that? I thought neighbors were supposed to look out for one another."

For the remainder of the interview, Calasso half-listens. Madeleine Connolly's story has remained consistent since the first uniformed officers responded to her call. As has her insistence that her son was a good boy, not mixed up in any trouble, working part time at Home Depot and taking classes over at HVCC. It's the stereotypical parent's response to questions about their child's extra-curricular activities. No matter that, in Calasso's experience, the vast majority of serious crimes are committed by criminals upon other criminals, mom and dad maintain their denials. He doesn't hold her belief in her son's innocence against Mrs. Connolly. Were he to be placed in the same position, he knows he would utter similar protestations on behalf of his children. At the same time, it slows the investigation into Richard Connolly's apparent abduction. He and Alter will have to track down and speak to the missing boy's friends and co-workers, which adds time to the investigation that he's afraid young Richard does not have. When the uniforms arrived, located the super, and convinced him to open the door through which the boy had been taken, they were met by empty rooms. Aside from dust and mouse droppings, the apartment's only content was in the center of the kitchen floor, an antique china plate on which sat a slice of liver, bloody and warm. While the lab results have yet to return, Calasso has a sinking feeling the organ will prove human, and specifically, Richard's. Thus far, he's succeeded in keeping the most sensational details of the boy's abduction from the local media, but it's still early days, and so only a matter of time before reports of the cannibal kidnapper fill the news.

"Anything you'd like to add, Tom?" Alter's question returns his attention to the interview.

He's about to say, "No," and thank Madeleine Connolly for coming in, tell her they'll be in touch, offer a word of reassurance. Instead, he says, "Just one thing. Those movies—the ones with Hannibal Lecter—what do you think they are?" He isn't sure what he's asking.

The woman doesn't hesitate. "Why," she says, "they're documentaries, aren't they?"

2. Calasso: *Per Una Selva Oscura*

Detective Thomas Calasso of the Albany, NY, Police Department is not a happy man. If, aided by a bottle of decent single malt, you were to ask him the reason for his unhappiness, he would tick off the causes on his fingers. His cholesterol continues to be high, which means he is going to have to return to taking the medicine he insists makes him tired, although his doctor swears that this is not one of its side effects. Despite several years of daily exercise, he has been unable to shrink the belly that pushes down the front of his pants. His sex life has dwindled to practically a seasonal event, as his wife, Theresa, has been harrowed by a menopause that has lasted the better part of two years and has withered her desire. Even when she has been receptive to his advances, as often as not, he has been unable to perform the act to its conclusion.

Nor are his complaints limited to the physical. His career, whose early, upward trajectory was so steep as to be almost vertical, leveled off a decade ago, and has maintained a pretty much constant altitude since. More men and women have clambered around him on their way up the departmental ladder than he cares to remember, many of them pausing to take what instruction they could from him, then continuing without a backward glance. He's contemplated retirement—after twenty-seven years, he's served well past the minimum requirement—but last week's mail brought a letter accepting his youngest to Bard, her top choice, while his oldest is contemplating returning to college to earn her degree as a paralegal, and his wife is insisting that the bathroom needs to be not just painted, but completely gutted and redone—in short, there are plenty of bills headed his way in the short term, the long term, and no doubt the longer term. If he could figure out a path from police work to another, more lucrative career, he would likely take it; a few former colleagues are driving Mercedes and living in Loudonville. But he cannot map a route that will lead him to a five-bedroom, two-and-a-half bath McMansion with a German car in its long driveway and a hot tub on its bluestone patio.

Those who have known him the longest—his younger brother, Mark, a cardiologist who practices in Boston; his cousin, Felicity, an entertainment reporter for *People* magazine—would say that he has inherited the dour fatalism of their Sicilian grandmother, for whom every happy occasion was a promise of imminent calamity, and every calamity a herald of further disaster. Theresa is convinced that he is clinically depressed, and has been urging him to speak with his primary care physician about a prescription for something that would help to lighten his mood. If ever it amused her, his answer that this is what the liquor cabinet is for has ceased to do so for some time. And if he were being honest, with Theresa or with anyone else who cared to ask and had poured him two fingers of Talisker, neat, he would admit that the booze doesn't help whatever is wrong with him, anymore. There is still the loosening in his chest once the whisky warms his stomach, the psychic equivalent of tugging down the knot in his tie, opening the top two buttons of his shirt, but it is as if, underneath his white dress shirt, he is wearing another garment, a vest woven from thick, coarse hair, a relic of his *Nonna*'s austere Catholicism. Here he is, midway through his life's journey (and that's speaking optimistically: his father died at fifty-eight, eleven years beyond his current age, while his father's father lived only ten years after that), and he cannot shake the dread, the outright conviction, that his adult life has been nothing. The feeling is more than the typical policeman's cynicism, the awareness that basically everyone is an incipient criminal, that whatever victories he has won have been local and temporary. No, what plagues him is the sense that his part in everything in which he has been involved, from his marriage, to his children, to his job, might have been played by anyone with as much if not more success. He is a blank, a space around which his life has happened. It's no wonder, he thinks, that he has wound up working missing persons, because that's what he himself is.

Midlife crisis is the diagnosis of the therapist he's consulted on the sly, a pair of words so generic as to be meaningless. (Strangely, it put him in mind of the tumult of his adolescence, which his favorite aunt used to assure him was normal, symptom of a phase he was going through; his mother offered almost identical counsel when he and Theresa hit a rocky patch when the girls were young and seemed to monopolize her time. It's as if life is a series of phases to be endured until the final, phasing-out from it.) The phrase brought with it a set of images equally banal: Calasso with a woman twenty years his junior, her most noteworthy features her vacant smile and the breasts filling her bikini top; him seated behind the wheel of cherry red sports car, a Porsche or Corvette; him, walking hand in hand with his new companion on a tropical beach, the tip of a wave foaming around their bare feet. He is sufficiently honest with himself to admit some measure of truth to the therapist's assessment. In the last few years, a surprising, almost frightening number of the friends of his youth have divorced, started new careers, moved vast distances, embraced religion, quit drinking, battled cancer. (This last he recognizes as no one's choice, yet he cannot help listing the disease amongst the trials to beset what he continues to think of as his class, decades past their high school graduation.) In spite of this recognition, he is convinced that there is more to his feeling than midlife *noia*. It is as if, after a promising start in a couple of moderately-successful films, he is one of those actors who is constantly mistaken for another actor. Like a film, his life possesses the illusion of depth; shift perspective, however, and it flattens out to nonexistence.

3. *Mostro* (Xenomorph)

"I don't know how you expect me to draw this," Maxwell, the sketch artist, says.

"Try a pencil," Alter says.

"Look," Calasso says, "just do the best you can, okay?"

Maxwell shakes his head, but returns to the office where Judge Marcus Ryan is waiting. Once the artist is out of earshot, Alter says, "You know what he's going to come back with, right?" Although Calasso nods, his partner continues, "A picture of the Goddamn monster from the *Alien* movies."

"The xenomorph," Calasso says.

"Whatever. The point is, you'd be as well Googling a photo of the thing and copying that."

"You know who the judge is, am I right? You understand how miserable he can make our lives, and by 'our,' I mean everyone in the Capital District. It's important—it's essential—that he feels like we're pulling out all the stops for him. So allow me to tell you what I told his honor. Obviously, this was someone in a costume. Maybe the costume came from a store, or maybe it was home-made. If the judge can give us a picture of what he saw, then it should help us to figure out what kind of costume the bad guy was wearing. That will aid our investigation."

"You don't think that's taking the long way round this? It's not as if we have the manpower to spare. Shouldn't we concentrate on the judge's driver, find out if he had his fingers in any pies he shouldn't have?"

"Once the Commissioner hears that Marcus Ryan's personal driver has been kidnapped, we are going to have more warm bodies at our disposal than we'll know what to do with. The Captain's going to tell us to leave no stone unturned—you can imagine. We might as well get a head start on some of those rocks. Based on what Ryan's already told us, I'm guessing the suit was put together by the guy inside it. Could be he has some experience in costume design. I don't know where he'd get the material for it, maybe a junkyard, maybe online. Once Maxwell's done, we'll tell one of the uniforms to start researching what you'd need to construct something like this, and then we'll go from there."

Alter nods. "I'll put Vargas on it."

"She's sharp."

"You think this is connected to that other kid, Connolly?"

"Hard to think it isn't, what with the movie references. On the other hand, it's a pretty big jump from dressing up like Hannibal Lecter to making your own xenomorph suit."

"Like you say, it's a hell of a coincidence."

"Nah, it can't be, can it? What's the alternative, though? A single kidnapper with a closet full of horror movie costumes? A gang whose members dress as their favorite monsters?"

"Sounds like something out of Batman."

"It sounds ridiculous. Maybe this is all some kind of elaborate practical joke."

"Tell that to the Connolly kid's liver."

"I know." Calasso sighs. "And I'm afraid that blood is going to be the driver's."

"Yeah," Alter says. "I'll go find Vargas."

"Do that."

After Alter has navigated the maze of desks and chairs to the exit, Calasso glances at the windows of the office where Judge Marcus Ryan sits on the edge of one of padded chairs, his massive forearms on his knees, his hands clasped, while Maxwell moves his pencil over the page of the sketchbook open on the coffee table between them. The judge's tie hangs unknotted around his neck, his shirt collar is unbuttoned, his sleeves are rolled up to his elbows. A pewter flask stands uncapped on the table to his right. Through the strands of hair combed over his scalp, his skin is flushed, shining with sweat. Calasso's dealings with the man have been mercifully few and far between, but each time, the judge has conducted himself with an almost Olympian reserve, as if his legal authority is indicative of power more profound. The abduction of his driver, however, has deflated him, reduced his long, perfectly-formed sentences to jagged and jumbled fragments. Calasso interviewed Ryan upon his arrival at the station, and struggled to make sense of his story.

The judge had been on his way out of his house on New Scotland to a fundraising dinner for St. Peter's. He instructed Mario (Navarro, his driver) to bring the Cadillac around to the carport. When Judge Ryan stepped out of the side entrance and turned to activate the alarm, Mario was waiting with the back door open. As the judge descended the side stairs, he saw something moving above his driver, descending from inside the carport's roof. "Uncoiling," Marcus Ryan said, "unspooling, unrolling itself from itself." Black, glossy, its skin was more like the surface of the car than the flesh of any warm-blooded creature. He saw arms and legs too, too long, like the limbs of a giant spider, a tail like a string of bone, an oblong head whose face was all mouth, a nest of silver fangs. It was the way it moved, the judge said. He could not tear his eyes from it. Mario saw him staring at a point directly above him and tilted his head back. What was lowering itself towards him made his mouth drop open, the front of his trousers darken. His head lolled on his neck, his body went limp, but before his faint could carry him to the driveway, the thing grabbed Mario by the shoulders and lifted him into its embrace. Once he was secure against it, the creature retracted up, under the carport's roof. Too frightened to move, the judge stood where he was, until a shower of blood slapped the roof of the car, startling him into action. The uniforms who answered his call went so far in their search of the carport as to climb amongst its rafters, but the structure was clear, as were the roof of the main house, the garage, and the branches of the old oaks scattered around the grounds. The only evidence corroborating Judge Ryan's account was the one to two liters of blood drying down the windows of his Cadillac.

Calasso offered to interview the judge at his house, as a courtesy, but the man insisted on coming to the station. "The way it moved," he said. "If you could have…Like nothing…You would understand…Turning…Like nothing you want to see…Twisting… Corkscrewing…Nightmare…Like a nightmare."

4. Calasso: *Città Irreale*

Detective Thomas Calasso of the Albany, NY, Police Department is not a happy man. Sometimes, he blames this on the city where he has lived since moving there to attend the State University when he was eighteen. From the start, he was aware of a certain, odd quality to not only the capital city, but to those around it: Rensselaer across the Hudson, Watervliet to the north, Troy across the river from that. As a college freshman, snug in the self-contained world of the campus, he was not overly concerned with the surrounding community except as a destination for the occasional party, or trip to the movies, or late-night excursion to the diner. Once he had a car, during his junior year, he took to exploring Albany, venturing downtown, to where a cluster of tall buildings gave the impression of a slice of another city, Boston or Manhattan or Chicago, lifted from its setting and deposited on the long hill that led up from the Hudson. Sometimes, he continued towards the river, in amongst the forest of concrete pillars that raised a network of roads into the air. He'd been majoring in American History, with a focus on New York State, and he had read that this place had been the original downtown, a collection of homes and businesses built along the Hudson's west bank. When the spring thaw raised the river, it had flooded the streets, sometimes to a depth of several feet. Now, it was flat, bare earth, in the shadow of the elevated roads whose construction had provided the rationale for the neighborhood's destruction. He would steer to the shoulder of one of the local streets that wove through the support pillars, shift into Park, and try to imagine the place as it had been, to reconstruct the flat brick façades of its buildings, awnings lowered over shop windows, people entering and exiting their front doors. In the rush and boom of cars and trucks passing overhead, he could almost succeed in projecting the images he had seen in old photographs onto the shadowy space.

If there was time, he would return the car to Drive and, depending on traffic, head north or south. North brought him past a short building atop which a giant model of Nipper, the RCA mascot, socked his head to one side. He was charmed by the enormous dog; it seemed like a detail from the old Batman comics, one of the oversized ads that crowded Gotham's rooftops, made real. Not long after Nipper, the road straightened and broadened, its margins empty of everything but a diner at which he liked to stop for a Coke and the gyro platter. (He'd dated a Greek girl who'd dumped him for a rich French guy but left him with a taste for her country's cuisine.) If conditions were right, heavy fog would roll up from the Hudson over the road, forcing him to drop his speed to almost a crawl until, ahead on the right, the diner appeared luminous in the mist. Something about the stretch of road reminded him of a runway; he wasn't sure what. Its emptiness, perhaps.

Driving the opposite direction, the impression was oddly similar. There, faded brick buildings and two-family homes lined streets that led down to Albany's port, an expanse of warehouses and empty lots surrounded by sagging chain-link fences. It wasn't so much that he expected a plane to drop out of the sky as it was an underlying sensation of imminence, as if all this open space was needed for the arrival of…he didn't know what, something vast, sublime. Struck by the symmetry of his responses to the northern and southern reaches of the city, he was on the lookout for any such parallels between its eastern border with the river and its less well-defined western limit, where he had his first off-campus apartment, in the former attic of a large house. That he could discern, the horizontal compass points were opposites, the east a site of absence, the west a site of presence, of new construction as the shopping centers and malls and office buildings replaced stands of trees and meadows. Although he supposed the stores that populated the malls and plazas were their own kind of blank, national and international chains whose connection to the surrounding community was accidental and contingent.

Not until he had completed his Bachelor's and was working towards his Master's, also at SUNY, did it begin to occur to him that his understanding of the city, of the entire Capital Region, was in error. Rather than take on any more student loans, he had found a job just up the river in Troy, working as the office manager for an eye surgeon. Every morning, he rose early to chip away at the week's reading for his classes, showered, and drove to work. If he was running late, he headed for 787 and raced to the exit for Route 7; if he was on time or ahead of schedule—which he generally was—he took a local route, either along this side of the Hudson to Watervliet and the bridge, or over the river to Rensselaer and north along the Hudson's eastern shore. On his return from his job, he followed another set of local streets home. He viewed the exercise as an extension of his textual research into the area, a way of seeing history on the ground, as it were.

When he decided to leave the Master's program and the Ph.D. for which it was presumably laying the groundwork in favor of the police—a career shift facilitated by his then-girlfriend's revelation that she was, in fact, pregnant—his knowledge of the side streets and out-of-the-way pockets of Albany proved a considerable asset. Indeed, it developed into a running joke, amongst both his fellow officers and his family members, that he was never lost, was incapable of becoming lost. "Mr. Map," they nicknamed him. In the time before widespread GPS, he was frequently consulted by other cops for directions to unfamiliar and hard to reach locations. Even after everyone could look up the best route to an address on their phone, he was asked to evaluate the information, refine it, suggest shortcuts. It was as if he carried a replica of the area in the folds of his brain. It was one of the reasons, he suspects but has never been told outright, that he was assigned to missing persons, because he knew all the places the lost might be found.

He knows something else, too, something he started to learn during those early drives between Albany and Troy. At the time, he interpreted the impression the region made on him as one of openness, of readiness for some great event. Especially once he graduated the Academy and began his time as a patrol cop, he realized that what he had taken for openness was in fact emptiness, that what he had viewed as readiness was actually exhaustion. As he moved from patrol to robbery, then from robbery to homicide, then from homicide to missing persons, what he experienced daily of the city and its surroundings aligned with what he had studied of it before dropping out of graduate school, namely, that its best days had been lit by the sun of years long past, and that since the end of the nineteenth century, the area had been on a steady decline, its only real growth industry the legions of office workers required to keep the state bureaucracy from complete paralysis. Yes, the region had its cycle of booms and busts, but from the long view, these were only the shifts and lurches of a ship that has already slid beneath the water's surface. Years, decades prior, the damage was done, and now, the place was in a kind of living death.

5. *Demone* (Krueger)

Through what Calasso supposes must be some species of luck, he receives the call for the third kidnapping while it's still in progress, at four o'clock on a Thursday afternoon. While he and Alter are speeding to the Catholic charities soup kitchen in Arbor Hill, he's on the radio, calling for roadblocks to be set up at the nearest intersections. Although the initial report is jumbled, with no mention of any vehicle spotted leaving the location, there is no way for the kidnapper not to be behind the wheel of something (Calasso's bet is on a van). If, for some foolish reason, the perp has tried to hoof it, so much the better: the army of police he's about to unleash on the neighborhood surrounding the soup kitchen will find the guy in even less time. It wouldn't be accurate to say that Calasso feels good—there's far too much that can go wrong—but there is satisfaction in thinking that the odds have finally started to favor him.

Three hours later, as the uniforms continue their search of the houses, yards, and lots around the Catholic charities building, and the Captain heads for the press conference for which Calasso and Alter have done their best to prepare her, Calasso struggles to hold onto the feeling that the case has turned in his direction. It was a mistake for the kidnapper to strike during the day, and a bigger mistake to do so at a location as crowded as the soup kitchen.

Calasso is familiar with the institution. When his oldest was fulfill-
ing the service hours required for her membership in the National
Honors Society, she volunteered here during the Christmas sea-
son. He tagged along—to lend a hand, he said, and did; although
both of them knew it was to keep an eye on her. Ten years ago, the
soup kitchen was busy, and that was before the economy collapsed
in the Great Recession, from which this area seems to have taken
particularly long to recover. There are regulars at this place, men,
women, families, who witnessed the abduction of Sr. Lucy Grace
and in one case attempted to intervene (for all the good it did).
Calasso has witnesses to spare, and surely one of them has noticed
something, some incidental, seemingly-inconsequential detail that
is going to unravel this case.

Because what they have from the principal witness, Sr. Christine
Aquin, is not terrific. When Calasso pushed past the groups of
agitated men and women choking the hallways, to the kitchen,
he found a woman younger than his oldest daughter, her face
streaked with tears, her wimple gone and her brown hair in disar-
ray, the front of her habit spattered with spaghetti sauce. Her eyes
were wide, her face preternaturally still. *Shock*, Calasso thought.
Voice trembling, the nun said, "It was the Devil. You must know
that. He was the one who took her. We were boiling the water for
the pasta. Thursday is spaghetti night. He stepped from behind
her. There were four pots on the stove. I said we needed a fifth.
The dining room was already crowded. Sr. Lucy said four would
be plenty. I couldn't find the sauce. We had a donation of sauce on
Tuesday. There was no one there, and then he stepped from behind
her. Newman's Own, the sauce, the one that gives the profits to
charity. Cabernet marinara. I searched the cupboards and all the
cabinets. We had to start the meatballs. I spent the morning making them with Mrs. Allan. Sr. Lucy said one of the volunteers must
have put the sauce in the pantry. His skin was burned, all the way
through, as if he'd stepped right out of a fire. It smelled like pork,
like burnt pork. I heard her in the pantry. The jars clinked together

as she shifted them. 'Here it is,' she said. She walked out of the pantry. Her arms were full of jars. Eight of them, at least. He was wearing a hat, one of those hats…a fedora. It was brown. Sr. Lucy didn't see him. He grabbed her by the shoulder, her right shoulder. He used his left hand. He couldn't use his right one, because it wasn't a hand, it was metal. A claw. Sr. Lucy looked over her shoulder. When she saw him—the Devil—she screamed and threw her arms up. The jars of sauce went everywhere. One of them smacked the counter in front of me and exploded. I put my hands up, to shield myself from the glass. The Devil had his arm—his left arm—around Sr. Lucy's throat and was dragging her backwards, out of the kitchen. A number of the volunteers appeared in the hallway. They'd heard Sr. Lucy screaming, the jars bursting. One of them, a young man—I don't know his name, I'm sorry—charged the Devil. Wasn't that brave? Foolish, but brave. One flick of that claw, and the Devil laid him open. No one else tried anything after that. Who could blame them? I'm sure Sr. Lucy didn't."

The nun's story remained consistent through Alter's follow-up; indeed, she repeated it pretty much verbatim. The half-dozen men and women who responded to Sr. Lucy Grace's cry corroborated the latter details, adding that the kidnapper hustled his victim out the front door. None of them followed because they were all busy tending to the young man who had been half-disemboweled. A couple of the uniforms followed the trail of blood the kidnapper's claw left, but it diminished after a hundred yards or so. The perp appears to have been heading east, but that may be where he parked his vehicle.

After they turned Sr. Christine Aquin over to the EMTs, and assigned the last of the search areas to the final uniforms to arrive, Alter said, "You know who she saw, right?"

Without looking up from the screen of his laptop, balanced on the trunk of their car, Calasso said, "Freddy Krueger."

"Mr. *Nightmare-on-Elm-Street*, himself. Doesn't seem to have recognized him, though."

"Kids today: no respect for the classics."

"Is Freddy K. a classic?"

Calasso shrugged. "He's what we have, instead."

"Our boy certainly likes him."

"He likes all the bad guys from that time period, doesn't he?"

"You're thinking…?"

"Nothing. I don't know." Calasso folded the laptop shut. "Actually, you know what I can't figure out?"

"You mean, aside from what an eighteen-year-old, part-time college student, a thirty-nine-year-old Dominican immigrant, and a forty-two-year-old Catholic nun have in common that could make them the targets of a kidnapper who likes to dress himself as horror movie icons?"

"Yeah, aside from that."

"I haven't the foggiest."

"It's the effect his costumes have on the people who see them. Remember Judge Ryan? Even Mrs. Connolly was convinced her son had been grabbed by *the* Hannibal Lecter. And now this young woman. From the way they act, you'd think they witnessed an actual monster in action."

"So you're thinking what? The guy sprays some kind of psychoactive chemical into the air before he makes his move?"

"I don't know what I'm thinking. It's just weird, is all."

"Well, file that under duly noted. And speaking of weird: you know what I found out?"

"What?"

"Something unnervingly similar to this—the kidnapping, the costumes—took place in our beloved Capital District a little over a hundred years ago—hundred and three, I think."

"Seriously?"

"The wonders of Google. Four people with no apparent connection to one another were abducted by a man dressed as different Catholic saints. The papers called it the Communion of Saints kidnappings."

"Did they get whoever did it?"

"They got someone. A Polish guy, worked at a junkyard, which was how they figured he was able to come up with the costumes. Reading between the lines, maybe he did it, and maybe he didn't. No one else was grabbed after his arrest, which did seem to settle the matter."

"What about the victims?"

"Far as I could tell, they were never found."

"Huh," Calasso says. "All right, that is weird. In fact, it's God-damned spooky. What the hell were you searching for?"

"'Kidnappings in Albany.' It took me a while to find it."

"I never heard of it, and I have a degree in the history of this place."

"You think it means something? Like what? Our boy's a true-crime buff who decided to stage his version of Albany's strangest crimes?"

"Nah. I mean, could be, but how likely is it? It's probably a co-incidence. Which doesn't make it any less spooky."

What else can it be but coincidence, one of those moments when the present puts on the garb of the past? Madness to believe anything else; he might as well call in the psychics, break out the Ouija board. He might as well try to answer Sr. Christine's final question to him: "What is the Devil doing loose from Hell?"

6. Calasso: *Noi Crediamo Che Presto*
Le Cose Che Avrebbero Creduto

Detective Thomas Calasso of the Albany, NY, Police Department is not a happy man. Lately he has been spending time in local Catholic churches, St. James on Delaware and Blessed Sacrament on Central; once in a while, the Cathedral downtown. On his way to work if he's early, or during lunch if he isn't working through it, or on his way home if he isn't too tired, he slips through the front doors into the vestibule, and from there into the church proper, dipping his fingers in the small bowl of holy water affixed to the doorframe and crossing himself as he goes. Inside the church, he genuflects and slides into one of the pews towards the rear. Sometimes, he reaches down, lowers the kneeler, and eases forward onto his knees, resting his elbows on the top of the pew in front of him; other times, he remains seated, but hunches over, as if in prayer or contemplation. He does not attend daily mass at any of the churches, nor does he attend mass on Sundays or holy days of obligation. Though raised Catholic in a devout household, he has not been to mass on a regular basis since shortly after his youngest made her First Holy Communion, a decade ago.

The immediate cause of his first missed mass was, ironically enough, an Act of God, in the form of an early-morning thunderstorm that knocked out the power to the house and left the alarm clocks mute. He and the rest of his family slept right through their usual Sunday wake-up of eight A.M.; in fact, by the time he opened an eye, saw the clock radio's blank face, realized what must have happened, and fumbled for his watch, it was one minute to ten o'clock, much too late for the nine-thirty service. Eleven o'clock mass was not absolutely out of the question, if everybody hustled, and there was a twelve-fifteen service, too, but as he considered the face of his watch with its round of Roman numerals, another possibility occurred to him: brunch at the diner on Central he and Theresa used to frequent when they were first seeing one another. Initially, the girls were wary of his suggestion that, this Sunday morning, they do something a little different, and go out to eat. Of their parents, their father was without doubt the more religious, the more invested in their faith and what it meant. They weren't sure if this was some kind of strange test; for the matter, neither was his wife.

While they had cheerfully described themselves as recovering Catholics early on in their relationship, the moment Theresa told him she was pregnant, he tacked hard towards the faith whose headland, it turned out, was not that far away. It was for the baby, he told Theresa. It was important he or she grew up with the structure religion provided. Although she hadn't shared his sudden change of heart, Theresa hadn't argued with him. That first Sunday he had resumed attending mass, she had accompanied him. She had enrolled in the Pre-Cana classes that were required for them to be married in the Church, and at their wedding, she had promised to raise the baby swelling the front of her dress Catholic, along with any siblings the child might have. She had kept her vow, through Christenings, First Penances, First Communions, and in the case of their oldest daughter, Confirmation. If she had balked at sending the girls to Catholic school, it was as much because of the expense, and because their local public school had a good reputation. Questions of Church doctrine the girls raised, she referred to their father, who never seemed to lack for an answer. Whatever concerns she had about the religion, she kept to herself; although, when whichever priest was delivering that Sunday's homily lashed out at Planned Parenthood, as they did on a semi-regular basis, there was a certain tightness to her mouth that suggested she was holding in an opinion she very much wanted to share. Once, about two years into their marriage, Calasso had asked her what she got out of their weekly visits to the church. She shrugged, said, "It's something we do as a family," which he supposed was as good a reply as he could expect. He was the one who found satisfaction of a less tangible variety in religion.

Until one day he didn't. Cautiously, Theresa and the girls went along with his suggestion that they skip mass in favor of brunch. The following Sunday, they repeated their visit to the diner. He had to work the Sunday after that, so Theresa took the girls to church, but the next weekend, they were back at the diner, and a new pattern replaced the old: Sunday mornings were for sleeping in, then family brunch. At separate moments, surreptitiously, each of the girls questioned the change in their collective behavior; he justified it with as much subtlety of reasoning as he had their questions about Original Sin, the Incarnation. Theresa was less interested in his rationalizations, more concerned that the sudden change in his attitude was symptomatic of other psychological troubles. With her, he was direct. "I don't believe it, anymore," he said. "Any of it. I'm not sure I ever did."

At the time, the admission felt bold, liberating, a step into a new, more honest existence. With the passing years, however, whatever authenticity he seemed to find has proved flat and dull. The faith around which his and his family's life used to revolve has not returned, and while he suffers an ache at its absence whenever his obligations to his nieces and nephews bring him under a church's roof, his nostalgia is usually curdled by the priest's sermon. The child-abuse scandals, the clumsy cover-ups and self-righteous justifications have done nothing to bridge his distance from the religion, but he has retained the ability to differentiate between the actions of the clergy and the tenets of the faith they are supposed to exemplify, and while the corruption is a convenient rejoinder to any sibling or in-law who criticizes his departure from the Church, it is not the root of his problem. What he said to his wife is true: his current lack of belief has brought with it the sense that he never believed, that his return to Catholicism, his setting it at the center of his family's life, was fundamentally panic at shock of Theresa's pregnancy, an overreaction that continued for years.

Were you to suggest to him that his recent visits to local churches seem to argue against so absolute an interpretation of his history—to hint that his past devotion was not entirely a lie—he would likely shake his head. Churches are quiet places, he would say, they're *still*, a combination he finds conducive to reflection, which this current string of kidnappings demands from him. Dipping his fingers into the holy water, genuflecting, are camouflage, ways to guarantee he'll be left undisturbed for the fifteen to twenty minutes he devotes to turning over the details of the abductions. Sometimes, he would say, an unfamiliar location can help to loosen your mind, allow you to make connections you wouldn't have, otherwise. He would allow a certain irony to his selection of churches as his preferred location for the examination of a mystery, but he would caution you not to place too much faith in it.

7. *Madre di Lacrime* (Crone)

When they breach the shack, Alter goes first, even though Calasso is holding the shotgun. His sour thoughts about his partner's ambitions are interrupted by a flock of balloons that pour through the doorway, red white yellow, up to the underside of the overpass above. Alter raises his left hand to guard his face, and that allows the hulking figure waiting inside to step forward and chop off his right hand. Calasso sees the machete—practically a short sword—flash, his partner's wrist spout blood. He registers the hockey mask hiding the assailant's features as he pushes Alter down and unloads the shotgun into it. A flash, a thunderclap that stuns his eardrums, the kick of the stock into the meat of his shoulder, but he's already pumped the shotgun and fired a second time at the shape that's staggering backwards. He chambers a third shell, but the perp is on his back, the hockey mask and what lay beneath it a ruin. Calasso circles him to ensure that he isn't breathing, kicks the machete away in case he's wrong, and retreats to where Alter lies writhing. Keeping the shotgun trained on the kidnapper's form with his right hand, he unbuckles and unleashes his belt with his left. He holds out the belt to Alter, who takes it. As his partner is tourniquetting his right forearm, Calasso radios for backup, for aid for a wounded officer. He locates Alter's hand, still clutching his pistol. *At least he held onto his weapon*, he thinks, and has to stifle hysterical laughter. *Keep it together*.

There is no sign of any of the missing individuals in this front part of the shack, but at the rear, the dirt floor slopes steeply down. Calasso should wait for the other officers to arrive before investigating back there. At most, they're two minutes away. If *Friday-the-13th* here had any friends, they've been alerted to Calasso's presence, to put it mildly. Best to leave them to SWAT. He has nothing to prove. If it hadn't been for him noticing the shack on his and Alter's drive past it, and what's more, the grooves leading through the dirt outside its front door, as if a body had been dragged to it, they wouldn't have discovered the kidnapper's lair. Granted, it was more happenstance than the result of arduous investigation, but he was the one who told Alter to pull over. Whatever else takes place, he is the one who broke this case.

Except, he cannot stop his legs from carrying him deeper into the structure. It's as if he's caught in the grip of something larger than himself, part of a narrative that demands he fulfill the requirements of his role. He is the lead detective working this series of crimes, this mystery: it is incumbent on him to see the thing all the way through to the end. Light enters the rear of the shack from a hundred tiny holes in its siding, making the air glow. In front of him, the floor drops almost vertically. A series of planks jammed into the dirt one under the other forms a treacherous set of stairs. He takes them almost on his side, half-sliding under the ground, the shotgun muzzle up and ready.

The space into which he emerges is a pocket in the damp, dank earth. Layers of muddy trash carpet the floor. Muddy posters and papers decorate the walls. In the center of the room, a basin dug out of the ground holds a dark liquid whose coppery stench makes his gorge rise. On the other side of the basin, the sculpture of a woman kneels gazing down into it. Executed in gray clay, with the rough technique of either a beginner or amateur, the statue suggests the Virgin Mary, its head draped, its body robed. The face, however, is no maiden's; the opposite, in fact. It suggests profound age, a lifespan of such length that the various features are subsiding into a sea of creases and folds. The kidnapper dabbed blood on the lips, the eyelids. No doubt, it's some private fetish, a replica of the guy's mother or grandmother or great-aunt Rose.

The sculpture sighs. Calasso starts, aims right, aims left, shotgun ready for whomever he's missed camouflaged in the garbage. His eyes dart to the statue's face, where bubbles froth the blood smeared on its lips. His weapon trained on the sculpture, he steps toward it. Its eyelids open amidst the blood across them, and what looks at him through that crimson film causes him to lower first the gun, then himself, until he is prostrate before it.

Later, long after the backup has arrived, and Alter been sped away to Albany Med, and the crime scene been secured, and Calasso debriefed by the Captain, herself, he will attempt to put the sensation that swept over him to words. He will be sitting on the back porch of his house, a sizable glass of Talisker mostly untouched on the arm of his chair. After asking him again and again if he's sure he's okay, his wife and daughters will have heeded to request for a little time by himself, to decompress.

Staring at a night sky hung with low clouds, he'll think about other nights he's been out taking the dog for the last walk of the day, and an enormous wind has blown up, a change of weather moving in, with such speed and such force that it feels as if all the night is rushing against him. Only, what streamed out the crone in the mud was a torrent of sensations, images. Chief among them was the feeling of time, of decades, of centuries, time laying on him like a robe made of lead, time bending him down to the ground. If only he could let his burden carry him the rest of the way into the soil, from which he has the impression of having emerged, drawn forth from it by means he does not understand. (He had a vision of a hazy, firelit stockade that a distant version of himself recognized as Fort Orange, the settlement the Dutch raised on what would become Albany's location. The hewing of these walls, the laying out of the streets they enclose, the hearths around which those streets were planned: he has the sense of all of this as having summoned him and birthed him.) Exhaustion dulled his limbs, his thoughts. (He saw a succession of bowls scooped out of the earth, some filled with water, some with wine, some with blood. Reflected in the liquids' surfaces, a panoply of faces, the stylings of their hair a gauge of the passing years, their expressions united in desire.) Here is a *noia* to dwarf Calasso's own experience of the emotion, the disgust of a divinity, or of something near enough, a *deus loci*. Buried within the weariness, the boredom, he is aware of a bright thread, a burning seam that might be teased out, channeled to the accomplishment of deeds extravagant and extraordinary, violence of a real and of a figurative sort. All that would be required is an acolyte of sufficient vision, someone more than a high-school drop-out with power fantasies and a fixation on the monsters of his childhood.

That is what he offered her, the crone, the muddy avatar of the place where his life has run aground. The city revealed herself to Calasso, parted her robes, her flesh, to display to him the worn, leathery bag of her heart. In exchange, he promised her himself, mumbled into the dirt and refuse his pledge of something else, something better, he doesn't know what, but it will be more than mere costume-ry, a re-enacting of tired plots. Was his offer accepted? SWAT found him alone. Tucked into the breast pocket of his dress shirt, Calasso later noticed a tiny wooden figure like the miniature replica of a saint. It was her image, the hem of its robe dark with what he is reasonably certain is dried blood. He turns it over in his hand, his pulse quickening with something like joy.

For Fiona

EXIT STRATEGIES

BRIAN KEENE

nyway, where was I, Frank, before we got sidetracked? Oh, yes. Now I remember.

I arrived here in Uniontown just after sundown, which was good. Darkness comes early on these cold December evenings, but true night would not fall for a few more hours. That gave me time, and time was something that had been in short supply until then. I felt one of them, the others, out there in the place that isn't here—traveling the path, looking for an entrance. At some point that night, it would merge into our world. I needed time to make sure that didn't happen.

You see, Frank, I am an exit. What that means is that I close doors before they open.

Have you lived here all your life? On maps, Uniontown is nestled in a mountainous area on the edge of the Forbes State Forest. If you studied that map a while longer, you'd notice that the town is in the center of a region surrounded by Interstates 68, 70, 76, and 79. What you probably wouldn't notice is that the intersection of those roadways forms the rough outline of a magical glyph used by a race of humanoids who were in the final throes of extinction when the human race was still trying to figure out the basics of fire. It's okay that you don't know that. Most people wouldn't.

But I do.

While looking at the map, you probably also wouldn't notice the ley lines running through that glyph. Again, this is excusable. You wouldn't see the ley lines because they aren't on the map. But they are there, just as real and tangible as the highways that intersect with them, and the fast food restaurants, shopping malls, hotels, bars, truck stops, and housing developments that sit atop them. Do you know what ley lines are, Frank? No? Well, ley lines are like the blood vessels of the planet, carrying energy throughout the world-body. The Interstate Highway System is like that, as well. It pumps through the heart of America, carrying us throughout the nation's body.

According to the Internet, the Interstate Highway System is a network of freeways built to aid in our country's defense, by providing an expedient travel method for our troops. The system was championed by President Dwight D. Eisenhower. Construction was authorized by the Federal Aid Act of 1956. The original portion of highways was completed thirty-five years after that, but it has since been extended to a total length of forty-seven thousand, seven hundred and fourteen miles, making it the second longest such system in the world, exceeded only by China's.

I often wonder if there is someone like me in China, traveling that system, turning entrances into exits, and making sure the doors are sealed.

The Internet will tell you other things about the Dwight D. Eisenhower National System of Interstate and Defense Highways—better known as the Interstate Highway System—if you take the time to investigate. It will tell you, for example, about the General Motors streetcar conspiracy, in which General Motors, Firestone, Standard Oil, Phillips Petroleum, Mack Trucks, and the Federal government conspired to gain control of the nation's transit systems, spelling the end of streetcars and rail travel, which led to a rise in automotive sales and gasoline stations. They did this through the proposal of the Interstate Highway

System—bankrupting mass transit and the railroad companies all in the name of keeping the American people safe should we be attacked on our home soil. And in truth, it's not a conspiracy theory. It's a conspiracy fact. Don't look at me like that, Frank. It's a conspiracy fact. Consider how streetcars were replaced with buses and taxi cabs, and railroad tracks were paved over and replaced with vast spans of concrete and asphalt. And while passenger rail service still exists, albeit to a much lesser extent, have you ever considered why we are the only industrialized nation on Earth that does not subsidize its passenger rail system? Conspiracy fact, Frank.

Have you ever been driving along the interstate and seen one of those road signs with five silver stars in a circle? According to the Federal Highway Administration, this is the "official symbol commemorating the vision of President Eisenhower in creating the Dwight D. Eisenhower National System of Interstate and Defense Highways". But according to some users on various Internet conspiracy forums, it is an occult symbol. These theorists aren't wrong, but they don't understand the significance of what they've found. They blame Freemasons or the New World Order or Black Lodge for this design, without understanding that its origins are far older, and not of this world.

Time spent with Google will give you other theories, as well—that Route 66 was designed by a secret occult group to hypnotize masses of American automobile passengers; that the highways are designed to represent the symbols of Anubis/Sirius, or Satan, or one of the Thirteen; that the highways were laid out in the shape of a giant magical glyph that will enable the Pentagon to summon demons to protect us in case of an attack; and something about Aleister Crowley and Henry Ford teaming up with the Bush family and a secret post-war Nazi order to design a giant swastika across the nation's landscape which will somehow allow Lucifer to reign supreme.

All of these theories are obviously the concoctions of crazy people. The thing about crazy people, Frank, is that they don't know they're crazy. They speak earnestly of their beliefs, secure in the absolute knowledge that they are right, and the rest of us just can't see it. Now I know that, at first glance, I must sound crazy, as well. But I'm not. How do I know I'm not? Because I'm willing to allow for the possibility that I might be wrong. I'm willing to admit that the whole thing is in my head, and that maybe beings from outside our reality aren't bleeding through into our world via dimensional portals along the Interstates. And that I'm not really closing doors before they arrive. That I'm not really turning entrances into exits. And that all of the things I've done…that they're really just point-less atrocities.

That's a terrible thing, I admit, but the thought doesn't keep me up at night, Frank. What keeps me awake at night, what terrifies me, is that I'm right. That these things really are happening, and that sooner or later, I won't be in time to stop it. That a breach will occur.

I've dreamed about that happening. Many times. The dreams—nightmares, really—are different, but they all begin the same way. I don't get there in time, and a door remains open. Then a living darkness engulfs the world, devouring anything with a spark of life. Or the dead come back to life, not like the zombies from that television show, but as vessels for something else—something as close to evil as I've ever seen. Or the world is flooded with a great deluge, and at its center is a great, squid-headed beast who views us like we are nothing but gnats. Or something that I can only describe as sentient static electricity spreads itself across our wi-fi signals, broadcasting a signal that drives everyone mad.

Hang on one second, Frank. I need to check outside. I thought I heard a car pulling up.

***

Okay, sorry about that. It was a family. Dad got out to pee. Mom and the kids stayed in the car. They just pulled back out onto the highway, so no worries. We're good to go. It won't be much longer. We just need a few more minutes before it's time.

Here's the thing, Frank. I'm not crazy. Are you a religious man? No? Neither am I. Or, perhaps I should say I'm not an organized religious man. I have spirituality. I can't do what I do and believe what I believe without some sense of the spiritual world beyond this veil. But I have no use for organized religion of any sort. There is a bible verse I'm quite fond of, though. Isaiah 35:8—"and a highway shall be there, and a way, and it shall be called The Way of Holiness; the unclean shall not pass over it; but it shall be for those: the wayfaring men."

I'm not insane, Frank, and I'd appreciate it if you'd stop doing that and hear me out on this. Because here's why all the theorists and crackpots on the Internet are wrong. It's not the Interstate itself.

It's the missing interchanges.

This country's highway system did indeed have an occult origin. If it had been completed as originally designed, I wouldn't have to keep doing what I do. There would be no need for it. But the Interstate was never completed. Not entirely. They told us it was finally finished, back in 1992. You're old enough to remember that, I'm sure? No? Well, they made a big deal out of it at the time. But it wasn't finished, Frank. Not exactly. Two of the original interstates, I-95 and I-70, are missing interchanges, because of local opposition and political pressure. There are very few things on this planet that can be more powerful—or ugly—than local politics. In New Jersey, the local community were able to force the cancellation of the Somerset Freeway, leaving sections of I-95 disconnected from the others. And here in Pennsylvania, there's a missing interchange near Breezewood, where motorists have to hop off the turnpike and I-70, cluster onto Route 30 for a few miles, and then get back on the interstate.

So, you see? The actual Dwight D. Eisenhower National System of Interstate and Defense Highways is not contiguous. That's why things keep getting through from other worlds. The walls between our reality and all of the other realities are thin in the Mid-Atlantic region. Pennsylvania, Maryland, New Jersey, Delaware, Virginia, and West Virginia—these are where those things from my nightmares get through. It's because of those missing interchanges. If the system was complete, this wouldn't happen. But it isn't, and it's never likely to be because of politics, and so, I have to do this.

I'm a wayfaring man, Frank.

Anyway…it's time now. I think I'd better leave the gag on until I'm finished. I'm sorry about that, but it's for the best.

Stop that. You're only hurting yourself, Frank. Those handcuffs are much stronger than your wrists. I got them off a West Virginia State Trooper who, years ago, found himself in the same position you're in now. Look, you've cut your skin, thrashing about like that. Now you're bleeding. We have to be careful of that, Frank. I need the rest of your blood to help seal this doorway. So stop making yourself bleed. I'll handle that for you.

Listen, I need to be honest about something here. I lied to you earlier. When I said that your wife…what was her name? Beth? When I said that Beth was in the other room and she'd be safe as long as you did what I told you? Well, I lied, Frank. I don't feel good about it, but I really had no other choice. This is not my first rodeo, so to speak. I needed a way to control you. Plus, in looking at the two of you, I was fairly certain that she would give me more trouble than you. The truth is, Frank, I killed Beth right after I took her into the other room. I want you to know that she didn't suffer. It was quick.

And I also want you to know that I'm sorry. This isn't something I like doing. I take no joy or pleasure in it. At times, it still turns my stomach.

But I have to do it anyway, Frank.

Because I am an exit.

I am a wayfaring man.

I wish I could tell you that this wasn't going to hurt—that, like Beth, you wouldn't suffer, but that's not true. Pain and suffering are part of the ritual. I'm going to need both from you, along with your blood.

Okay, let's get this over with, Frank. Let's close that door.

You have been reading...

GIALLO FANTASTIQUE

Directed by:

ROSS E. LOCKHART

And featuring the talents of:

Adam Cesare
Garrett Cook
Ennis Drake
Orrin Grey
Nikki Guerlain
MP Johnson
Michael Kazepis
Brian Keene
John Langan
Anya Martin
Cameron Pierce
E. Catherine Tobler

Cover art by David Palumbo
Cover design by Scott R. Jones

A Word Horde release

COPYRIGHT ACKNOWLEDGMENTS

TITLES AVAILABLE FROM WORD HORDE

Tales of Jack the Ripper
an anthology edited by Ross E. Lockhart

We Leave Together
a Dogsland novel by J. M. McDermott

The Children of Old Leech: A Tribute to the
Carnivorous Cosmos of Laird Barron
an anthology edited by Ross E. Lockhart and Justin Steele

Vermilion
a novel by Molly Tanzer

Giallo Fantastique
an anthology edited by Ross E. Lockhart

Mr. Suicide (July 2015)
a novel by Nicole Cushing

Cthulhu Fhtagn! (August 2015)
an anthology edited by Ross E. Lockhart

Painted Monsters (October 2015)
a collection by Orrin Grey

Ask for Word Horde books by name at your favorite bookseller.

Or order online at www.WordHorde.com

ABOUT THE EDITOR

ROSS E. LOCKHART is an author, anthologist, editor, and publisher. A lifelong fan of supernatural, fantastic, speculative, and weird fiction, Lockhart is a veteran of small-press publishing, having edited scores of well-regarded novels of horror, fantasy, and science fiction.

Lockhart edited the anthologies *The Book of Cthulhu I* and *II*, *Tales of Jack the Ripper*, and *The Children of Old Leech: A Tribute to the Carnivorous Cosmos of Laird Barron* (with Justin Steele). He is the author of *Chick Bassist*. Lockhart lives in an old church in Petaluma, California, with his wife Jennifer, hundreds of books, and Elinor Phantom, a Shih Tzu moonlighting as his editorial assistant.

Visit him online at www.haresrocklots.com